THE DEMON OF LONGING

short stories

Gail Gilliland

THE DEMON OF LONGING

short stories

Gail Gilliland

Carnegie Mellon University Press
Pittsburgh 2001

Acknowledgements

I thank the Trustees at Yaddo and the Institute for the Humanities at the University of Michigan for time and space provided.

Most of all, I thank my parents for giving me their stories. I keep them among my treasures that no thief can ever steal.

Book design: Sean Mintus
Cover design: James Mojonnier

Library of Congress Control Number: 2001091296
ISBN 0-88748-362-3 Pbk.

10 9 8 7 6 5 4 3 2 1

*For Mama and Suz and Bill and Sonny
and in loving memory of H.W.L. Gilliland,
the greatest Texas Ranger of them all.*

"The Demon of Longing" originally appeared in *Apostrophe;* "News of the World" in *Passages North;* "When Amelia Smiled" in *Sextant;* "Purple Heart" and "Kindnesses" in *Sonora Review;* "The Sturbridge Tale" in *Thirteenth Moon;* "Witches" in *Colorado-North Review;* "Dog Stories" in *San Jose Studies;* "Permanence" in *Object Lesson;* "Berkeley" in *Rackham Journal of the Arts and Humanities;* "All Their Secrets" in *Yankee;* "Freedom" in *Dark Horse;* and "The Texas Ranger" in *Swallow's Tale.* First drafts of a few of these stories were in a manuscript that won a Hopwood Award at the University of Michigan.

Brief excerpts or mentions are from the following works: Nathaniel Hawthorne's "The Gentle Boy," in *Hawthorne's Short Stories* (NY: Dodd, Mead, and Co., 1962); "Babette's Feast" by Isak Dinesen in *"Babette's Feast" and Other Anecdotes of Destiny* (NY: Random house, 1986); "Il Plœ:r Dã Mõ Kœ:r," by Hortense Calisher, from *The Collected Stories of Hortense Calisher* (NY: Arbor House, 1977); Dante's *Divine Comedy*, translated by Allen Mandelbaum (NY: Bantam Books, 1980); *Deceit, Desire, and the Novel: Self and Other in Literary Structure*, by René Girard, translated by Yvonne Freccero (Baltimore, MD: The Johns Hopkins University Press, 1965).

CONTENTS

I have found…from reading my own writing, that my subject in fiction is the action of grace in territory held largely by the devil.

—Flannery O'Connor

I will sing…while I have any being.

—Psalms

For where your treasure is, there will your heart be also.

—Matthew

THE DEMON OF LONGING

Three men—two business executives and the train conductor—keep precarious balance between two cars of a commuter train. The men all went to high school together in the approaching town, were pals clear until the two who have become businessmen went off to college, then got jobs downtown.

"I bought a three-family in Attleboro," the conductor says. The men are still young, maybe thirty, but the two who have jobs in Boston belong to a sports club, where they get together every few nights or so to play basketball, or go upstairs to the weight room to work out, while the train conductor is already getting a little paunchy, a little bald. "Place is maybe five, ten minutes from the Attleboro yard," he tells his friends.

The businessmen nod. One asks, "You ever take the Providence run?" He's wearing an Italian designer suit, gray with a metallic thread that shimmers in the long light of the suburban Boston summer evening's setting sun.

"Once in awhile," the conductor says. "I can take the Providence run if I want to. Or not, you know. I got enough seniority now to choose."

A woman is walking toward them as he speaks. She isn't one of his regulars. She is wearing a simple sweater and skirt, white pearls at her throat, and she has nice brown hair that brushes her shoulders. She carries a leather briefcase. A good-sized book is tucked beneath one arm. The conductor tries to read the title of her book when she stops beside him at the door. This is a woman with dignity and class. A woman like the one he'd like to have, but knows he can't.

He isn't married, and he should be. He still lives at home with his mother, and he knows people say things about a man like that. *Man lived with his mother*, they'll say if he ever does something crazy. *Man was a loner. Didn't go out much, and didn't talk. Come to think of it, now that ya mention it, there was always something about the guy that was a little off.*

But he's not weird, just picky. Problem is, no one really good enough has come along. His mother asks him his intentions every time he takes a new girl out.

"I like variety," he tells his two old buddies as the train pulls up. "Sometimes this line, sometimes Attleboro. That way, I don't get in a rut."

His friends chuckle. They've also seen the woman. There is no more talk.

Yesterday, the train conductor was supposed to do this run, but some old man got hit in Wellesley by the 4:53 Amtrak to Chicago, just before the commuter rail was pulling out. An announcement came on at Back Bay telling everyone on the train they should get off. The train sat in the yards for at least an hour.

The old man was eighty-six. Someone saw him put a hand up to his eyes before the hit, so the papers suggested that the old man had been blinded by the setting sun. But his daughter said he had always been an avid walker, said her father knew those tracks and walked there everyday. *I cannot understand this*, is what she said.

The train conductor swings down to the platform, extends one hand to help the commuters off.

"Have a nice weekend now, Charlie," his friends call out.

"G'bye youse," he shouts after them. His fingers sink into the flesh of the new woman's arm. He watches her walk up the stairs behind his friends, then looks down the platform, making sure everyone is clear of the train before he climbs back on.

* * * * *

Make sure you always have a book along, the woman thinks. In Hawthorne's story, "The Gentle Boy," a Quaker child tells stories to a deformed boy. "His tales were of course monstrous," the narrator reports of the child's paltry efforts at fiction. "Disjointed, and without aim; but they were curious on account of a vein of human tenderness, which ran through them all, and was like a sweet, familiar face, encountered in the midst of wild and unearthly scenery."

The scenery would be of untouched forests, deep and dark and full of demons. Hawthorne's forests were those of New England, after all.

Maybe I'll call the course "Paul and Frances: The Book Between Us," the woman thinks. Include contemporary texts *re-visioning* the situation of the two lovers whom Dante sent to hell forever for reading books. I will show that, as with the medieval love-tract which Paolo and Francesca were no doubt reading when they began their tryst, it is still the province of the book—any book at all, it seems to me—to seduce our longing selves. Like Paolo and Francesca, we discover the spiritual intimacy we have in common with those who read. We *desire* to talk. The serpent in the Garden of Eden was a *talking* serpent, after all.

But then, the woman thinks on her more practical, less academic side, why send two people to hell forever for falling in love with their heads together over a stupid book? In Dante, the book is the serpent that brings them together in the first place, as well as the obstacle that separates them in the end. The French critic René Girard asserts in his seminal study of the triangularity of desire that romance depends upon the existence of an obstacle between the lover and the object of his desire. For some, the love of country. Think of Goethe, for example. Or Verdi. For others, as with Tolstoy, society with its awful conventions. And for still others, as in Stendhal perhaps, religious duty, the love of God.

But it all goes back to Dante, it seems to me. All the questions of Christianity—nay, of humanity itself—are in that book.

And so now, the woman thinks, I just may have the substance of my course. Let's hope to God they buy it. I've never thought of myself as teaching in a women's college, but I need this job.

* * * * *

The artist invariably produces from the experience at hand.

So: A young man works for the headquarters of a small, revolutionary American church, where he writes letters to all the affiliates that are closing down. The remaining governors, the kindly old people from the heyday back in the Fifties who run the place, don't have the heart to tell the aging membership that the church itself, the main one, is closing down.

In the meantime, a love story has unfolded between the revolutionary American church's business correspondent, a young man with a degree in English from Harvard who couldn't find a job, and the venerable old woman for whom he writes, a great-granddaughter of one of the church's four original founders, and therefore a dyed-in-the-wool nineteenth century New England Romantic, though not a man.

The old woman has almost succeeded, through her integrity alone, or perhaps just through the brute strength of her human will, in keeping the church from going bankrupt, its modern corporation-minded leaders from going off to jail. She wears her thick white hair in a lustrous bun. Her face shines with the luminosity of holiness. *The lines are fallen unto me in pleasant places. Yea I have a goodly heritage. Amen.* If the old woman had not inherited this Puritan Protestantism from her father, she would be a nun.

The correspondent is a strong, good-looking boy, and he has surprised himself by falling ludicrously in love with the old woman whose business letters he has been hired to write. *Letters to the Field from Naomi Brand,* he will someday entitle this collection if called upon.

Some of the letters the correspondent writes are in response to memorial donations. Checks come in from contributors in memory of a member. $5. $10. Never very much. Often, the donor includes some little anecdote from the remembered person's life. The correspondent receives on a regular basis, for instance, Letters-To-The-Editor that various deceased persons have written to their respective local newspapers over a spate of time. Most of these are dated around 1945. An elderly spouse, or a middle-aged daughter, though most likely themselves not members of the church, will be going through the deceased's belongings, when they will happen across a cache of these letters, and, hesitant to dispose of such intimate proofs of passionate opinion belonging to the loved one, will pass along the task of disbursement to the deceased's chosen place of worship.

But who do the relatives think is going to read these epistles, the correspondent wants to know? Who do they think will write them back?

So the correspondent does. He picks up his pencil and begins to write. *Dear Friend. Thank you so very much for sending us your loved one's cogent reproaches to the Daily Press!*

Some of the memorabilia, however, is quite a bit more interesting than that. Once, the correspondent received a yellowed copy of a citation that had been issued by the French Foreign Legion to the one who'd died. The citation was signed in beautiful black script, *C. DeGaulle*, and was accompanied by a photograph of a dashing young man wearing jodhpurs and a crisp, long-sleeved shirt with *épaulettes*. The soldier in the photograph sported a *képi* atop his trim head, and shiny, knee-high boots on his smallish feet.

I will celebrate his life, the correspondent thought, *even if no one else in this place will.* So he took the soldier home with him, along with the yellowed citation from the French Foreign Legion, and hung the two of them side by side on his kitchen wall. Every night for several months, while he was eating his solitary dinner by candlelight, the correspondent spoke to the soldier about his day at the office in the church, and about his growing, overwhelming, and—he knew this, but he'd be damned if he was going to let *her* know it—*forbidden* love for Naomi Brand.

One day, the old woman called him into her office. She told him how very, very much she admired his work. She told him that his letters had made her cry. They were the most compassionate letters she had ever read. She had sat weeping over his beautiful letters for hours and hours, she told him. She thought them quite as good as Paul's letters to the Corinthians.

Naomi Brand was particularly fond of a letter the correspondent had written to an affiliate out on the Arizona desert, in which he had employed a quote from Isaiah. *And there shall be a tabernacle for a shadow in the daytime from the heat, and for a place of refuge, and for a covert from storm and from rain.*

The affiliate wrote back: *Hallelujah! We have never heard such inspiring words before! It is as if your words had come directly to us from the Book of Revelation! Could this mean that it arriveth, the grace for which we have been praying for, lo, so long?*

Because, of course, the Arizona People had been given to believe that it was she, this eighty-year-old virgin, and not the graduate of Harvard, who had penned the hymn of thanks. He was only her correspondent. Which is to say, her *ghost*.

But after awhile, the members of the church to whom he had been writing, thanking them in florid prose for the generosity of their contributions and the gracious magnanimity of their souls— eventually, these people started to notice something wrong. Although Naomi Brand continued to sign the letters, they had begun to sound a little odd.

A 93-year-old Portuguese man who had found the sect in his twenties while he was a merchant marine, sent the church $500 from his pension, explaining on a dirty, crumbling slip of paper he attached to the check that he had jumped ship in Honduras when he was twenty-three to find the truth. *And you see*, the old man wrote to no one in particular—he had opened the letter simply with *Dear Friends*—*I have continued to love the truth these 70 years.*

The correspondent knew he should have written a simple

thank-you letter to the old seaman. *Dear Nonas Bartone*, it should have read. *Thank you for your generous gift of five hundred bucks.* He should have closed with another quote from Isaiah and been done with it.

But by now the correspondent knew he was in love with Naomi Brand. And he was more than a bit rebellious against this fact, for he was beginning to believe that a tremendous joke had been perpetrated upon him by a fickle God. In whom, by the way, he did not believe in the first place. Maybe this God was punishing him for his unbelief. Or just for going to Harvard. In any case, the correspondent wanted Naomi to notice him once and for all. Then, if worse came to worse, she could kick him out.

So, instead of a simple expression of gratitude to Nonas Bartone, the young man effused. *Many thanks for your tremendous tokenism, brother,* the correspondent wrote. *Here now, as in Philadelphia, flowering plants walk into our church offices every day, whilst an unusually sunny February turns apocalyptically toward the darkened sky. What doest thou, friend? How goes it? Quibble with us, won't you, as to how it actually feels to be 93?*

Now the venerable founder's great-granddaughter, her eye well-trained to perceive *the substance of things hoped for, the evidence of things not seen,* immediately intuited the correspondent's verbiage as the language of suffering. More specifically, she glimpsed that her poor, anonymous employee was bearing witness to the vagaries of unrequited love.

So one evening, when the young man took the elevator up to the office of Naomi Brand, to pick his letters up as he was wont, he found the old woman waiting for him. She sat on the edge of her desk, arms crossed over her thin, flat bosom, her tiny legs dangling over the wooden sides. She fastened the correspondent with her bright, black eyes and said: "Young man, I detect that you believe yourself to be in love with me. Is that the truth?"

"Yes ma'am," the correspondent answered. And then, feeling very much like the young George Washington must have in that

apocryphal story about the cherry tree, he had to check himself
from saying, *I cannot tell a lie.*

Naomi Brand burst out laughing. Her fragile head shook as
she went on chuckling. "Your timing is outrageous. What a farce."

* * * * *

At this point in the story, stop and read Isak Dinesen. It will
do you good. See "Babette's Feast," for instance, with its life-saving
insistence that *an artist is never poor.* Which is a nice sentiment,
really, because artists always seem to get themselves in trouble
when they have to work.

Or try something more on the lines of, say, *Harold and Maude.*
Because if you're not quite up to literature, a cinematic approach
just might suffice. But that's film, you see. And I don't *do* film.
All I have ever wanted to do, all I am longing to do this instant,
even more than the nagging human longing for whatever, whom-
ever they, he, it, was, were, is just *to write.* And eventually, I will
have to outwit the demon of longing to get back to that. Which
is of course why I am writing this story in the first place. To cast
the demon out.

* * * * *

One day, the correspondent goes to work, where he sees big
trucks parked outside the church. Eight-wheelers, like the ones
he used to long after out on the highway in New Mexico when he
was growing up. Men in blue jumpsuits are carrying oak desks
out of the church and up big steel ramps, on into the silvery
caverns of the idling trucks. The trucks purr like kittens. The desks
are the kind his elementary school teachers used to sit behind.

He stands on the sidewalk, watching the men load the trucks
with chairs, computer equipment, even the fixtures from the
orange and black and green art deco tile bathrooms that he loves
so much. For awhile, after he knew for certain that he was in love
with Naomi, he would go into those bathrooms many times a

day to try to hide. He would latch the bolt on the doors of the black marble stalls, and sob into his own dark reflection: *Why me? Why in this particular place? Why now?*

Across the plaza, where the bronze fountains, cast in Italy at great cost to the church during World War II, now lie derelict and broken among mossy stones, the correspondent sees Naomi Brand, her wonderful white hair curled up neatly in that eternal bun. He can imagine how her hair must have looked once, long ago, as it hung loosely around her hips. For he has heard the rumors. That she had a lover once, someone high up in the church, a married man. But she had not been willing, as had been wise Solomon, to split the living child, the church, right up in two. As if it were a peanut butter sandwich, or a Hershey bar! *There you are, my little pretties, one bloody half each for the two of you.* It was said that Naomi, too, had gone daily into the black marble toilet stalls to cry, and that this became a form of sacrament she continued to this very day. As for the happy ending, she herself became a pillar of the church. The Mary Magdalenes always turn out to be the holy ones.

The correspondent waves, and the old woman's veined, translucent hand waves back, her ripple of pale life reflected in the polluted pond. Once, when he went to visit her in her office after hours, she sang for him, bubbling old tunes from the Thirties and Forties in her crackling voice. *The winds of March that made my heart a dancer! The telephone that rings, and who will answer?*

What will happen to him now he doesn't know. *O King*, Daniel said to the man who tried to have him eaten by lions. *Live forever!* Just remember, though: All the other Hebrews were burned alive. And the correspondent is not sure he would want that. He is not even sure he wants to go on longing for this old woman all his life.

Naomi has not stopped looking at him from across the pond. He waves again. His hand takes on a desperation of its own. She is so very, very far away. Finally, giving in to the insatiable demon of longing, he begins to walk.

* * * * *

All we really have here is the need to talk. Sex is only a cheap substitute for that. The girl sitting beside me in the pick-up truck says, *I'm never with anybody when I'm with them. You know what I mean? I'm, like, riding along in the car, you know, listening to Janis Joplin, or Vivaldi, or Bach, or else the Stones, anybody really, and I'm still alone.*

"What? Would you say that again?" I was thinking about the man with whom I believe myself to be in love, and I've missed it all. I can't write. I don't listen.

I mean, like, love is the next earthly accident I must resolve. The one that took place in the Garden of Gethsemane. The fear that we'll find everyone else asleep at two in the morning when we need to talk.

Thus she gives me a starting story line: *Oh, but then, flight's the expected outcome for a girl like me!*

* * * * *

For the last six months, I've been playing angel to an older couple at the train stop. When I first started watching them, he was always there waiting to meet her when she got home. He would watch from the bridge as she climbed the stairs with the other commuters, and he would take her bag from her when she reached the top. I could see it had been a May-December romance once, but the scandal itself—his leaving his wife, his children, maybe even his grandchildren, for all I know—hadn't occurred recently. More like ten years ago. In the meantime, the old man had retired, and the younger wife had kept working. An office, possibly, where they saw her as a nice, middle-aged woman who seemed content, and who cared about her looks, because she kept them up.

She dyes her hair, I've noticed. An auburn. Almost red. And from the looks of her flat stomach and slim legs, she diets, maybe even belongs to a gym, where, like the two businessmen and the conductor, she too works out. In any case, she is well past May, though pliable. A little like Edith Piaf, I want to say.

After awhile, the older husband, if that's what he is, started walking down the steps to the platform with her in the morning, in addition to meeting her in the afternoon. He would wait with her there in the morning, the two of them talking and talking, their heads together, talking low, until the train came and took her away from him. I imagined him standing there, long after we had pulled out of the station, looking longingly down the tracks as we sped toward town.

One day, I noticed he was riding all the way into town with her, talk talk talk. They were magnets for each other, as the saying goes. At least, she was for him. I don't know what he did when he got into the city, when she went to work, how long he stayed before he took the train back out to the country. But at the end of the day I would notice she rode home alone.

Then for awhile he was on the train with her in the evening, too. Whether he stayed in Boston all day, or just rode back and forth, I didn't know. Always talking, the two of them, their eyes into each other like there was no one else. And I thought that if I could manage to catch even a few of the words they were saying to each other, I would have the answer to the question I have been asking almost all my life. And that is, *What is your life like if you are granted your desire?* Say the obstacle is removed and you have it, whatever it is. What is your life like when there is an *after that*?

Yesterday morning as I passed, I heard the woman with the red hair reading a restaurant menu aloud to her older man—a daybill some enterprising local *cafe* owner was passing out. Perhaps the commuters would be too tired to cook tonight, the owner suggested in the advertisement. If so, they could come to his restaurant. The menu varied. There were expanded hours. The owner had his own variety of hopes.

Now the woman was reduced to humoring her older man. *Hmm*, she said. *Sea food. Fried entrées. Sounds pretty reasonable, doesn't it? Yes, you're right.* They got onto the train together. But she was bored.

Last night, I saw him waiting for her on the bridge. We all

filed up the stairs silently together, one at a time, not so different from nineteenth century factory workers responding to the whistle that ends the day. I could see the old man searching the crowd for his beloved. But she wasn't there. As he walked slowly to his car, he kept looking back over his shoulder to make sure he hadn't missed her. He seemed so lost. Maybe even a little frightened. What had she done?

This morning, when I saw her waiting for the train, the woman with the red hair was alone. She stood on the platform, staring at the ground, chewing her lip, never looking up.

* * * * *

Once, when I was driving east from California in an old blue Plymouth station wagon during one of those moves back and forth across the country I kept making by myself, I stopped in Albuquerque to eat at a restaurant I like in Old Town, on Central Street, the old Route 66, where I can choose *hot* or *mild* on the menu, depending on how long it's been between my drives.

After lunch, I came out of the restaurant, my lips blistered, and sat down on a bench in the square long enough to smell the sage, and to listen to the wind in the cottonwoods, and to hear the Rio Grande river cicadas squawking in the noonday heat.

As I sat there, I watched a girl who looked a lot like I had once—brown hair to her waist, a flowered gauze skirt and sandals, maybe even a beaded Indian band around her head—as she gazed up longingly into the face of an older man. I heard her shout at him, "If you leave, don't you know you'll never in your whole life meet anyone like me again? My whole being is love! All I am is love!"

The man to whom she was speaking was wearing black perma-crease slacks, a neat, short-sleeved white shirt, and polished shoes. He had short hair, a little gray at the temples, and he was freshly shaved. He was probably fifteen, maybe even twenty, years older than the girl, but he had a nice tight waist, and a healthy tan. Still, he didn't look like anything out of the ordinary, compared to her.

"I can't just leave my life behind and quit my job," he was saying. "People don't really do that. People have responsibilities in life."

About fifty feet away, the man's business partner leaned against the rental car and looked off toward the distant desert, his lips pursed in the silent whistle of some Sixties tune. He was destined to be a minor, forgettable character, trying hard not to ask too many questions, as people who are just along for the ride in those situations usually do.

"If you leave," the girl repeated, "you will never again find anyone to love you the way I do."

The man said, "Then that's a chance I guess I'll have to take." He kissed her on the cheek and walked over to the rental car and, signaling to his partner to get in quickly, he drove away. I waited for a little while, holding invisible guard over the girl. I wondered how long it would be, or if the time would ever come, when the man would realize what he had done, what a terrible mistake he'd made.

The girl never looked up. She never saw me. Today, this afternoon even, when she thinks of that moment—because there will never be a day in her life that she does not—I won't be there to help her when she cries.

* * * * *

Yesterday, after not seeing the May-December couple for about a month, I saw the woman again. She was with her teen-age daughter at The Gap. Lunch hour. When we all leave our offices to wander through the air-conditioned mall with its chain stores, built indoors for office people like me who no longer know how to go outside. Our identities have been erased by the work we do, that has little or nothing to do with what we are.

It surprised me that the woman had a daughter, but there was no doubt that this was indeed her daughter, for they looked alike. The girl was slimmer and taller than her mother, with beautiful, curly, auburn hair she didn't have to dye. She was standing in front of a mirror, wearing big, baggy pants and an oversized plaid wool jacket she dearly loved. She did a little Charlie Chaplin dance and clowned around.

The woman laughed. "That's great," she said.

The salesboy laughed, too. "You could roll the trousers up a little," he suggested, trying to be helpful. The girl did what he said, glad to have some practical advice.

* * * * *

And here is yet another story about the demon of longing I can tell.

At forty-eight, the woman remembers the incident as if it were last summer. That day in Nice. She'd only been married for about ten months, and she and her husband were on the honeymoon they hadn't been able to take right away, because they were married in November, and he taught school. But the summers, he'd told her, would be lovely. She'd see. They could have their delayed honeymoon in Europe at the end of June.

The husband was still sleeping in their cheap hotel, and the young wife was looking through the grimy window at the rain. She saw all the dreams she'd ever dreamed before she married him, back when she'd traveled all over Europe by herself, and now her dreams were pouring down the sides of the dirty gray buildings that were her only vista, and she was sad.

She pulled on her jeans without waking her husband, and ran down the street to a bakery she'd noticed the day before. As she approached the bakery, she started singing in French, an old nursery rhyme she'd learned in elementary school. *Il pleut, il pleut, bergère, c'est ron ron ron, petit pat-a-pon.*

The baker came out from behind the counter as she stepped inside. The shop was warm, its windows steamed over. The lovely, pungent smell of fresh yeast swept over her like—she has said this over and over again ever since then with frustration, knowing that everyone says this, that we are all alike—*the scent washed over me like a tide.*

Like a tide, I tell you! He was an old man, maybe in his seventies, and he was wearing a spotless white apron and a black beret. His thick white hair curled out over his ears, and his wonderful pink cheeks puffed up as his face broke into an enormous smile.

He shook his head with the recognition, and reached for the three-foot baguette he already knew that she would want. He took her by both hands and kissed her narrow forehead still wet with rain. "But where have you been all my life?" the old man asked. "I've waited all my life for you to come in here, like this, one day when it is raining, singing just as you are doing, with that song."

He took her into his arms and began to dance. She moved to the rhythm, her slim legs following in perfect accord with his accomplished steps. Pressing his lips to her hair, he sang the rain-song into her ear as she matched his waltz.

She felt the old man's tears upon her face. "Now you've finally come," he said, "and I'm too old."

* * * * *

Another first line: *She had started playing the organ again.*

They were old songs. *Through the Heather on the Hill. These Foolish Things Remind Me of You. They Can't Take That Away From Me.* The kinds of songs she'd been forced to learn years ago as a teenager, when her parents decided that what she really needed to help her get over her disappointment at being the only one in her group not to be elected cheerleader, was to learn to play a musical instrument.

They decided which instrument, too. An organ. A Hammond. The best of its kind for the day.

"You've got a nice touch," her father would say. Her three-year-old nephew, her wayward older sister's only son, would beg her to *play the orgie* every night when he went to bed. "You can always make your living playing dinner music in a nice restaurant," her mother said. It was supposed to be a compliment. When that was not at all what she longed to do.

So when the married man at work spoke to her obliquely of some lyrics to a song that he had heard—they were in a crowded conference room, among people who didn't know, and couldn't be allowed to know, about their affair—she went home to the old book of pirated love-songs her mother had insisted on passing along to her, and, after a twenty-year hiatus, she dusted off the Hammond, and she played the song.

A tinkling piano in the next apartment.
Those fumbling words that told you what my heart meant.

She practiced the melody over and over and over, with the Upper Drawer bars and Vibrato on, pretending that someday the man would find a way to come to visit her at her house. She would make dinner for him, and after dinner, he would sit down in her living room, and she would play.

"You have a nice touch," he would tell her. But he would sound just like her father. "You could play in some nice restaurant," he would add. But she would hear her mother speaking.

And she would have to laugh when he said those things, and so the affair would be over before it began. The flames of the demon of longing would be quenched by the humor she had long since developed to stay alive.

* * * * *

From the train, she can see evidence of families who have perished from this earth. Only their longing for something more than they were given still remains. A tree-house weathered into gray with middle age. Concrete stairs that lead nowhere. A fence trailing its broken lace among knotted weeds. A flower vase, Italian *majolica*, tossed down the embankment late one autumn afternoon, its hardy enough red geraniums having finally given in to the bitter frost.

Or a perfect ring of rusty holes on a purple and white sign that says *Wellesley*. The holes are the last vestiges of a small boy's

BB gun practice on that sparkling morning when he first refused to go to Sabbath School thirty years ago.

But then, what was it that you wanted if it wasn't *that*?

When David *went in unto Bathsheba*, as the Bible says, what was it he thought she could give him? The book says she was a woman who was *beautiful to look upon*. But there are lots of women, even now, who look like that. Better even. So what was it about Bathsheba that David loved? Why did he have to fall in love with someone who already belonged to someone else?

Imagine Bathsheba sitting across from David in an office. They can't even look each other in the eye. His pretext for calling her in here is something she has written for the company. A newsletter for her division perhaps. She's written a clear, precise summation of the facts.

"Do you pray about this, David?" she asks, drumming her little fingers on his desk.

He looks up, interested. Circumstances do not allow him to speak aloud, but she can read what he has to say right on his face. *Pray, Bathsheba? About falling in love with the wrong person at an inconvenient time?* He doesn't remember seeing anything about this in the Book of Psalms! Which, incidentally, he is about to *appropriate* so thoroughly that no Biblical scholar on earth will ever be able to prove definitively that most of these inspirational lyrics were really written by someone else.

"Because I do pray, David," Bathsheba says. "I surely do." She leans forward. "And you know what I prayed all day today, David, as I walked through the corridors, and as I went up and down on your elevators?"

The King is getting nervous. He shakes his head.

"I prayed, *Dear God, wash me clean,*" Bathsheba says. "I prayed, *Let me be more aware of You as infinite Love itself than I am of this very confusing love I have for your shepherd king.* And I prayed, *Please don't let me see this man today if I cannot be a blessing in his life.*"

But does this change the story? Does it keep David from setting Bathsheba's husband—poor, dull-witted, though devoted

Uriah—at the front of the battle so that he will be killed? Everything might have gone back to normal if the characters in the story had just been willing to leave well enough alone. Bathsheba and Uriah might have gone on living together happily enough. At least she knows that he will be faithful. He likes fighting battles for the King. He likes coming home every now and then after the various wars to climb into his nice, clean bed with his attractive wife. Nope, Uriah won't go off and leave B. when she gets a few wrinkles, or develops arthritis, or can no longer produce the warmth of a hot, young virgin—like the one who will eventually be assigned to the aging David by his advisors, one Abishag.

How about a new house for Bathsheba, for starters? *She has always enjoyed gardening,* someone says.

But that isn't going to do it, either, all by itself. Because Bathsheba knows that she and her husband were never *wild*. And that's what she wants, now that she's met David. What Bathsheba wants is to be very wild.

Let us consider another entry from her diary. *The problem with the human imagination is not that it is too wild. The problem with the human imagination is that it is never wild enough.* The story has its little possibilities, of course. Girl meets boy. Boy gets girl. Or else, does not. One or the other dies as a consequence. In any case, suffers. But does not go on.

I want to write Bathsheba's story so that it goes beyond that ending. I want to show the demon of longing to be a fraud.

But then that is always a good question, isn't it? Maybe even the one big question of our lives. After the longing. Say you get him. Or he gets you. Anyway, you both get what you thought you wanted. You get divorced. Or he does. You move away, someplace far from the office where you were the ultimate scandal for all time. Because that's all it ever was to anyone else there in the office, you know. It was never *love*. You move out to California where it is nice and warm. You buy your own place, just the two of you, in Carmel. Gradually, you make your own new circle of friends. People who know vaguely that you have some sort of past, but they don't care. You're the nice new couple who have moved here now.

What *then*, is what I am asking. Now that the obstacle has been removed, now that there is no reason for the longing, will you still love each other forever? Or will the dissatisfaction—he has halitosis, she lets the laundry go too long—will all the things that happen every day to all of us kill that now?

Would it ever be enough just to know that he loved you? Or will that, too, just end up in some silly song?

* * * * *

The correspondent never saw the old woman he had written letters for again. After the day that became known to the old church members as The Day of the Trucks, Naomi Brand is said to have disappeared. Some say she took the Friday night Concorde to Paris, just as she had been threatening to do for years, to live the libertarian artist's life that had been hitherto denied her, given the peculiar zeal of the family into which she'd been born.

Still others say that she fell asleep beneath the desk in her office that afternoon, after sharing the long-awaited consummation with her correspondent, and that she lies buried, a permanent relic, like Saint Cecilia, beneath the great stone floor of the demolished church.

As for the young man, her correspondent, a few years later he met a nice, educated woman and settled down. He wonders every now and then what might have happened if things had been different—if, for instance, Naomi had returned even one of his desperate messages that last day when he saw her across the pond.

For he had gone back to his office later, after everything, including the very building that contained his office, had been sold, and he had whispered into the voice-mail system that still miraculously functioned, as though from a distant galaxy: *Star me back! Star me back! Star me back!*

* * * * *

But then, why must the longing always be between a woman and a man? Why not a woman's longing for ballet? Ballet defies gravity even more than love. And in the end, we are not longing for each other, anyway, but for the power that will remove us from the ground.

If that's the case, my parents chose to bind my older sister to the earth.

I remember her tantrum after the recital. How angry she was in the car as we were coming home. She'd been cast as one of the principal Willies in the graveyard scene from *Giselle*, and somehow the orchestra leader—an amateur, after all—had skipped over an entire page of the music and left her out.

"That's it," my father said in a quiet voice.

For awhile, she paid her way at the dance academy by teaching the younger children Fundamentals of Classical Ballet. A few little boys looking bored or naughty. Hundreds of little girls, though, each of them wearing identical black leotards and pink nylon tights and miniature pink ballet shoes with instep straps.

I don't know what happened to that arrangement. Maybe with no time to do her homework, she began to fail in school. That would not have been acceptable to them. Or perhaps she became ill. She was often ill. Hot fevers that took her to places where she was small and kind because she could scarcely think. I would stroke her beautiful, thin, bare back for hours, with cool alcohol soaked onto cotton wool.

In any case, the teaching stopped, and therefore her own advanced tutorials at the ballet school. And, as my parents pointed out whenever people questioned their decision, she survived.

But I have seen my sister, a grown woman, her feet deformed from going on *pointe* long before she should have many years ago, as she wept within a darkened theater. Alarmed, I asked her: *What's wrong?* She shook her head. And there was no man with her. Only those lithe young bodies leaping from the earth.

* * * * *

And still another story, if allowed.

A couple who have known each other since high school, marry, have two children, separate for awhile, then come back together and have another baby, then get divorced. She remarries first, again to an old friend. But the husband meets someone new and falls in love.

Even after their divorce, they have remained good friends. "I never understood what you meant," the man tells his ex-wife. "Once, in high school, you said you knew you had fallen in love. And then you married me instead, and so you said you would never know what it would be like to have married someone you loved like that. And now here I am, about to marry the one great love of my life, so I'll let you know."

They laugh about it together. The absurdity of a middle-aged couple finding love!

The following Thanksgiving, for the sake of the children, they all come together for dinner. The wife and her new husband. The husband and his lover, soon to be his wife. All of the children, hers and his and theirs.

After dinner, the husband's great love of his life stands up on a chair in the dining room to give a toast. She is tall and elegant and lovely. She has a wonderful sense of humor. She is even kind. The ex-wife is happy for her old friend and former husband, because he's in love.

But just as his fiancée is raising her glass, she has a stroke. She falls down, dead, in front of everyone there at the table. In front of the ex-wife, their two teen-age children, and the little girl they had when they were still trying to make a go of their marriage, before they both reluctantly agreed to get on with the divorce.

"And she was no older than you are," the ex-wife tells me. "She wasn't even forty."

* * * * *

Or why not just the longing to be alone? The longing not to need, or long for, anyone other than oneself? The sound rain makes on a roof, or on an umbrella, and on the self inside. *I don't need anyone. I don't want anyone. I only need to long to need to be alone.*

Why not the longing of a mother for her child? For a daughter who has run away from home. Think of the letters of Mme. de Récamier, I believe it was, to her only child.

"Mommy," my daughter said to me once, "he loves you because you're cute and funny. He loves you for your sunglasses. But if he knew what was at the source of your buying those sunglasses, he would be scared to death."

When she was little, I told my father, "Daddy, all the passion I ever had for a man is in this child."

My father looked at the sleeping toddler I had draped across my arm. "I can see that," he said. "And I want you to know that I understand."

"What I mean, Mommy," my daughter said. "This man at work? The one who thinks he's in love with you. He isn't. And he is going to be very, very frightened when he gets to where he thinks he wants to go. Get rid of him. Get rid of Daddy. Get rid of all of them. Because none of them will ever know just who you are."

* * * * *

She stood in front of the office window, looking out.

She was wearing jeans, because even though she was the manager of her own division, she was planning to help her employees purge the files. She'd added her Indian jewelry to make up for the jeans, though. The men on her commuter train had approved with a nod and smile.

Rain was falling, and lightning struck while she was looking out the window. The man who is always in the story approached her from behind. "Watching the rain?" he asked. He slipped his slender hands beneath her arms.

These lines between them, whenever you try to write them down, just make you laugh. They're the stuff of bad novels, of *purple prose.* What is this hubris, this self-importance, that dares to make us think we are the first? *There is one thing I have always wondered about you,* my best friend said to me last December when she flew clear over from Europe to pull me out. *Why do you always have to think you are so different from everybody else?* She told me to quit, cold turkey. *Don't even tell him you're going. You can't afford to see him anymore.*

"This is my weather," the woman standing at the window tells the man. She points with a perfectly manicured finger at the purple sky.

"It's a good day to be watching the sea," he replies. "The bashing storm. Such power!" Is he suggesting they run away together, that they take a ride? As he sinks his lips into the flesh of her neck, he whispers, "A day to watch the lightning crash beyond the sea."

And of course they laugh. They cannot love each other under these circumstances. The human condition is too hilarious for words. Holding their aching sides they laugh until they cry.

* * * * *

Lately, the men on my train keep looking at my face. Whenever I catch them at it, I don't look away; I smile. I can see the longing in their eyes. What is it they think they are longing for? Not sex. Not with me, anyway. Are they longing for the woman they think they could have talked to? The one they missed when they settled down with the one they thought would help to keep them safe? Am I the one they left on the square in Albuquerque when they drove away?

Taking a break from the office, I notice two young guys at a table in my espresso bar. One's got his cello with him. He has Byron's hair, a rich, chestnut brown, long below his ears, with a little curl. A ruddy complexion. Obviously spends a lot of time outside.

The other one is non-descript, the one I never would have looked at for myself. He's wearing a baseball cap turned around on his head like they all do now. And he's saying to Byron: "Then when she started telling me how much she loved me? I thought, *Wow!*" He pushes the chair straight back about three feet, spreading his legs as he goes. "I was, like...." He motions, his hand between his legs, the fingers pointing straight up.

Byron laughs. I cannot like him anymore. "I've got something for that," he says. He means this as the line his baseball cap friend is supposed to deliver to the girl. More laughter.

But in the end the baseball cap wearer shakes his head. "I'd be *afraid* of that," he says.

And at the risk of *simple reductionism*, I think, *that's it!* That is the difference between us. He *would* be afraid. They are. We're the ones with the courage to lose our minds.

One summer when I was a teen-ager, I sang in the chorus of a local production of *Brigadoon*. For the first few weeks, I watched as two girls longed after the leading man. One of the girls had been raised in an Eastern European home. Her mother wouldn't let her date. But that didn't seem to be a problem at first, because the boy wasn't interested in the other one, who was very American, and very sophisticated, and who talked too much. He wanted the one with the quaint little kinky knot of ash-blonde hair. The one with the fresh pink skin and the peachy cheeks. He wanted the one with the dainty amethyst tear-drops on her ears. The one who was different from everybody else.

Then, one night during a chorus rehearsal, just after the young man had finished singing his love song, and was standing on a darkened stage with his arms outstretched, the calculating American girl managed to dance by and leap into his embrace. She kissed him fully, and at great length, right on the lips. Right in front of everyone in the cast.

And as she pirouetted away, the leading man stood there, his eyes fixed upon her retreating back. She got him for the rest of the summer.

Questions here: Could he talk to her? Could she to him? Where is the Eastern European girl at this point in time? Is the leading man one of the men who is looking at my face now on this train?

Listen. I'm not alone because I didn't marry the man I was in love with, or because the one I did marry doesn't understand. Nor because my older sister and I still don't see eye to eye, in spite of the fact that I understand her mourning for ballet. Nor because my mother and father are living somewhere else. I am alone because that is what it means to be alive.

* * * * *

But back to the story that started all of this.

Now that he thought about it, the train conductor believed that the old man had been considering the possibility for years.

The newspaper said that those who had witnessed the accident thought the old man had not been able to see what direction the 4:53 was coming from. But the old man had been known to take the same walk every afternoon, and the same trains had been running on almost exactly the same schedule, going the same direction on that track, for at least the last fourteen of his eighty-six years.

And so, the train conductor reasoned, the squinting had to be due to something else. A kind of concentration perhaps. As when you have been left with only two choices, and neither one of them can make you happy, but you must decide.

The last enemy that shall be destroyed is not, then, death, but the demon of longing. The one thing you have always wanted that is just beyond. In my case, what I wanted was to talk. I thought I had a great deal to tell someone, and for some reason I decided that was you. As it has turned out, you weren't who I thought you were. That's all that has happened. Please don't be sorry. It is very simple, really. It is not your fault.

In the end, there isn't anyone to tell.

NEWS OF THE WORLD

This morning. In Ethiopia? It rained.

I heard that while I was sitting at the breakfast table, just after Leonard had left us to go on maneuvers, and it was raining *here*. I was having me another cup of that real fine-ground coffee, you know the kind you can get here, I mean not at the PX, but if you go in town, and if you know how to tell the round blond German ladies at the Konditorei—*Hand-filter bitta shern and danka,* which many of the GI wives over here cannot but which I can. Meanwhile Shana, our first and so far only, who I had on base in Monterey before we came over this time last year, was dribbling Gerber's all over her high-chair with the pull-out tray.

But to explain the rain in Ethiopia and how it came? I have to back up.

Monday night Leonard and I had this huge enormous fight when we went to bed. Leonard grew up on the south side of Chicago, and I met him after he moved up to Michigan, when the two of us were working swingshift on the assembly-line at the General Motors plant outside Detroit. Leonard's and my *individualized sociological problem*, as the bleached blond welfare worker used to describe things to my mother whenever she came to visit when I was growing up, is that Leonard was born black, and I'm a white. It wasn't until after we got married and lost our jobs we started having fights.

This time it was about why he signed up with the Army for

four years in the first place, and didn't even ask me, just came on home, saying he'd gone into that Army storefront office in Detroit, where a skin-head pimply white-faced kid from Tuscaloosa, or from who knows where else, did a real job on Leonard. Says to Leonard, *Sure we'll help you, Mister.* Says, *There's always a place in the Army for a good man like you who's had it rough. Car industry been going down the tubes a lot lately now, ain't it. You got yer goddamn Japs and Germans, all yer import cars. Well, we got us a lotta good honest men like you here, Mister, good men who just come in here yep like you did, and sign up yep like you are, make sure you make yer name real legible there now won't you, on the top, and yep they come in here just like you did, cause they need a job.*

Guy in the recruitment center says that's really great we got us *a mixed marriage.* Says to Leonard, *Yessir, Mister, that is just what this wunnerful wunnerful country here of ours is all about. Races living together in harmony, just like you and yer little woman. Why, right there between you? You and yer wife and yer little brown baby? You got yer basic American dream, you got yer meltin pot.*

And he says to Leonard, *We got us a lotta mixed marriages here in the military, Mister, we got a lot.*

A few days later, they told us Leonard was going to Germany as a sergeant, and that I could go along. They have all these transportation vehicles over here to take care of, and I have to hand it to Leonard, after all that time at GM he's pretty good with trucks. They kept telling us, *Everybody's equal in the U.S. Army, People! And over there in Germany, too, People, as you'll soon find out, why, they don't know one race from another, nope they don't. Ah, they mighta hated a few Jews and such in their time whiles they was at it back in the old days there with Hitler and those old guys. But nowadays? Shit. The New Germany? Shit. When it comes to colored folks and white people living together, People? They don't give one fuck.*

It wasn't true, was what I found out. Not about me and Leonard, and not about other people, either. As for me and Leonard, I seen them eyeing us, middle-aged blond German couple out walking on a Sunday, say along the Rhine. I seen them stare at the baby in her stroller. Then I seen them look at me, and look at Leonard, up from the cocoa baby there in the stroller, with just a lift of eyes. I seen that almost invisible twitch the German lady couldn't keep herself from making with her tight red mouth, like she knew we were U.S. Army and everything, and so she knew she was supposed to be grateful for what the Americans did for the Germans when the war was done, and maybe we did have a lot of it among us, this marrying each other, she'd be thinking, just so she could give us all the benefit of the doubt, but she sure as hell wouldn't mix the races if she was in charge, nope, she would make damn sure if it was up to her, nobody would do such a mean thing to a little child.

And as regards the other people, there was this little Jewish man, getting on the bus downtown with me and Shana one day when Leonard was working, and I couldn't get any other wives to leave the base and go into town. Shana was in her stroller, and we were coming back from a Happy Meal at McDonald's there in town, getting on down there at the Bahnhof where we catch our bus, and this old Jewish man who was getting onto the bus with us helped me with Shana's stroller. He was wearing one of those little beanies on the back of his head like they wear them, not right on top, and he was smiling and saying, *Bitter bitter ick kan zare garn innen helfen,* or something like that, but I knew enough from the course I take at the base to know he'd like to help.

And I was so grateful I said without even thinking, just burst right out in English, *Thank you! Thank you very much!*

And he said, *Oh! You ah speaking English?* And I could tell he wanted really badly just to talk. But while his hands were busy helping me with Shana's stroller he wasn't looking behind him, and some skinny German kids in black leather jackets took his beanie off the back of his head, just tore it off, and threw it into the wind as the bus was leaving, so that he couldn't possibly go back and get it, or else he'd stop the bus.

Well, last Tuesday morning, after Leonard and I had this nasty fight, he left the bed real quiet to take care of Shana. I could hear him in there changing her out of her night diaper and into her

Pamper. Shana was saying, *Daddy, Daddy*, all happy and laughing, and all of this was going on while I was still in bed, deciding, when you come right down to it, if I should at all get up. Leonard is good to Shana, and that means a lot. But I seen plenty myself as a kid, some of it between my mother and father before he left her, because he was always drunk. So I don't forgive very easy. And on Tuesday morning, with a split lip that might pass as a blister, but with an eyesocket blue as a kid's summer evening when he can leave Detroit, I wasn't much in the mood for forgiving. I'd already been thinking of leaving anyway. And as I was lying in bed there, I was mad as hell.

I was remembering what Leonard said to me during the fight, that it was a good thing one of us had enough sense to be working, even if it was for the Army, because it was a cinch one of us had to have the brains to realize you don't have a place to live, or food for a baby, if you don't have a job.

And I remembered saying back to Leonard, *Okay you shit-faced nigger, you think we need you? You think for one minute I can't take that baby Stateside and stick this blond ass of mine sideways in the door of some rich white businessman's office and get a job? 'Cause if you think that, Leonard, I'll go where you'll never find us. I hear there's places out west they don't even have niggers, Leonard. Just white folks and Indians, Leonard—maybe a Mexican here and there, but no goddamn black-butted niggers, Leonard, not even one!*

Then Leonard was saying, *But I didn't do that to you, did I, Baby, Baby*, and he began to cry.

And me yelling back at him, *Of course you did it, you stupid nigger!* And then me falling, falling, falling over the edge of the bed and rolling off. And my mouth in the end like one of those punctuation marks some English teacher I had in high school kept yapping about one day when I went to class. This teacher kept saying, *A long stroke for emphasis, you see that, don't you, about the exclamation point now don't you, don't you, class.*

And now I had a long stroke for emphasis all right, and a dot just below the stroke that was caking blood. And Leonard saying during the night, *But I didn't do that, did I, Baby*. And him crying, and me crying, and him saying, *Oh why did this have to happen, how can it happen when we love each other this much.*

And he covered me up like I do Shana, with all our blankets, like he could keep me warm. And he touched my hair with his nice long fingers that are creamy smooth dark on the outside, like good German chocolate, but pink on the inside, very pink and soft. And the two of us went to sleep together like that, me folded in half against him all small the way I used to sleep against my sisters when we were growing up.

Even when I woke up sore on Tuesday morning I was in his arms. I stayed in bed clear until Leonard left us, because I knew he was going out in the woods on maneuvers, where they play around, them and the local German army. That is, if the local German army wants to come.

I waited there in bed till I knew for certain that Leonard left feeling awful, and till I knew it would be too late for him to be coming back inside the house.

I got up and went in to Shana. I wish I could say what I feel about Shana. When I look at her. When I come into her room with the *a-little-child-shall-lead-them* wallpaper, all those lambs and soft-mouthed lions sleeping together on the wallpaper from the PX that Leonard and I pasted up all by ourselves. I take one look at her, and no matter what it is I've been thinking—maybe it's how much I hate living in Germany, with nobody else here to talk to, just the other stupid wives, and him being here in the Army without even asking me, and how all our fights remind me of all that stuff I saw while I was growing up—and when I look at Shana, I give up. I see her over there holding onto the siderails of her Hasbro, doing these deep knee-bends, kind of up and down. She's got her fat little olive-colored legs bowed out in her stretch suit like a cowgirl over her corduroy t.v. boots, and she's just smiling and jumping when she sees me, and her dark brown hair is silky and fine like mine is, but with Leonard's curl. She sees me and she's laughing, and she loves me, that's all. She loves me, and she loves her daddy, and love is all she has for anybody, anywhere, in the whole wide world.

On Tuesday morning when I went in there that is what I saw. She didn't even notice the way my face looked. She just saw me. And I saw that her seeing had nothing to do with what her eyes were seeing. I saw both of us were seeing something else.

I think I said something like, *How's my little girl this morning?* I went over and put my arms around her, and nestled my nose and the sore part of my face into her hair that smelled even more like Johnson's than usual, because I hadn't used enough water when I rinsed it out. I just kept my head there against hers for a minute, just breathing in real slow and easy while I held her, till I got myself together, and then I picked her up.

I went out to the kitchen and put her in her high-chair. I walked over to the counter. I put some of that coffee I like into the filter cone, and I put my little Melitta on top of my blue-and-white Delft china mug.

This mug was a gift from Leonard when we rented a car last spring and drove up into Holland to see them raising tulip bulbs. Something about the wind-mill on the mug and the scene of these kids skating on the canal above the blue Delft ceramic ice, and the fact that we had a good time up there in Holland, me and Leonard and Shana, is why I always call it my favorite mug.

While the water was on the stove and I was waiting, because you have to have your water really boiling to make this coffee, to make it right, without even thinking I flicked on this portable radio we keep in the kitchen, because I usually listen to American Forces in Northern Europe Radio in the morning, no matter what. I do get tired of all their history lessons, though, their patriotic facts, say about maybe the American Revolution or Vietnam. And they have these little security slogans. Like, *If you think you know something important, don't take it home.*

First, the announcer just read the domestic disasters, all of it delivered in this neutral voice. Thousands of families were homeless in Ohio. The Mississippi and Missouri, like two great armies, had joined ranks and were invading people's fields and houses and driving everybody out. The governor of Ohio was flying to Washington and was going to visit the White House to ask for help.

Meanwhile, an Army truck on maneuvers in the Arizona desert had overturned. Dead was Private First-Class Henry Ludlow and an as yet unidentified female passenger on the right-hand side.

Then there was a report about a convict on death row in some prison in Oklahoma, a famous mass murderer, somebody I hadn't ever heard of, but a man who had gone berserk on a three-day spree back in the Sixties, while he was doing drugs. And now this man in the prison there in Oklahoma had just been stabbed.

I was looking at Shana in her high-chair and loving her till I could hardly stand it anymore. I knew I could forgive her for anything, anything at all, and that nothing could stop me from loving her, not even if she was that famous mass murderer in Oklahoma who had just now died.

Once, I was pushing Shana in her stroller through the PX, where I always shop, and this dressed-up officer's wife comes up to me and she says, *My, what a beautiful baby!* I could tell she was an officer's wife because she'd had her hair dyed black at a beauty parlor and she was wearing a lot of make-up with that dark brown lipstick and she was all dressed up, and she says to me, *Such a beautiful baby, honey! Why she's just the color of itty-bitty cocoa now isn't she, such a nice light brown.*

And I say to this officer's wife, *Thank you,* and I keep on pushing the stroller right on by. Because people come up to you and say that sort of thing about babies all the time.

But then she follows me and she says to me, this officer's wife says to me in this sweet, high voice, *Are you sure you wouldn't let me take her home with me, this itty-bitty cutesy, maybe just this once?*

I look straight at this woman, and I can't stop myself. I say to this woman, *Lady, can you love this itty-bitty when she's thirteen and wearing braces, and chewing gum, and swearing left and right at you, calling you a stupid selfish old bitch and a liar and a fuckin asshole and a lot of other stuff?*

This woman stares back at me wide-eyed, like she wants to run.

And I say to her, *Because I can, you know, lady. I can love this baby forever. I can love her even if she slits my throat and divides my bloody body into a hundred parts and sticks me out in the garbage, if it comes to that.*

And so on Tuesday, standing there looking at Shana in my kitchen, I was thinking about that man in Oklahoma who murdered all those innocent people, and then one day all those years later while he was waiting in prison to be put to death he got stabbed himself. And I got to thinking about that man's mother, how she must have felt. And all of a sudden, I got to wondering why I couldn't stretch it, like it was some kind of elastic, that kind of love. Maybe right up, say, to Leonard, for starters.

That made me think about Leonard's mother. A couple of years ago, there where she lives in Chicago, some door-to-door preacher got to talking with her, and now she prays a lot. She'd written me over here how much she loved me and how good she thought I was for Leonard, and she didn't mind it quite so much anymore, she said, me being white. She said she prayed someday God might send us home from Germany, and maybe, she said, God would have us settle right there in Chicago beside her, or else if we didn't want that she'd be happy, if invited, she said, to find a place and come live near us, in Detroit.

And I kept thinking as it dawned on me, *Babies, that's what.* Everyone was some mother's baby. I saw this long line of mothers and babies. Leonard's mother and him. Me there in the kitchen with Shana. And there's this long string of mothers nobody's heard of, but we're the ones who know how to do it, how to bring it off.

I must have looked pretty strange just standing there staring, because Shana started looking worried. She said one of her two words, *Mom-0?* With that little upturn at the end she's learning, like a question, that is in her voice. And then, because she looked so worried, I pulled out the tray of her high-chair and I picked her up.

And I was walking around and around my kitchen, holding Shana against me, my baby, arms wrapped around. And I was thinking, *Why can't I just hold all of them, Leonard and the Jews and the Arabs and Russians, the Afghans, and the former Yugoslavs, and the murderer out in Oklahoma, and the people down there by the rivers, and all of the others I've never heard of, just as if I were holding Shana, but go beyond?*

That's when the radio announcer said the people in Ethiopia were still going hungry. There was a drought and nothing was growing. Food was pouring in from America and other places, out of the goodness of people's hearts, but it still wasn't enough. The different groups couldn't agree on a plan of delivery. Each group was stopping the others so they could be in charge. And anyway, the announcer said, even if they did all get it together, what the people in Ethiopia really needed more than anything else was a little rain.

Rain. So they could get something growing. So they wouldn't have to depend on everybody else and could help themselves. Because even with all the donations, and even if the different factions could all *comply*, the announcer kept saying, as long as it didn't rain in Ethiopia, the people would just go on starving, because there would still be drought.

I stood there holding Shana. I stood there holding Shana in my arms.

Start small, I said. You can do this. Maybe you can't quite do the Russians, or the Yugoslavs, because they've been killing each other off now for a long, long time. But food is something a mother can handle. Focus your attention on this thing with drought.

And I thought:

A mother would make it rain in Ethiopia.

A mother wouldn't let her children die or go hungry.

I began to feel love pouring. All those children, all their mothers. Pouring out.

And then I thought:

But then how could this happen in the first place? Is there no mother in Ethiopia? Is there no mother in Ethiopia to stop this drought?

And so I thought:

Hush now, hush now. You'll get in the way of what I'm doing. Hush that doubt.

And for a few minutes. Just a few minutes? I loved clear down into Ethiopia. *I felt it.* I was standing there holding Ethiopia in my arms. And I wish I could describe it, blue and round and weightless-heavy, how it felt.

And that's what it was, what happened.

Because this morning. In Ethiopia. It rained.

PURPLE HEART

Early morning was his favorite part of the day. No matter how late he'd turned in the night before—and most likely he'd spent the evening having a few beers with the other guys from Nam, down at that old place on Fourth Street that had just been taken over by the U.S. Government and donated anonymously to the Veterans of Foreign Wars, only everybody knew about it— no matter how late he'd stayed up, his eyes would snap right open at four-fifteen.

It had started in Nam. This one day they'd been checking out reports of the enemy, wading through rice paddies and worrying about traps, not knowing if one of their legs'd get blown off in the process, and these two guys on his left had tried inching their way across the territory *together*. Jesus. It seemed to him afterwards that he'd heard the thing click, and then that the two guys had stopped and turned to each other, and had looked into each other's eyes, intimate as an old married couple, before blowing up. But even though it all played back to him like that over and over in slow motion, the click, the look, the rise, he knew the whole thing really had taken place in a split second, the two guys shooting into the air like rockets, holding hands.

For some reason, the C.O. wanted to list those guys as MIAs. Nobody could exactly argue with that, since just about everything was missing you could identify. But somewhere a couple of women were probably still badgering Washington about those men who were *missing in action*, hoping maybe they'd show up as some of those Americans a newspaper reporter had said he saw working up in some hell-hole in Cambodia as captive slaves. *Tell the world about us*, the men had supposedly shouted to the newspaper reporter in Cambodia. When he could've told them there wasn't a hell of a lot of sense to that, since no one cared.

On the morning he saw those two guys go up, he had happened to wake up at four-fifteen. Everybody else was still sleeping. He raised himself up on his elbows and he couldn't believe how pretty the whole thing was. He sat and stared. There was a ground fog rising and everything was pink—the earth around him, the birds flying over the paddies, the faces of his sleeping buddies, the goddamn *air*. It was then that he knew he'd been chosen to survive. You stay in an environment like that long enough, in all that Oriental mind-stuff, and some of it is bound to rub off on you. And something told him that morning, waking up early like that, that he was going to make it through this and go home. So when the two guys got blown up like that, not fifty feet away from him, with him still left standing there with the others, he knew he'd been given some kind of message. From then on, he wasn't afraid of anything. He knew he had only to get up early enough every morning to *listen*. Nothing would get him if he got up first and *knew* it wouldn't get him. It wouldn't dare.

Nowadays, even though he didn't need to protect himself so much like that, he still got up early from habit. Every morning, he would go over to the kitchenette in this motel room he was renting by the week, and boil himself some water and have some tea. It would kill the guys down at the bar to know what he drank in the morning. Twining's Lapsa Oolong. Something to put him in touch with all that mind-stuff of the Great Far East. Later, about seven-thirty, he would take his usual walk down to the Circle K convenience store, and he might have a cup of coffee with the Spanish woman who ran the store at that hour of the morning. But when he first woke up he liked the Oriental, smoky flavor of that Chinese tea. It sort of brought the whole thing into focus for him. He'd sit down with the tea in a mug and watch the lights of Albuquerque against the mountains. He could just see the lights over the top of his bathroom window. He got a weekly rate here and with the kitchenette he could fix himself coffee and Campbell's for supper, and it was a hell of a lot better than the place he'd rented in South Dakota near his parents when he first got home.

They'd wanted him back the way he was before the war. They hadn't wanted him to talk about it, and deep down he could understand that, he really could. But then right away they wanted him to just pick up and take some kind of job, and he hadn't known right off what he wanted to be. *What ya wanna be, kid?* It was the same thing people had always asked him when he was growing up. Back then, it was a baseball player. Or a fireman. Nowadays, maybe a cowhand on somebody's ranch. He couldn't quite make his mind up, though. He wasn't sure. His parents suggested he could go back to school on his GI benefits, then come into the lumber business with his father. But he guessed he waited around too long trying to decide on that one, too, because after awhile they told him they didn't want him hanging around there anymore, so close to home.

So he drifted down to Albuquerque, where he had a sister. She'd gone to school at the University of New Mexico, and been in some sort of club for women, and ended up in the same social set as the wife of the mayor's son. She lived with her ex-football-star husband in Corrales, to the west of town, with three or four different kinds of show horses and a bunch of dogs. Her house was built all adobe, the genuine clay bricks hand-made by the locals, not the fake plaster kind, and she made it very clear to him, the first time he showed up at her place for dinner, that he wasn't going to wear his old Army issues and his beard and ponytail and gold-rimmed glasses, not in *there*. That era was over, she told him. He didn't see *her* still wearing her sandals and long skirts and Indian headbands, did he? Not anymore.

Though he hardly ever had any contact with his family now, he thought he'd seen his sister yesterday, when he was on his usual seven-thirty walk to the Circle K. He'd been walking along Fourth Street, wearing his Army issue parka because it was cold, and carrying his sleeping bag on his back because he'd got to talking with the Spanish woman at the store and he'd told her how the seams on his bag were splitting and she'd told him to bring the thing over and she'd fix it up for him between customers in nothing flat. That was when he thought he saw his sister. She was driving a red sports car, maybe one of the fancier Toyotas, but that was something else that didn't seem so important, knowing the names of cars now, anymore, and she was alone, her dark hair flying, sunglasses on at even that hour of the morning, her lips shaped with something dark, some kind of terror, in a big red O. He couldn't figure out why she'd be out at that time of the day, because she didn't work. She stared real hard at him, her mouth open like that, as she drove by, but when he raised his hand in a greeting, she didn't seem to know exactly who he was.

Funny he should think of that again this morning, boiling his water and making his Lapsa Oolong. Like there was some significance to his seeing her down by the Circle K on Fourth Street, driving by. Orientals would know exactly how to *listen* to such things. They knew how to hear the messages that every one of us gets inside our heads. Westerners didn't develop that power the way Asians did. That's something he'd really noticed in Vietnam. That day the guys went up, for instance, they'd had reports of the enemy in that section, and so they were checking out the paddies. But the Viet Cong had already known somehow they were coming, and they'd disappeared.

That was how it always was. You'd arrive at a village that was supposedly full of sympathizers, and the whole thing would be deserted. All you'd find was an eerie silence. Maybe a few baskets hanging outside a hut, or a pair of shoes. They knew what it was they were doing. You didn't. He was sure it came down to *listening*. They were just better at it than we were, that was all.

He'd had a lot of fun, when he first came home, hearing his father go on and on about the Russians and how his own son

with all his isolationist anti-American bullshit was just proof positive
that the goddamn rooskies was gonna bring us to right where they
had in mind for us to be, which was on our goddamn knees.

He would wait till his dad finished, till his dad really thought
he had him, and then he would sit back in that Barcolounger
that was his dad's, in his parents' playroom, and he would sort of
smooth out his battle jacket and sort of stretch his limbs out a
little, and then, settling his hands behind his head, he would tell
his dad, *But ya see it ain't the goddamn rooskies ya gotta look out for,*
Daddy. 'Cause you can see what the goddamn rooskies is doing.
They're right there in plain sight where the CIA can see em, all their
bomb factories and tanks, and their KGB. No, what you really gotta
worry about now, Daddy, is the enemy that's got a mental *weapon.*
And we Americans don't know shit about it. Yer Asians is the ones
gonna have us under their power. Not the rooskies. And it'll all just
be by thinking. *What you better look out for now, Daddy, are yer*
goddamn basic gooks and Japs and Koreans, and yer Red Chinese.

It was during one of those talks they kept having that his
father said he was crazy and threw him out. *And you a Purple*
Heart veteran, his father shouted. *I never thought I'd see the day*
it'd come to this.

* * * * *

But that was a long time ago. Life really wasn't treating him
so bad. He got his check every month from the government, and
it was enough to cover his room here and his soup and coffee and
the Lapsa Oolong, plus a round every once in a while for all the
guys he knew down at the bar. He cashed his check as soon as it
came, down at the Circle K with the Spanish woman who liked
him. And if he ever needed anything more than that, more than
what his government check gave him any single month, then he
just signed up to work for a couple of days with one of those
companies that were putting up all those tacky little houses on
the new west side. He'd just hammer a couple of nails in some
pre-fab walls and collect his pay.

Now he pulled on his clothes and sat in the hard, greasy blond chair they provided for him here in the motel, and he drank his Lapsa Oolong and watched the lights of Albuquerque through the bathroom window as they all went out. What he'd like to know was, how many of those lights kept shining throughout the day, but you just couldn't see them. That was something else that just might hold some kind of meaning here this morning, but he could not think what. If only he could be just a little bit more like the good ole Asians, and could just plain *think*.

The money that came from the government had been another thing that had bugged his father when he first came home. "No son of mine is going to claim he's crazy and get paid for it by the United States of America!" he'd heard his father shout one morning at his mother. His mother, always a religious woman, had answered softly. *A soft voice turneth away wrath*, she used to say. Now even his mother seemed to have her doubts. "But he *was* injured in some way, wasn't he, Martin? Didn't they use to call it *shell shock* when you were a soldier, what he has? And they *did* give him a Purple Heart for *something*, didn't they, Martin? I mean, the government must know what they're doing, Martin, or they wouldn't pay."

He had a chance once to make a little more than he already was with the government, but he never followed up on it. A letter had come with his check saying some Senator was sponsoring an inquiry into Delayed Stress Syndrome, and they felt perhaps he would be willing to help them in their research, and they would of course pay him for his assistance, and the Senator personally wanted him to know he was personally planning to inform the public of this problem, because he was personally aware. . . .

He got up from his chair, closed the bathroom window, rinsed out his cup in the kitchenette and brushed his teeth. It was nice of the Spanish woman to fix his sleeping bag. His bag was like an old friend, and he was eager, more eager than he wanted to let her know, to get it back. So he was going to set off a little earlier than usual this morning for the Circle K.

He pulled on his jacket and picked up the check that had

come yesterday. Two rounds on him tonight could come from that. He closed the door to his room and stepped out onto the hard red clay surface of the parking lot. It cracked him up, what they called *landscaping* here. A few dusty juniper bushes stuck in a kind of island out in the middle of the dirt. Probably they'd had decorative gravel around the bushes at one time. That's what they called what they put in the yards in front of all those ticky-tacky houses he helped put up on the new west side. Decorative gravel. The decorative gravel in front of the motel had long since succumbed to the wind that came when the seasons changed. After twenty years of fifty-mile-an-hour winds, all the decorative gravel had been covered up.

As he walked, he glanced at the restaurant a few places down from his motel. He always passed this restaurant called the Cowboy's Friendly Grill and Steak Café. This hour of the morning no one was in there. They didn't open up till around ten o'clock. He went behind the restaurant to see what they might have left over in their garbage pails. He'd looked through there once when there was a perfectly good T-bone somebody had ordered and hadn't even touched. He took his time eating it, too, enjoying the congealed grease on the surface and gnawing his way right down to the good pink bone.

But this morning there wasn't much in the garbage. He went back to the front of the restaurant and took some stock. People were all starting out for work now. Some of them would probably stop at the Circle K, and he'd exchange a few words with them over a cup of coffee. *You were in the service were ya fella? Where ya from?* It was a nice enough way to pass a couple hours. It was funny how a place got to mean something to you.

As he approached the big red and white plastic sign of the Circle K, he had the oddest feeling of coming home. He thought about the fact that some people might be coming into this store this morning maybe just this once. Maybe they were on their way out to California, for example, just driving through. And yet to him it was the place he most liked to visit every day. The people who ran it changed pretty often, and they all had different reasons for working there, so he was always getting to talk with someone interesting, someone new. The Spanish woman who was fixing his bag had been the most steady. She had four kids at home and she could come down here at night and work through the early hours of the morning while they were still asleep. She'd leave them their breakfast, she told him, and then the two older ones could dress themselves and help each other get off to school. By ten, she would be home again for the little ones. Then if she could get them to take a nap after their lunches, she'd get back in the sack herself, she told him, laughing, and get some sleep. It seemed to him she was a very conscientious mother, trying to raise those children all by herself. She'd tell him, whenever he talked with her, exactly what she'd left her kids to eat.

He saw as he entered the Circle K that she was there. But she had some customers. He waved to her and stepped over to look through the magazines. He crouched on the floor and thumbed through a motorcycle magazine that showed a big guy on a Harley-Davidson. He was wearing black leather pants and a jacket with silver rivets. He had his hands on the bars of the chopper like he was shifting, and he was grinning out at the world through his big white teeth. Behind the motorcycle rider, there was a young girl with very blond hair down to her shoulders. She was wearing clean pink shorts and a clean white T-shirt that had little cat-paw designs all over it, as if a little cat had jumped up on her pretty shoulders and walked down her front.

He looked more closely at the girl on the back of the chopper in the picture. There was just barely the trace of a smile on her fresh, sweet lips. He thought he'd like to meet that girl, she looked so sweet. *What is it? What is it?* He felt something leave him, make him empty. Now the Asians, hell, they would know exactly what that meant.

He heard a loud voice and turned back to the counter where the Spanish woman was working. Some kind of problem was going on. She was arguing with some kid, shaking her head and yelling at him. "You kids don't got the slightest idea, do you, what it means to work! I got four kids to home I gotta feed with the peanuts I'm making in this place, and I still gotta put up with the likes of you! I told you, kid, there ain't even ten dollars in here, 'cause of the lock-box, and I don't *got* a key."

The only other people in the store were two men wearing business suits. They were inching slowly backwards, away from the counter, their eyes wide. It seemed to him he almost saw those two guys he'd known in Vietnam, and that in a moment they would be going up all over again, just two little kids in trouble, facing whatever it was out there on the playground, holding hands.

"I don't want no problems here, lady," the kid was saying. He had his back towards the magazine rack. "Just give me the cash that's in the box that you can get your hands on, and shove it over." His long black hair was tied back with a piece of leather. Two holes in the back of his jeans revealed his butt. "You just give it to me quiet and there won't be any trouble."

It dawned on him, standing there watching, that this kid didn't even know he was in the store. He'd been crouching low by the magazines when all of this started. If he moved forward little by little, he could get behind the kid and surprise him, maybe pull back his arms and pin him till they could get some help.

The Spanish woman had her hand in the cash register, pulling out some bills. "So what you gonna do when you use *this* up, asshole?" she was saying. "You know you ain't gonna get away with it twice in this goddamn town. Kids like you, they think they. . ."

The businessmen seemed frozen to the gray tile floor. One of them was clutching a refillable mug of coffee, a white plastic mug filled to the brim with coffee and marked real big in green with *Circle K*. The businessman's hands were shaking so bad that some of his coffee was spilling out.

He thought maybe that one businessman noticed him moving, as he slowly made his way up behind the kid, because the guy's eyes got even wider and then rolled back up in his head a little, like he was passing out.

The Spanish woman handed the kid the money in a bag. By now, she'd stopped talking, because she'd seen him sneaking up behind the kid, and he could tell she was worried. He shook his head to signal her she should not let on. But just as he caught her eye the kid noticed what was happening and whirled around and faced him, holding the knife and the bag with the money. The kid started for the door, to run away.

He threw his whole weight into the kid's body, his hands around the kid's middle. But his battle jacket got caught up on his shoulders, and the kid was beating on his head and kicking, and holding onto the bag of money and shouting, "You better let go, Mister, or I'll hurt you, I swear I'll hurt you, and I wouldn't wanna, I wouldn't wanna. . . . "

So he used his knee. The kid doubled over in two, and swung the knife.

From then on it all went in slow motion. He heard the pocket on his jacket as it caught and ripped. It was like that whole scene all over, the two guys rising up together in the slow, pink air, and him there watching, as if it had nothing to do with him, from far away. And not feeling it, either, just watching the whole thing and sipping his Lapsa Oolong, and the kid pulling his knife out of the ripped pocket of the Army jacket and saying, "But I told you, didn't I, Mister. . . ."

And as he slipped into the red-running pink sky, going up like a rocket, holding someone's hand, he heard a voice saying, "They're coming, they're coming to help you, can't you hear me, please oh please will you stop bleeding, will you, honey, oh please, will you just, wait."

He saw the lights of Albuquerque going out over his bathroom window, one by one, and he thought again how he had been chosen to survive, and how those Asians knew a whole lot more about survival than we did. How to listen, how to go with it. And he drifted on out the window with the lights.

WHEN AMELIA SMILED

There is still a question, of course, whether she ever went down at all. The last time I took my father, Will Massey, silver-haired, stately, tall and healthy at seventy-eight, to one of the Search for the Truth About Amelia meetings, there was even a heretic who insisted that Amelia Earhart was a spy, and that she had landed perfectly normally in Japan and then gone on to live with Emperor Hirohito and his wife, to whom she personally delivered America's top-secret military plans.

This particular theory had the American government forgiving Amelia for her betrayal and letting her return after the war to live out a life of solitude. Her betrayal was not without its consequences, though. Amelia had to return as a nun on a Red Cross ship and, furthermore, she had to agree to submit to shock treatments that would make her surrender her pilot identity in the States.

"That's bullshit," my father told me the night of the conference in our motel. "Amelia would never have agreed to such a thing. And give up everything she ever knew about flying planes? I feel sorry for the guy, sweetheart, and I'd like to help. But Jesus. A *nun* for Christ's sake? No, not Amelia. Not on your life."

The heretic, Benny Overfield, a pale, middle-aged little man in a wheelchair, had told my father during breakfast at our motel that he'd been suffering from ill health. He said he'd already undergone four blood transfusions in the last eighteen months.

And so, because he couldn't hold down a regular job anymore, he was hoping to make his living going around the country giving these talks about what had really happened to Amelia Earhart and her plane.

"I am hoping very much that you will support my findings," Benny told my father at breakfast. "And to that end, I'd like to pay for your accommodations here at the conference—your room for you and your daughter here, and all your meals, and whatever else will make you have a pleasant stay."

He produced from his briefcase an old photograph he'd found in some archive in Southern California. "Look, Mr. Massey," he said. "Over here by the left engine. Is this not you?"

My father peered into the photograph, fascinated as though with an image in a crystal ball. He let out a soft whistle. "Well, I'll be damned!" He turned to me, enraptured. "I remember the day this was taken, honey," he said, hardly able to contain himself. "The day I've always told you about. When Amelia smiled."

I reached for the photograph and focused on the spot that the heretic was pointing at with his fat, pale forefinger. The picture showed my blurred but unmistakable father, standing among perhaps thirty other young airplane mechanics, all of them proudly posed in front of Amelia's plane.

"All I'm asking," Benny said, "is, let me say my piece at the conference this afternoon. I know you think you can't go along with my theory, Mr. Massey, but if you'd just agree to, you know, just keep your convictions to yourself and let me talk."

On that note, Benny picked up our bill for breakfast and we left.

I grew up with Amelia. Not that we went to school together, or were chums, but that her life, and her attempt to become the first woman pilot to fly around the world, became one of the stories on which my father brought me up. "You can be anything you choose," he would tell me. "Look at Amelia, honey. Women just weren't flying in those days."

My father was an aircraft mechanic at a small airfield in Southern California in the Thirties, even before he and my mother were married, and his connection with Amelia Earhart was that he once had serviced the Lockheed Model 10 in which she crashed.

"Not on that particular trip, mind you," he always added, as though if he had been servicing Amelia's plane when she set out with her dashing male co-pilot, then the two of them might have had a little better luck.

"She was everybody's darling," my father said. "The photographers dogged her. The newspaper men and the photographers followed her around every goddamn place she tried to go."

One day, the newspapermen and photographers followed Amelia Earhart out to the airfield where my father, along with a lot of other young mechanics, was servicing her plane.

"We had work to do," my father said. "And here were these guys swarming around with their cameras and notepads, see, and they didn't know zilch about airplanes. They were just out there on that airfield in our way."

Then my father told me how it happened that Amelia smiled. "Well, sir, I guess she could see we could've cared less about all those photographers and writers. And I guess, being the professional she was, she caught, shall I say, our *irritability?*" Here, my father always chuckled, a small *heh heh*. "Because," he would continue, "just as she was letting those guys get one more shot of her stepping up to the cockpit, she suddenly turned to them and said, *This'll be it, boys. We've got to let these fellas do their jobs.*"

At this point in the story, my father inevitably stopped the plot. A massive sob lay waiting. A permanent state of mourning, an ongoing wake, floated at the bottom of my airplane-mechanic father's romantic heart, like Amelia's plane on the floor of the ocean.

I waited while my father remained with his head bowed for a few minutes before going on with Amelia Earhart and her plane.

"And then there was that useless playboy husband she left behind." My father's worship was rich with the self-righteousness of one who knows that the pure and innocent object of his worship has been wronged. "I will never forget the day Amelia came to see us out on that airfield," my father whispered through the stricture of his sorrow. "How, as she turned to walk away from the plane with the reporters—oh, sweet Jesus, but she was lovely—she tossed her head, like this."

In the story, my father *became* Amelia Earhart, a tow-headed, high-spirited girl who tossed her curls. "She caught my eye over her shoulder," he said. My father moved one muscular shoulder forward in a seductive shrug, and looked back at me with a little smile. I imagined succulent bow lips, slightly tinged with red. "Then she smiled directly at me, right at me, I'm telling you, honey, as though we were this close."

Most of the people who've invested any time in Amelia still say that her plane was lost, and that she and her co-pilot nose-dived into the deep blue waters of the Pacific at a rate of speed that would have buried them in over two thousand feet of water in nothing flat.

"Still," my father would argue. "Still. If she did plummet into the water like they said, why didn't the divers find the wreckage beyond that reef?"

It was probably this last remnant of hope still left in my father that attracted the heretic to him in the first place. If my father was willing to listen to other theories about the possibilities of Amelia's whereabouts—the theories about the extra plane, for instance, the one that goes that she was really flying a second Lockheed Model 10 that was far more experimental than the first—then why not his?

And my father was always a gentleman. To me, he might have said about Benny's theory, *That's bullshit.* But that was well after the conference, when we were alone. At the conference itself, when all the people gathered there asked him if he thought Benny's nun/spy theory was even a possibility, he just said, very quietly, "No, I don't."

The conference people, none of whom were at all interested in the heretic's theory anyway, did, on the other hand, want to hear everything my father, an eye-witness of sorts after all, might have to say.

"Were there really two engines?" they asked him. "The one

she usually flew with, and then this other top-secret governmental thing she stowed away?"

My father, whose airplane stories had met with more and more of my mother's disinterest, and finally her disapproval, all their married lives, had learned to look to me for the signal to go ahead.

"It's all right, Daddy," I said. "I think these people *want* to hear what you have to say."

My mother had issued edicts about subject matter and length whenever my father started in with his airplane tales, especially the one about Amelia. My mother didn't yet know my father that day out on the airfield when Amelia smiled, and over the years, as she herself went from the tall, raven-haired beauty she had been considered in her day, to a fuller, rounder-figured woman who unabashedly used Loving Care, she grew tired of the story about Amelia Earhart. She had no room in her house for that slender, tow-headed, romantic, rebellious girl, who never got any older, and who never died.

And in that way that is peculiar to daughters, I could see both sides. "He's got to stop living in the past," she told me once by way of explanation after she'd been particularly rough on him. "I've had to."

When it came time for my father and me to check out of the motel after the Search for the Truth About Amelia conference, Benny Overfield was there to pay our way, just as he'd said he would. My father wouldn't hear of it, of course, but the effect on the poor man and his theory was the same.

"I had thought, Mr. Massey," the heretic said, looking up sadly at my father from his wheelchair, "that you had come to support my efforts to keep our hopes for Amelia's possible whereabouts alive." He laughed and made a friendly but futile swipe at my father's side. "I thought," he told my father, "you weren't going to talk."

* * * * *

My father told that story about Amelia for the last time about a year after that particular Search for the Truth About Amelia meeting. My mother had arranged to have a realtor come appraise their condo in Dexter, where I'm still living with my daughter Julie after my divorce, and where my parents followed me and my ex-husband Howard and Julie six years ago, after my father retired from making planes, so that, as my mother put it, *We can learn to be grandparents for a little while.*

But Michigan is frigid in January, and my father, a third-generation Westerner, hates the cold. Meanwhile, my mother, a third-century New Englander, had outright refused ever to set her foot down out West again. So they compromised. They decided to sell their place in Dexter and move down to West Virginia, a state where no one on either side of their families had lived before.

"That way," my mother said cheerily when they announced their plans, "your father and I will be even. Neither one of us knows anybody there who knows the old stories. So both of us will be obligated to give our lives a brand new try."

I didn't understand the choice for West Virginia, and I didn't understand why they waited to move there till I needed them in a way I never had. But I did understand everything they had to say about the cold. Every year, if you compare the obits in the local newspaper in Michigan in January to those in, say, July, you'll see that an inordinate number of old people, even some not so old, give up and die in January, just because they know that Michigan's spring still has to be another four months off.

The visit with the realtor turned out to be a kind of oddly predictable family disaster. Right before the agent arrived, my mother coached my father on what he was to do and not to do, and particularly what he was supposed to say and not to say.

"Now don't you start talking about airplanes," she warned him, wagging her index finger in his face. "You let this woman do all the talking. She has to get on to other things when she's through with us."

But the realtor happened to be married to a pilot who flew in and out of Detroit with Northwestern, so my father naturally had to tell her his story about Amelia's smile.

"I was *fuming* inside when that real estate woman left!" my mother said. "It was all I could do, while your father was sitting there in our white living room with his dirty feet up on my coffee table in his old blue socks, and with this poor woman, this agent, this poor captive audience sitting there going, *ooh really?* and *ahhh!* It was all I could do just to remain *polite!*"

"So what did you do?" I asked. "You didn't stop him right in front of the woman, did you? That would not be nice."

"Oh, no," my mother said cagily, her lips red and tight. "Oh, no, I didn't do *that*. I waited until the agent left. And remember now, I'm so mad at your father I can barely speak. And your father says to me, he says, all jaunty and happy because he's got around me anyway and told his tale, *Well, Jeannine, what do you say we drive over to the mall to Burger King and get a bite?* So I go. I go with your father to Burger King. I don't say anything, understand, but I just go. And then we're sitting there in Burger King, and by now he's figured out I'm mad, because I'm not saying anything, and probably it shows, because my lips are squeezed."

Pursing her lips, she gave me a little demonstration. "Just like this."

"So Daddy asked you what was bothering you," I said.

She forced a strangled laugh. "Your father says to me, *Well, sweetheart, I guess from the way you're not talking to me, you're pretty pissed.*"

I shivered. I knew my father had to have been worried if he'd used a word like *pissed* with my mother. *Your mother is a lady*, he always said.

"Then I let him have it," my mother said. She smacked her right hand into her palm several times, like a baseball pitcher working a glove with a tightened fist. "I said to him right there in Burger King through my smashed closed lips, *Look, Willard Massey, I am sick to death of your shirt-tail relationship with Amelia Earhart all these years.* And I told him, *'Because that's all it is, you know, Will. It's a shirt-tail relationship, that's all it is, and I have been listening to that one goddamn, worn-out story about your wonderful Amelia all this time. So why didn't you marry her, I want to know? I don't ever want to hear that story about Amelia and her goddamn plane again!"*

By now, I was holding onto the armrests of my chair, my back stiff and upright, in exactly the same terrified position I assumed the one time I was ever really inside any of the airplanes my father serviced, and it was taking off. The plane I was in that once was a Lockheed 1011, and I got in it after Howard left me a note saying that he'd fallen in love with a man he'd met on one of his sales trips to New Jersey, and that the two of them were going to live together in Florida for awhile. I took a few days off from my receptionist job at the Dexter Sheet-Coating Company, and I arranged for Julie to stay over at a friend's, and without telling anybody, including my parents, I flew down to Florida, not in order to talk to Howard, mind you, because I didn't really much want to talk to Howard at that point, but just so I could have an idea what he might be thinking. I rented a car and drove around a little, and I got out and walked on some beaches and picked up shells. And so when I got back, even if I still didn't understand Howard, at least I had something tangible I could show to Julie, this bag of shells.

"So what did Daddy say after all of that?" I asked my mother.

"Well, he was quite contrite," my mother said. She twisted her hands and looked off in the distance. I could see it dawning on her, what she'd done. Amelia's smile and airplane, after all, made up a life. "Yes," she said, as though she was still trying to convince herself. "Yes, I'll have to say he was quite contrite."

And I guess that was true enough. Because for the next three months, during the whole process of my parents' move, I never heard my father mention Amelia Earhart, or her Model 10-A, or any of the current theories about what had happened to her, again.

And so, when the heretic from the Search for the Truth About Amelia group called me up to find out how he could get in touch with my father, whose phone had of course been disconnected by that time, I wondered what my father would have to say.

Julie had to interrupt her Suzuki practice to get the phone. I was in our bathroom, looking at my face. It was pale green, because I had an awful cold. Next winter, I vowed to myself, I would be out of Michigan if it killed me.

"If that's some telephone solicitor," I growled at Julie when she came to get me for the phone, "you're going to watch Mommy tear somebody's head off. I'm going to pluck out his heart and his gizzards and eat them raw before your very eyes."

Julie stood there with her violin tucked up under her arm in that way they teach in Suzuki. She looked worried. "How would you do that?" she asked. "Would you do it a little piece at a time? And what if the man has some children? Or a real nice wife?"

I stomped on by Julie and picked up the phone. "Hello?"

At the other end of the line, I heard a slow, weak voice. I wish I could describe that voice. It was a voice that contained the entire Michigan winter, thick and white and flat the way it was falling outside my window from the winter storm watch that had been scheduled for all that day. It was a voice that had a whole history of unfulfilled dreams in it, and missed opportunities, a lifetime of projects given up.

"Amelia?" the voice said. It was a voice that lay at the bottom of an ocean floor.

"Yes," I answered. "This is Amelia." Because, although I don't know how my mother ever let my father get away with it, that is my name.

"This is Benny Overfield," the voice said. "I met you when you came with your father to the Search for the Truth About Amelia group last year. I was the one in the wheelchair. I've been trying to get in touch with your father. Is he there?"

"Hello, Benny," I said, my voice softer now. Julie smiled and gave me a thumbs-up signal from the hall. "Yes, I remember you," I said. "My parents have moved, Benny. To West Virginia. And we're having a winter storm watch over here."

"So are we," Benny said. Spare words, as though he were saving up his breath for something else. "Here in Milwaukee, six, maybe seven inches for the day."

"Well," I said, "I can give you their number, Benny, if you like."

A faint wheeze escaped across the wires. "If you please," he said.

I gave Benny Overfield my parents' number, and he was about to get off the phone to call my father, when I remembered the four blood transfusions. "How are you doing, Benny?" I asked. "I mean, your health?"

"Not well, thank you," he said. He took a struggling breath. "They said leukemia. Weeks, a couple of months at the very most."

I thought of Amelia's plane, that frail shell that had delivered her who knows where. "I'm sorry, Benny," I said. I wanted to say something about immortality, or his lifelong quest to find the truth about Amelia, but something about his voice, and my bad cold, and the snow outside my window stopped me short.

"Your father and I got along," Benny said. "I just wanted to tell him that. We didn't agree about Amelia, but I just wanted to talk to him about her for a little while."

"Sure, Benny," I said. "He'd love to talk to you about Amelia Earhart. You call him up."

After I got off the phone with Benny, I stared into the solid sheets of snow outside my house. I saw the blurred image of my father out there, just as he'd appeared in Benny Overfield's photograph, the one taken on the air strip in Southern California when Amelia had smiled at him all those years ago. Lean and sinewy, a sort of James Dean of the Thirties, my father leaned into the shade of the plane's belly in the blowing snow. Everything but his stance had been obscured.

My father began to move. Slowly, hips swaggering, grease-stained hands opening and closing in anticipation, the young airplane mechanic who was not yet my father, nor even the adoring husband of his lady wife, made his way past all the other mechanics, past the reporters, past all the photographers crowding together around this celebrity in the swirling snow.

Till at last he stood directly in front of the first woman pilot to have almost flown around the world. *A smile's nothin', babe*, I heard him say. *You're gonna have to do a whole lot better than that goddamn smile.*

Amelia Earhart's white silk pilot scarf blew behind her in the wind. Running her little tongue over her open lips, she peered with unmistakable longing into Willard Massey's face. I could feel his hot young breath as it filled her mouth. *He has a job to do, fellas,* Amelia said.

Then, scooping up Amelia Earhart in his arms, my father carried her out of the picture, outside the Michigan winter, clear into some warm and sunny place I will never go. Unaware of my existence, my father didn't even stop to say good-bye.

STONES

The radio station Pam and Richard have tuned in up in the front seat of the Taurus only comes from as far away as Las Vegas. But Leah knows she might receive just about anything, driving across the desert like this at night. *If you don't know me by now,* the Drifters are singing, *you will never never know me.* But Leah is expecting more than the music of Solid Gold.

She squeezes her fingers around the quartz lying like a tiny dagger in her palm. *What do you have for me?* she asks the stone as she rubs her thumb along its inexplicable extra crystal at the top. Last month, the Leader at the retreat in Sedona told her that the stone's greatest power lay in this additional crystal that has grown over the centuries, atom by painstaking atom, like a patient wart.

Leah is on her way back to Albuquerque from California with Pam and Richard and their nine-year-old daughter, Katie. Pam and Richard used to live in Albuquerque, and they were driving out to Richard's conference in LA from their home in Chicago where they live now. For some reason, when they reached Albuquerque they phoned Leah to see if she would like to ride along. Apparently, a mutual friend had told them about Shawn.

"Aren't the stars beautiful?" Pam asks, just as the quartz sends Leah an image of her son. Shawn's face appears on the inside of the car's windshield, along with reflections from the dashboard's pale green lights. Leah leans forward, struggling to see whether

her son's expression is perplexed or peaceful. But Shawn only stays for a moment, just long enough to run his hand across the single patch of albino hair he inherited from her. Then he disappears against the backdrop of desert night.

"Has Katie fallen asleep?" Richard asks.

"Of course I'm not asleep," Katie replies. She is indignant. The child has stretched her lanky little body across the back seat, so that her head rests like a fragile melon in Leah's lap. Her voice is slightly muffled by the afghan Leah has tucked around her neck. Leah's mother knit the afghan six or seven years ago for Shawn.

Pam turns around to look at the two of them, and laughs. "I should have known you wouldn't be asleep, Katie Andrews!" Leah feels the tenseness in the child's thin shoulders as she shrugs. Why is it mothers think they possess their children in this way? She wants to tell Pam that her child is a stranger who will someday surprise her. Leah has come to see things that the mothers of living children don't seem to know.

She would like to tell Pam that this child is very much like the son she lost. A few days ago, before they all set out on I-80, they stopped to pick up some things for the trip at the shopping mall. She and Pam left Richard and Katie to wait by the fountain, while the two of them went into CVS. When they got back, Richard was reading the *Albuquerque Journal*, and Katie was dancing around the fountain, executing her own brand of gypsy choreography, set to a melancholy little tune she was making up. Shawn, too, had always entertained himself, inventing stories, talking to imaginary playmates. It had never occurred to Leah that he might be sad. As for her, she'd been so delighted with him that she'd never felt the need to have another child. He was three when his father died, and seven when she married Collier, and when Collier asked her to have her tubes tied, because, as he'd put it, he didn't want to be pushing a baby stroller when his own kids were grown, Leah had gone to her doctor without a thought. She had Shawn. And Shawn, wonderful Shawn, would be enough.

"Hey, everybody!" Katie cries from below Leah's breasts. "Did you guys see that humongous shooting star?"

Right away, her mother corrects her. "They're not actually stars, honey," Pam says. "They're meteors. Hot rocks that have broken away from others out in space. So really, all we are seeing is their light."

Katie smiles up at Leah. "We've got a secret," the child says. Leah smiles. Later, when Richard and Pam aren't monitoring her conversation so carefully, Leah will tell Katie that the shooting stars are vehicles for departed spirits. For now, though, it is enough that the child's hair spreads like a tender halo across her shorts. Katie's hair is exactly the color that Shawn's was once.

It's Oedipal, the child psychologist told her years ago when she went for help. *A boy's mother is his earliest love object. And so it is only natural that when you remarried, Shawn was a little jealous of your time.* The psychologist put down his pencil and peered at her over his shellrim bifocals. *But now tell me, Leah,* he said. *You say the boy and his stepfather don't get along well. Is there anything else you want to tell me? Are you sure there isn't something you are leaving out?*

Leah is holding the stone so tightly it begins to cut. *What do you have for me?* she begs of it. Collier's handsome face appears on the windshield, distorted with rage above the bare buttocks of her only son. She reaches out in vain to stop him. *You don't know how close I came, Mom,* Shawn told her when she finally found him hiding in the tool shed behind a neighbor's house. *I really thought I was going to get up off that bed and kill us both.* She sent him to Gallup to live with her parents after that.

"We've got a lot to see tomorrow, Katie," Pam says. "So you'd better go to sleep now, honey."

"Okay," Katie says affably enough. But she tugs at Leah's arm, and when Leah leans closer, the child says under the hum of the engine, "Tell me something more about the stones."

Leah looks at Pam and Richard up in front. Pam is resting her head against the window of the car, lost in the Oldies but Goodies that continue to cackle over the airwaves in the desert

night. She is singing along with the station, off in a world where
Richard can never come.

We'll sing in the sunshine!
You know we'll laugh every day!

Leah remembers giving herself over completely to the music
just like that. As a teenager, she used to spin around the corners
of Gallup in the Ford pick-up truck her father drove whenever he
went out to the reservation for the BIA. She would take his
F-100 out onto the dirt roads beyond the town and let its V-8
rev faster and faster, let the wind blow hot and dry and free across
her face, as the radio blared out its music and she sang along.

Standing on a corner in Winslow, Arizona,
I got seven women on my mind.
One she tried to stone me,
Two she tried to own me,
Three, well, she's a friend of mine.

Richard reaches over to run his finger along Pam's arm.
Leah knows that part of it, too, how a woman's escape into
the music can make a man afraid he will lose her. At the same
time, she knows that freedom in a woman turns men on. They
fall in love with a free spirit, then use anything they can find
at their disposal to tie her down. *"We'll sing in the sunshine,"*
Pam sings as she gazes at Richard with that little smile. *"Then
I'll be on my way!"*

Leah presses the quartz into the girl's small hand. "The stones
have different qualities," she tells her quietly. "You may have this
one for your very own. If you listen, the stone will speak to you
in pictures."

Katie holds the quartz close to her chest and shuts her eyes.
"Hm," she says. "Yes. Where is the picture coming from?"

Leah doesn't ask her what she saw. "No one knows," she
says. "The stones have been around longer than we have, though.
Many ancient civilizations made their greatest decisions based on
the pictures and messages sent to them by their deity through the
stones."

Katie nods. "We learned about Stonehenge last year in school."

Leah strokes the child's hair. "A people called the Druids worshipped at Stonehenge," she says. "The stones were part of their religion. And stones have played a part in almost all religions, for a long, long time. There is a story in the Bible about a man named Jacob who fell asleep with his head on a stone as a pillow and woke up to see angels climbing up and down on a ladder that led to an enormous throne. The angels told Jacob to go home and make peace with his brother."

But by now, Pam is listening, alert, shoulders back, nose pointed, like a watchful dog. "Oh yes, Katie," Pam adds, too sweetly. "And don't forget that story about the stones in the New Testament, either, Leah," she says. "You know, it's one of those little stories that Jesus tells. Let me see now, how does it go? Jesus is telling a crowd of people that God will always provide for them, and then to bring home his point he says something like, *If a son asks his father for bread, will he give him stones?*"

Leah doesn't answer *yea* or *nay*. She has been through this before with her parents. They appear to listen to her for awhile each time she's home, but sooner or later they always interrupt. *You have to face reality, Leah*, they've told her many times. *No matter how you think you failed Shawn, you need to move forward now. Shawn would want you to find a way to accept his death and to go on living.*

But who are they to know what Shawn would want? She left Collier the day after the funeral. She wishes there were a way to let Shawn know she is no longer afraid of his stepfather's rages. She has become a woman with nothing left to fear. She is also aware that this new courage makes her just a little bit dangerous, that it is hard to say what she would do, if it came to that.

"I think stones can work magic," Katie confides.

Pam flips off the radio. Leah catches the profile of her friend's face, and sees her frown. "All right, Katie Lee Andrews," Pam says. "Now it's really time for you to settle down."

* * * * *

Several hours later, Pam jerks awake. "Where are we, Richard?" she asks. She feels confused.

"Somewhere near Death Valley," her husband says. "I'm too tired to keep driving." He glances in the rearview mirror at Leah and Katie, both of them sound asleep in the big back seat. "I've been the only one awake in the car for the last hundred miles."

Pam reaches over and pats his arm. "I'm sorry. The funny thing is, I didn't know I was sleeping. I thought I was sitting here, watching the road for you, but I guess I was just dreaming. Do you want me to drive?"

Richard shakes his head. "I saw a highway sign awhile back that said the turn off for the Death Valley campgrounds was coming up. I thought we could go park there for a couple of hours and take a nap."

They pull into the camp after midnight. It's March, still a little too early for the tourist season, so the grounds are dark. A wind has come up, and the new moon is barely visible behind the clouds. Pam gets out of the car with Richard and strains to see what she knows must be a huge range of mountains off in the distance. But she can see nothing. The night closes in on her, black, enormous space, and she feels as if she is standing alone in the dark in a vacuum. She peers through the back window of the car at Leah and Katie, their faces illumined just enough by the lights from the dashboard so that she can make them out. As her eyes adjust to the darkness, she can see Katie's knees tucked up beneath her. Her head is pressed into Leah's stomach. Leah is slouched against the corner of the car, her head propped up with the pillow she brought along. One pale arm lies across Katie's shoulders. Her mouth has fallen open, and her eyelids are smooth and veinless and very white.

"Richard," Pam whispers, reaching for his hand. She is probably just tired, but she has been seized all of a sudden by a nameless fear. They are parked at the edge of a bottomless cliff, and if she takes a step in any direction she will fall for hours. On the way down, she will be surrounded by howling ghosts, each one shouting the name of an unanswered hope. "Richard," she says out loud. "I am so afraid."

Her husband puts his arm around her, this warm, good man, and brings her close. "What is there to be afraid of? It's just the wind." He pulls her in the direction of the car.

"Wait," she says, holding back. He places his big, firm hand against the small of her back. She presses into the warmth of it, the flesh that is proof of his existence, that he is with her now. "Richard," she says, "do you believe that someone can put a curse upon your child?"

"Come on," he says in his quiet, reassuring, familiar voice. "This place would give anyone the creeps. It'll all look different in the morning, when the sun comes up. Let's get back in the car and push the seats back and get some sleep."

Pam steps through the open blackness of the Taurus door. Richard is right, of course. After a few moments, her head lolls back reluctantly against the seat. But right before she drops off, she catches a glimpse in the mirror of Leah's hair, glowing like a specter in the dark.

* * * * *

Leah breaks off another piece of the Devil's Golfcourse at Death Valley National Monument. She and Katie are collecting specimens of the ancient salt crystals that make up the desert floor. After they all woke up around seven, they felt refreshed, and Richard suggested they spend a little extra time driving through the park.

Katie is delighted. "Let's pretend we're giants and we're stepping on mountains," she suggests. "Look, Leah! If we lean way over, we can look down at the little people in the canyons between our feet."

The sun burns through Leah's black cotton T-shirt to scorch her back. The moon must be like Death Valley, barren, gray, and dusty, but not as hot.

"Did you taste the stones?" Katie asks. "Try a little piece of this one. It tastes like salt."

Leah places a piece of the ancient floor of the sea inside her mouth. She thinks of potato chips, the thick, natural kind they sell in her health foods store.

"Did you hear the Ranger tell everybody back there at the Visitors Center why they call this place Death Valley?" Katie asks.

"No," Leah says. She busies herself with the crystals, arranging them according to shape and size. Her head and neck hurt, probably from sleeping in the car. She says to the child, "But Death Valley seems a logical enough name to me."

Katie rambles on. "Well, see," she says, "there was this group of pioneers on their way out west through the mountains? Only, they had their map wrong? And so they thought there was only this one set of mountains when there were really two? And then they couldn't travel over this rough stuff. So two men went out to try to find help and they were gone for like months and months. And when they came back, most of the pioneers were dead, or blind, and these two men helped lead the others out."

Leah stretches, reaching with her arms up to the sky.

"So that's why they call it Death Valley, see," Katie says. "Because when the pioneers got to the top of the second set of mountains? One of them turned around and said, *Good-bye, Death Valley!*"

Leah gives the child's shoulder a little pat. "Where are your parents?"

Katie shrugs with obvious indifference, then points toward her parents' retreating backs. Pam and Richard are holding hands as they return to the car, carefully picking their way over the sharp crystals. The Taurus is parked under the retreating shadow of the mountains. The sun is rapidly moving up over the entire range. They have all agreed they will be on their way by noon.

"They don't care about us at all," Katie says. "It doesn't even matter to them that we're here."

Leah feels a sudden tightening in her throat. "Your parents love you very much," she says. "Never forget that. You mustn't do anything that would hurt them."

The child looks puzzled. "What do you mean hurt them? I wouldn't be able to hurt them. There's two of them. And anyway, they're way too big."

Leah opens her mouth but no sound comes out. The hot desert air rushes in against her teeth. Katie doesn't wait for an answer. "It's no big deal," the child says. "They've never been all that interested in me. Not like you are."

Leah looks out across the desert. "Oh, I see," she says. "Well, everybody's got something different to offer. Your parents, too."

Katie sighs. "You mean like stone soup."

Leah tries to make the connection, but the child's brain has jumped from one electrical impulse to the next, leaving her standing alone on the other side of a great abyss. "I'm sorry," she says. "I missed that one."

"Stone soup," Katie repeats. She looks surprised. "You mean you don't know that story? Gee, I think I read that story as long ago as the second grade. You want me to tell it to you?"

Leah nods.

"Well," Katie says, taking her hand as she begins. "This guy comes into a town, see? And he's hungry. But all he's got is this big bucket. So he puts a big stone in the bucket, and he adds some water, and he starts a fire under it, and he sits down by the side of the road, and he just waits. Pretty soon, along comes this farmer.

"*What you got in the pot?* the farmer asks.

"Stranger says to him, *Stone soup.*

"Farmer's never heard of that kind of soup, so he looks inside. *When's it gonna be ready?* he asks the stranger.

"Stranger puts his finger in the pot. *This stone soup needs a carrot,* he tells the farmer.

"Farmer says, *No problem,* and hands him a carrot.

"*Great,* says the stranger. *This stone soup'll be ready by and by.*

"Farmer says he'll come back later and have some. Then he leaves.

"Pretty soon, along comes a chimney sweep, wants to know what the stranger's got cooking inside the pot.

"*Stone soup,* stranger says. Puts his hand in the pot and tastes it. *But it needs some rice.*

"Chimney sweep says, *No problem.* And he goes off and comes back with a bag of rice.

"Anyway, the story goes on and on like that till the soup is done."

Leah crouches on the ground and draws one hand over the pointed stones. When she turns the hand over, her palm is streaked with blood. She makes a sun visor for her forehead with the other hand. She can see Pam and Richard off in the distance, leaning in the shade against the car. "We should be getting back," she says.

"Don't you get it?" Katie asks. Leah looks up and sees the expression of total concentration on her face. It is an expression she remembers from her son. *So why do you stay with him when he hates me so much, Mom?*

"Okay," Katie says. "So if you don't understand, I'll explain to you about the soup. It's a story about making something out of nothing. And the funny part, see, is that the people reading the story know the truth. They know the stranger started out with an empty pot."

* * * * *

Just inside the Nevada border, about an hour after they've left Death Valley, Richard brings the Taurus into a gas station where two roads meet. Leah unfolds her legs and prepares to get out of the car. Her feet have swollen in the heat, and her ears are clogged.

"The guidebook says this area used to be a thriving metropolis," Richard jokes. "Sure looks like a ghost town now to me."

"Oh, goodie!" Katie says, sitting up. "Are ghost towns really full of a lot of ghosts?"

"This isn't really a ghost town, honey," Pam says. "People do live here. It's just that they live way off over there." She motions vaguely at the silver heat waves dancing several miles down the two-lane state highway in a wet mirage. "But I'd certainly have to agree with you that it isn't much."

Leah looks out the window at the combination laundromat, gas station and general store. *Hop Inn,* the sign says.

"I think I'll top off the tank," Richard says. The air conditioner gasps, a metallic sound. "We're not that far from Vegas, but I'd hate to try to push it out here on this desert and run out of gas."

"God no," Pam says. She sighs. "I'll go see if I can find some snacks to keep us going till we get somewhere decent where we can have some lunch."

"The casinos in Vegas maybe," Richard offers. "I hear some of them have a huge buffet. All you can eat for maybe seven bucks."

Katie leans over and places her mouth next to Leah's ear. "Will you go to the bathroom with me?"

"Sure," she says. But as she places one sandal on the hot pavement, something sharp goes through her foot. Too late, she sees the dry tufts of goatshead poking through the seams of the cracked cement. Shawn used to call it demon weed. It grew in abundance at the back of her parents' yard. She reaches down to pull a good-sized thorn out of her foot.

"Wow," Katie says, and before Leah can stop her, the child has taken the thorn, still fresh with her blood, out of her hand. "Look at that! It's got a face, just like a devil. See? Here are the two holes for eyes, and these are horns."

"Come on," Leah says. "We'll probably find the bathroom behind the store."

They are going around the side of the building towards the back when they notice a little boy about three years old waving at them wildly from the cab of a pick-up truck. "Hi! Hi!" He jumps up and down in the passenger seat.

"Gee, he's sure friendly, isn't he?" Katie laughs. "He better not get too excited, though, or else he'll fall."

The boy is small and dark, with big, black eyes. Leah walks over to the truck. "Hi, sweetheart," she says. "Where's your mommy?"

The little boy points across the heat waves in the yellow dust.

Leah looks in the direction the child is pointing. An enormous, scowling woman with badly dyed hair is waddling toward them. She's wearing huge blue jeans that don't quite cover her belly, and she has tied a faded red checkered tablecloth around her middle as a kind of halter top.

"Sit down, you little bastard!" the woman yells. She pushes past Leah and Katie, and yanks open the door of the dilapidated truck. "Didn't I tell you not to talk to anybody while I was gone?"

The woman gets in and starts the engine. The truck begins to move slowly in reverse. But then the woman stops the truck in the middle of the driveway and takes a newspaper off the front seat and starts to hit the little boy across the chest.

"What's that woman doing?" Katie cries.

Leah starts to run toward the truck. Amazed, she watches as though from outside herself, marveling at the way her arm stretches toward the window and reaches through to open the broken door and pull the woman out. She is like one of the all-powerful cartoon creatures Shawn used to watch on TV every Saturday morning when he was growing up. She is Plastic Man, or Spider Woman, a superhuman endued with superhuman powers.

"You cannot do this!" she shouts. Her fist closes around the extra three inches of flesh on the woman's arm. "It is against the law to do this, and you are going to stop!"

The little boy is whimpering as Leah pins the doughy woman to the ground. "I will not let you do this, do you hear me?" she shouts at the woman. "I will call the police to come and get you if you don't stop!"

The woman stares up at Leah from the ground. A lack of comprehension fills her face. "And just what exactly do you think the *police* will do when they get here, honey?" she asks Leah in a quiet voice.

Leah feels the woman's stomach rippling beneath her, as warm and fluid as the waterbed she used to share with Collier. She inhales the stink of the woman, sweat powdered over with Avon.

"This here happens to be the sheriff's son," the woman says.

"And for your added enlightenment, honey, I happen to be the sheriff's wife."

Leah watches, fascinated, as the red and white squares of the halter tablecloth alternate small, big, then small again, with the massive rise and fall of the moon-like breasts.

"That's right, honey," the woman says. "If anybody's gonna get arrested out here in this hell hole, it won't be me."

Katie puts out her hand to help Leah up. The woman struggles to her knees, and brushes her jeans off, then moves with injured dignity toward her truck. "Slide over, will you, Matthew," she says a little less roughly to her son.

Then she turns around and narrows her already small eyes at Leah. "Honey," she says, "you are in trouble. Deep trouble, too, looks like to me. I would even venture to say you need some help."

Leah stands there, watching the battered truck disappear into the desert like a sad mirage.

After awhile, the child standing beside her says encouragingly, "Well, we sure stopped *her*, didn't we!"

Leah doesn't answer. The heat of the desert is inside her now.

"Maybe the stones sent us a picture," Katie says. She is pulling at Leah's arm to get her attention, and as Leah tries to focus on her face, the child opens her fingers to reveal the quartz. "Maybe the stones sent us to this place so we could help."

But the stones will forgive nothing. Leah sees Shawn's face rise with the undulating waves on the parking lot.

"Hello?" Katie says. "Leah? Are you all right?"

Leah takes the quartz from the child's hand and brings the jagged edge of it against her breast. The additional crystal begins to write. Word by wicked word, the stone carves the dark confession on her heart.

I let him.

WITCHES

This is a ghost story of sorts, but only from Sally Spotted Pony's point of view. From my point of view, it's a kind of love story—not, you know, like *Romeo and Juliet* or something, but the kind of love story where somebody just goes on wanting something they can never have.

I met Sally Spotted Pony right after Shana and I moved out west to Albuquerque two years ago. I got a truck-driver who was on his way home to New Mexico to give us a ride out from this truck-stop where I'd been bussing dirty dishes for about a year. It's on I-94 just outside Detroit, and I saw all kinds of people coming and going, and meantime I didn't seem to be going anywhere myself, and one day while I'm pushing this dish cart I hear this old guy say he lives in Albuquerque, and I think to myself, *Albuquerque, huh?* And the name hits me like it's some sort of message from someplace else, and when I say it out loud it feels smooth and hard and mysterious, as if little pebbles of polished turquoise are in my mouth. And I know right there in the truck-stop that going out to Albuquerque is something I have to do for Shana, and for myself.

This is probably one reason I liked Sally Spotted Pony when I met her. Because when I told Sally how Albuquerque said itself clear out of the blue, out of all the general bzz-bzz-ba-hoo, all the cigar smoke, she nodded, *yeah*, like it all made sense, it followed. She told me she grew up with voices that spoke to her like that out of the trunks of trees and in the wind that blew on the tops of the mesas, and for awhile there she understood whatever I said to her, no matter what.

Sally was full-blooded Navajo, about my age, and she taught Native American Studies at UNM. Sometimes, she wore her long black hair braided up the back with strips of white cotton. I asked her once could she do my hair like that, but she was dead silent. When she didn't answer, I decided it was a Navajo secret, the way they did their hair, and I shouldn't have asked her. I said, real quick, "But maybe it wouldn't be right for me to wear my hair like that."

Sally raised her eyebrows. "Perhaps not, Eileen," she said coolly, and then she came back to me. But then, of course, there was that day she never would. I should have seen that at the beginning. You had to know right from the start you were just a ghost.

* * * * *

Anyway, I stop my cart full of dishes right in front of this old guy there at the truck-stop, this truck-driver who's just said the name of the city where I'm going to move, and I sit down next to him and plunk my elbows down on his table, and his fellow drivers there at his table look real surprised. I say to this old guy, "Take me with you, okay?" I say I'll pay good if he will.

Nobody moves for a minute. Then I notice one of the other men at the table sees my scar. Truck-stops aren't like they are in the movies. Drivers aren't all looking to pinch some woman's ass every time they stop. I'd been bussing at this truck-stop ever since Shana and I left Leonard over there in Germany on the base in K-Town—that's what the GIs call Kaiserslautern over there, for short—and flew home *military dependent*, and all I ever got when one of those guys looked at me was a kind of pity that said they were sorry for what had happened, even though it was sure as hell a pity I didn't want.

Now, in the movies, all that would be different. In the

movies, if someone who looked like me, but without this scar—
say blonde hair just a little bit frazzled, but decent enough to
look at when I let it out, and with a pretty good figure, too,
although I may be a little on the thin side because I don't eat
that much—anyway, if someone like me were to say to this
truck-driver in the movies—who'd be Burt Reynolds in the
movies, or maybe if he was older, Paul Newman, but not this
guy—"You wanna take me with you out there to New Mexico,
Mister?"—the guy who was making the movie would play the
next scene with me and the three truck-drivers really rough.
I've seen those kinds of movies. Burt Reynolds, or whoever it
was they had playing the truck driver, would laugh so you
could hear the dirty hotel room and the smiley face on the
condom in his macho voice, or maybe you'd hear Janis Joplin
in a voice-over of *Bobby McGee* as you watched the two of us
roll around together in the sleeping compartment behind the
driver's seat of his diesel truck. One of the other guys at the
table would say with a leer, "Jeezus, Maxie. You got you a hot
one there, buddy, and if you don't wanna take her up on it, I
will myself."

But like I say, it was never like that. This man, whose name
turned out to be Pete Morgan, had a face like I wished was my
father's. My father left my mother when I was little, and even
then I thought, *good riddance*, because he was always drunk. I
heard Sally Spotted Pony say once that one of the old men in her
tribe had a face like a road-map. By then I knew exactly what she
meant, because I got to be good friends with Pete Morgan, and
then his wife, and that described his face exactly.

Anyway, Pete Morgan says to me there at the table in the
truck-stop, "I don't usually take along any riders, young lady."
And it about makes me want to throw my arms around him, how
he's so polite. Then he adds, "You're sure you're not going to get
yourself into trouble by talking to truckers about leaving? You're
not running off, are you, running away from something?" And I
know right then he means *somebody* and not *something*, because
he looks around.

Leonard has never tried to come after me and Shana, not even once, not even when we were leaving Germany, after I decided he'd beaten up on me for the final time. I'm not really afraid of him coming after us. The funny thing is, I know Leonard loved us. I have no doubt. Maybe Shana more than me—he never once hit up on Shana—but he loved us both. He just didn't know how to deal with it, all the nonsense, and we didn't have it any easier there in the Army, either, the fact that Leonard's a black man and that I'm white.

I don't pretend to understand this. I don't know why there's all these races. I just know after that last fight when I called Leonard a fat black stupid nigger, even though I never meant it—it was always just something I seemed to end up saying when we had our fights—we would've had us a hard time saying I ran into another wall there on that post.

The stitches have healed real nice now. The military doctors did a decent, no-questions job when they sewed me up, and now when I look at myself in the mirror from one certain angle so that side's not showing, I'm like I was.

So anyway, I shake my head, *no*, at the truck-driver, and I tell him it's just me and my daughter. Pete Morgan sips at his coffee, a gray-haired, heavy-set man with a kind of paunch, and you can tell he's thinking about it. He's asking himself does he want this *young lady*, this maybe *desperate young lady*, for all he knows, sitting next to him for fifteen hundred miles while he drives his truck. He's still got the muscles for driving. You can tell by the big blue veins that run through his hands there holding the coffee that he's pretty tough.

* * * * *

Sally Spotted Pony told me a story once about a truck-driver younger than Pete Morgan who picked the wrong girl up. It was one of Sally's ghost stories. Sally believed in ghosts and witches, and that you had to watch out you didn't mistake them for human beings, even now. Anyway, her truck-driver was doing a first-time run from LA to Gallup, and he had a load of, I don't know, oranges or something, that he was supposed to deliver to the Safeway there in Gallup, in his truck.

"They say," said Sally Spotted Pony in her story voice, "that he had come all that way across the desert, that he had crossed the desert, as they'd told him, in the night, and that he was about twenty miles outside Gallup, coming up, when he saw a young woman walking alone along the last lonely stretch of highway. She was pretty and young, like you are, Eileen, and he was a good, kind man who had a baby back in Los Angeles, and a pretty wife, and so he wondered what this young woman could be doing, walking along the highway at five in the morning all by herself. So he stopped his truck to ask her if she'd like a ride."

Sally said the woman didn't say anything to the truck-driver, only nodded, and that when he opened the cab door for the woman, she got inside. He must have had a feeling something was wrong at that point, Sally said, but he could not know what. He didn't ask her anymore questions.

"They say they found his truck on a small road just outside Gallup," Sally said. "He was barely able to tell the story before he died. He'd been almost to the edge of town where there's a stoplight, when he looked over to tell the young woman he was going to stop, and to ask her where exactly did she want him to let her out. But of course, she was already disappearing in his cab."

Sally said the old people could have told the truck-driver all about that woman, who she was, because everybody around there knew her. Everybody around there knew better than to pick her up. But no one ever asked them. The white men who found the truck-driver just thought he was having some sort of hallucination before he died.

"Any one of the old people could have told him," Sally said. "That woman had died in an accident there on the highway. She was from the tribe. And now she walked along the highway in the early hours of the morning, trying to get people who didn't know any better to pick her up."

Then she added, "I knew who they meant, of course, because I saw her once."

Part of my problem might just have been that I never believed her. I just thought she was one hell of a good storyteller, was what it was. If I'd known all along she wasn't telling stories, then maybe I might have seen it coming. I asked Sally Spotted Pony about the young woman on the highway. "But was she Indian," I asked her. "Was she really an Indian killed in an accident, or was she white?"

This was one of the first times I saw the closing in Sally's eyes. "Of course she wasn't Indian," she answered, a shade too politely. "I don't think you get the point of the story. She wasn't an Indian *now*. She wasn't white, either. She wasn't anybody. She was dead. A witch. She had succeeded in making the truck-driver feel sorry for her when he first saw her, and so she could trick him into believing she was alive."

Sally sighed. "And anyway, Eileen, even from your point of view, the question as to whether she was a witch or not doesn't matter. Truck companies have rules about picking up drifters. The driver should have known not to pick her up."

* * * * *

Finally, Pete Morgan shrugs his shoulders back at this truck-stop. "All right, Miss," he says to me. "You can come along."

I see he isn't smiling, but I see what I know is kindness in his gray-green eyes. I saw this kindness in a picture of a very old Indian Sally Spotted Pony showed me once when she took me to the Rare Book Room at the University of New Mexico Library during my lunch-break. I'd never gone someplace just to visit old books before, but Sally said I would like the room if I saw it, and I didn't really have much to lose anyway because I had a whole hour off.

This room was on the top floor of the adobe library, with lots of floor-to-ceiling windows and WPA murals on the walls. There was one mural of a white guy in a Sears workshirt and

Levis, digging a ditch between an Indian wearing braids and a Spanish guy with a headband that I liked a lot. Sally and I had to go sign our names on a sheet of paper before the librarian would let us go into the room with the old books in it. I heard a hissing sound and a pop in my ears when the librarian closed the door behind us to seal us off.

There was a big shelf full of pictures by a man named Curtis. Something Curtis, Curtis something. Right after the government got New Mexico away from the Mexicans, they had all these Indians they didn't exactly know what to do with, and so the Bureau of Indian Affairs sent this guy Curtis out west with his camera to take pictures of all these Indians so the government would know exactly what kind of Indians they had out there, what it was they'd got. Sally showed me one picture of just the head of a wise man. He was a *shaman*, she told me, the leader of a tribe that didn't have any people anymore. "They say the shaman died right after Curtis took his picture," she told me. "The shaman believed that the black eye of the camera stole his soul."

I still see that brown face in its creamy-white background, the man almost smiling, but with pouches under his eyes like he hasn't been sleeping near enough. His head is cocked to one side, and he looks as if he is saying, *Okay, don't feel bad, I forgive you.*

Whenever I think of Sally, I see the face of that old man in that picture there in the Rare Book Room in the library, looking out. And I wonder to myself: If the shaman had seen the ghosts, or the witches, the dead people Sally told me over and over weren't really out there, but you think you see them, because they use some trick to pull you into their story so you think they're really real and you stop to help, but then if you stop you're as dead as they are—well, would he have just looked, real quick like that, *I'm sorry*, and gone right on by them, or would he stop?

* * * * *

So I go home from my job there at the truck-stop, and I tell my mother that Shana and I are leaving, going on out to New

Mexico, and I tell her she is welcome to come out with us if she wants to, but I know she won't. "You gotta have some sort of address that's permanent," she tells me. "I'll stay here and forward any checks you might get from the Army."

My mother lays her arms across my shoulders. I notice her arms don't weigh anything at all. I get Shana out of her crib where she's sleeping, and she's a heavy bag of sweet cocoa I'm lifting, little skittery black lashes fluttering like moths against the screens in the summer as I wake her up. And I love her. Oh God, do I love her. It's the one thing I know even when I don't know anything else.

"Give her over," my mother tells me. She puts out her two thin arms and I hand her Shana, and while she's nestling her nose into Shana's dark curly hair that I know smells like fruits and flowers, I pretend to be busy, so that my mother won't ever know that I see her cry.

I pack Shana and me one big suitcase between us, and I take one big box of Toddler-size Pampers, and I say, "Thanks a lot now for everything, Mama." And she nods in a way that means, *Go before I can stop you,* and we're off.

* * * * *

Pete Morgan, the truck-driver I drove out with to Albuquerque, really had a house. I knew those guys made awful good money, but when we got out to Albuquerque and he invited me and Shana home to meet *the Mother,* as he called his wife, I saw the spread they had on Rio Grande Boulevard, on the northwest side, and I couldn't believe it.

The house itself was all adobe—these bricks made out of local clay all packed by hand into wooden forms that look like ladders and then laid out for maybe a month or so to dry in the sun—and it was built ranch-style, this house, all on one floor. The rooms had arches for doorways, and black wrought iron was on all of the windows.

Mrs. Morgan trained horses, this breed they call Arabians.

She said these horses were born all black and then as they got older they got almost white. The stables and rings for the horses were on the front side of the property, sort of as an advertisement for the passers-by, but out behind the house the property stretched out along the ditch-banks clear into a stand of cottonwoods by the Rio Grand.

When I first saw that river, the low afternoon sun was sparkling on the fast-moving deeper water out in the middle like little coins, and I could see sand bars out there, as if a person could wade out there to the middle across the shallows and stretch himself out flat on the sand and take a nap. Shana and I had walked down there with the Morgans.

"Don't you ever try to go on out there by yourself now will you, honey?" Mrs. Morgan said to me. "That's quick-sand out there, and it's moving fast. Just when you think you've stepped onto something solid, you find out there's nothing under you but a current that's too strong to handle, and it will pull you down."

But it looked beautiful and peaceful enough there from the edges. I pictured pioneers crossing that river, their horses wading out clear to their bellies, and covered wagons out there in the middle, and men and women carrying their children in their arms. The women wore calico dresses with full skirts that floated around their bare feet and legs as they crossed over the river, and they were all wearing sunbonnets to shade their faces from a sun I could already tell was going to be different from any I'd ever got used to in my life. And in the background, I could hear some-body singing, *We're crossing, oh we're crossing, the Rio Grand.*

I was pretty damn glad we had moved there. I learned after awhile that the Morgans' place was only three acres, but for me, coming from a place like downtown Detroit, it looked as if their property went on for miles.

I liked Mrs. Morgan. "Mother," she said. "Call me Mother if you want to. Pete does." But I remembered the way my mother had hugged me when I left with Shana, and I didn't really want to call Mrs. Morgan *Mother*, because of my mother, but I said thanks a lot.

Mrs. Morgan had short silver-blue hair, and she was small and strong. She wore a lot of Indian jewelry, and her blue eyes, which were the same color as the turquoise stones in her jewelry, stood out in her oval face against a deep dark tan. When she first held out her hand and looked at me that day we got to Albuquerque, she had that expression on her face I have come to know, whenever someone focuses on me and they see the scar. Like, *Is there a God, I wonder.* She might have tried to hide it so I wouldn't feel bad, but I was used to that look and I saw it anyway—the lips all pressed together, the wrinkles across the forehead, the little frown.

Mrs. Morgan spoke softly and called me *honey.* They told me they had a daughter, who lived in town and was going to college. I could hear it in their voices, that they were proud. Mrs. Morgan said, "Come to think of it, honey, why don't you try over at the University tomorrow, see what sort of work they might have over there for you?"

They said Shana and I could sleep in their daughter's bedroom. Mrs. Morgan said she'd like to keep Shana during the day if I got a job.

"No, now you leave your baby to me," she said when I told her I thought maybe I could find me a day-care. "I hear they have the babies stamp time-cards in some of those places, as if children were day-laborers or something. No. She won't be any bother. I'll be happy enough to have this little girl around." She picked up Shana, and Shana's mouth opened up in a smile like a little cave, all pink and round. It was Leonard's smile, and I felt a current go through my middle that must have been like the one out there in the river, because it pulled me down.

* * * * *

I met Sally Spotted Pony my first day working. The UNM Maintenance people, where Personnel put me, sent me to Native American Studies with a vacuum cleaner and a rug shampooer and my supplies, because someone there had called up and complained that the University didn't care about them, and that nobody ever came by to clean the place or to pick up trash.

"Pick up their own goddam trash," said my boss, an over-weight, red-faced man, as he put my cleaning tools into one of the Maintenance vehicles and handed me the keys to what would be my truck. Maybe the winters were better here, he went on saying, but he sure as hell could do without these goddam sensitive *Hispanics,* as they wanted us all to call them, and yer same old injuns as ever, if he had his choice. He'd moved to New Mexico from New Jersey to beat the winters, he said. *Probably like yerself, little lady,* he said, though of course I hadn't. I told him I came from Michigan originally, but that I'd moved a lot.

"Michigan," he said. He looked east, toward the mountains. I could see he didn't know exactly where that was. "You got any children, little lady?"

I told him about Shana.

"You'll find out soon enough then for yourself," he said. "Around here, white man and his kids don't count for *nothin.*" He spit behind one shoulder and pointed at my truck. "Not even shitwork like this." He paused. "Ain't outright *blonde,* though, is she, like you, your little kid?" He sounded worried.

I shook my head, *no,* she wasn't. That seemed to satisfy him, that she'd be all right. I didn't tell him that Shana has her father's coloring.

"Good," he said. He threw a last-minute broom and pail into the back of my truck. "Could be then maybe your daughter's got half a chance."

* * * * *

I watched a lot of T.V. westerns when I was growing up. Re-runs of *Wagon Train* and *Bonanza. Have Gun, Will Travel* and *Gunsmoke,* that kind of stuff. You didn't see Matt Dillon dealing much with Indians, and Ben Cartwright and his boys were pretty much alone there on that ranch, but on the shows that had Indians, I always got the idea the guy making the show knew Indians had got a bad deal when the white men took over their country, and so in his show he was going to have a good white man taking care of all the poor Indians, sort of like all by himself he was going to try to pay them back.

The white man in these shows was always better off than the Indian, and he'd been to school. The first time I saw Sally Spotted Pony, she blew all that. I got to the Native American Studies building, a little two-bedroom adobe turned into an office about a block and a half from campus, and I knocked on the heavy Spanish wooden door and waited, because it felt more like I was going visiting at a little house. After a few minutes the door opened, and I found myself looking eye to eye with a pretty, thin-faced lady wearing a gray business suit and rose-tinted, gold-rim glasses. That first time I saw her, Sally's shiny long dark hair was pulled straight back into a braided bun.

She raised her eyebrows. "Yes?" she asked. Behind her, inside the office, I saw an Indian boy, straight black hair down to his shoulders, a red printed bandanna folded up and tied around his brow. He had a maroon backpack across his lap and he was wearing a T-shirt and Levi's and Nikes. He was sitting in front of what I decided was this woman's desk.

"I'm from Maintenance," I said to the woman. "Sorry we didn't get here any sooner." My boss at Maintenance had told me, *Whatever happens, say "we," not "I," so one person don't get blamed for every little thing that might go wrong.* I stood there in Sally Spotted Pony's doorway and tried to smile.

Now that I think of it, maybe it was the scar that put it off. My scar tends to pop out, ridge-like, a small mountain range across my cheek-bones if I smile too hard, and I knew right then that she saw it.

"Come in," she said. "They didn't tell me when you were coming. I'm Sally Spotted Pony, the director here." She stepped back from the door to let me pass, lowering her beautiful, shiny-smooth head in a kind of bow.

"Well, don't let me stop you, whatever it was you were doing," I said. I said it in the boy's direction, too, to include him, and again I smiled. The boy looked back at me, so I knew he heard me, but his gaze went right on through me, like I wasn't there. I dragged my equipment over to the center of the room and bent over and got out a pail and a mop and went and got some water out of the little bathroom and came back and started cleaning.

There's not too many people can beat me with a bucket and a mop. I'll always be able to make a living waiting on tables or cleaning up. Maintenance was happy to have me. Our family's not sure where we come from, but my mother used to say she thought the fact that we were all blond and so good at cleaning maybe meant there was a little German way back there. But when Leonard and I ended up on that base in Germany, I had to laugh. Germans don't really have much use for people who have to work for a living. So somewhere along the way, somebody very non-German must have got into my family's blood.

As I pushed my mop into the corners of the flagstone floor of Native American Studies, I overheard some of Sally Spotted Pony's conversation with the Indian boy.

She sounded angry. "Well, did you *try*?" she was saying. "Are you certain you've explained all this to your instructor? I can't do a damn thing for you, you know, if you don't even try when you come down here."

The boy muttered something back to Sally Spotted Pony that I couldn't hear.

"That's an excuse," she said. "You can't blame them for that. She's got a job. People she has to answer to. Work's no different wherever it is, and she's got a boss. But you came down here on a scholarship, son, and you can't just sit here now and tell me you aren't going to make the best use of it. You make the most of it, you hear me? So next week. When you come in here? You better have every one of those papers from her right here where I can see them. And don't you give me some Indian bullshit, either, you understand me, about how you miss the earth and the sky and the old people up at Window Rock. You don't care bullshit about any of that Indian crap, you're just goddam lazy, that's all. And you better stay here now and finish this, you hear?"

I peeked over at the two of them. Sally Spotted Pony had her gray-sleeved arms stretched across her desk, and she was pounding her right fist in front of the boy. She was wearing nicer Indian jewelry than Mrs. Morgan's, and I noticed she had long slender brown hands and bright red nails.

"Is that clear?" she asked the boy again. She was almost shouting. I felt sorry for him, and wanted whatever it was she was doing to him right then to stop, so I cleared my throat. Then I went back to my cleaning, but not before Sally saw me listening and caught my eye.

"Okay then," she said to the boy. "I'll see you next week. And next week when you come in here, you better make goddam sure you come in here right on time."

The boy got up and slipped out the front door of Native American Studies. I was on my knees, with my back turned, so I didn't see his face as he was leaving, but I heard the last little soft squeak of his Nikes walking away as Sally closed the door.

I felt her standing there, staring at me, her black eyes screwing right down into my back till they made a hole. "Okay," she said. "So I see you. So now that you've got my attention, why don't you go ahead and tell me how you got the scar."

I looked up at Sally Spotted Pony, who nodded. She had her arms crossed against her chest and she was leaning back, one high-heeled black leather shoe pressed up behind her against the adobe wall.

* * * * *

After that, I did a lot with Sally. Sometimes we both brought sandwiches and ate our lunch together down by the duck pond outside the library. Other times, I'd call her from Maintenance and ask her would she like to get coffee, and the two of us would meet at the Student Union for my break.

"Mind she don't cut your throat one day," my boss at Maintenance told me. "They don't like white people, that's all there is to it. And you're one of us, little lady, whether you want to be or not."

I told Sally Spotted Pony all about Leonard—how deep down I knew he'd loved us, but how once we got going, neither one of us could seem to stop. I told her that he didn't want me to leave him, and that he said he was sorry, and that he cried.

Sally shook her head, no, she didn't believe me, that Leonard could be sorry for what he'd done. "I don't know many African-Americans myself," she said slowly, using the word Leonard said white people used when they were uncomfortable, but still wanted to say what was polite.

"There have always been black spirits living among the people," Sally said. "They say the black man first came to this area as a soldier, and that because the people had never seen a black man before, they worshiped him. They took him in and shared their women and food, as though he were a god. But then the black men, whole troops of them, came in as soldiers, sent here by the white man's army, and they murdered off the people, entire tribes."

I was sorry to hear that about the black soldiers, what they'd done, but I didn't see how it had anything much to do now with Leonard, and I told her so.

Sally nodded, as if she could agree on that one point. "These were black spirits," she said. "Evil forces. They weren't real people. They weren't alive. If you ever go to watch the dances at the New Mexico Fairgrounds, you'll see them dancing, black-faced, wearing white feathers. These black spirits are witches. They're neither god nor man. They're only ghosts."

I told Sally I didn't think the thing that had happened between Leonard and me had anything to do with ghosts. I wanted Sally to see that it had something to do with men and women in general and with the stupid way that women loved their men.

"Don't your Indian men ever hit up on their women?" I asked her. We were sitting in the ice-cream parlor chairs in the Student Union, drinking our coffee and eating glazed donuts, which Sally had just told me were a little like Indian fry-bread. She said she was going to bring me some fry-bread one of these days, that I could try.

Sally took another sip of her coffee. "Our society is matri-archal," she said. "Women run all the families. They have the land. If an Indian man beats his wife, he has the whole council to answer to. Indian women's lives haven't changed much. It's the men who don't know what to do with themselves anymore. Like that boy you saw in my office the day I met you. He's supposed to be getting a degree in agriculture, so that he can go back and help his tribe develop new methods for growing corn. But he's wasting his time here. He hasn't made the grades."

"So what'll happen to him?" I asked her.

Sally Spotted Pony opened her long hands out flat and looked at her beautiful fingers with the painted nails. "He'll go back before he's finished," she said. "And he'll become a drunk."

It always seemed to me she was too hard on her own people. I didn't ever see her give any one of them there in her office so much as a handshake whenever I was there. And yet with me, she was different. She'd look up, whatever it was she happened to be doing at the time, and the minute I walked in there, she'd smile and say, "Just a minute, Eileen, I'll be with you." She always seemed to work me into her busy day.

Sally came from a little town up near Four Corners. After she got her degree from the university, she did not go back. "I go see my mother, of course," she said. "My mother's alone now, and I have to go up every now and then to make sure she's got groceries. I bought her a freezer for the back porch last summer. She never learned to drive, and, anyway, she refuses to go into town, even if somebody offers to take her."

Sally had two younger brothers who lived in Phoenix. An older brother had been killed in Vietnam. She'd met her husband, she said, when she was eighteen, doing Indian competition dancing at the Fair. She'd made her own costume out of deerskin and little glass beading, and her dancing and costume had earned her the highest prize. I pictured this business-suited Sally, dressed in a soft leather dress the color of coffee with thick cream in it, and wearing leather thongs and eagle feathers in her braided hair.

I could imagine that falling in love with Sally the Indian maiden had been pretty easy, judging from what Sally the director of Native American Studies looked like now.

But then, everything about Sally was interesting to me. Sometimes she read me the long poems she'd written about Navajo legends. Besides the story about the truck-driver, there was one about the Dead People along Highway 666, this road that's out near Shiprock, going north.

According to this story, you could be driving along in a snowstorm out on 666 all by yourself, and you'd suddenly see one or more of these people walking along the highway in the snowstorm, some of them children, depending on the kind of person that you were, and how vulnerable you were to children, and they'd start waving at you from the roadside, these Dead People, like they needed help. It seemed to me that whenever Sally read these poems she almost sang.

They say the Dead People walk by the highway
  and that they wave and try to get you to stop
  for them
  as if their truck has just broken down a little way
on down the highway
and now it's snowing
and they're on their way back to someplace just
  as you are
and they say no one ever comes along that stretch
  of highway except yourself
and you'll be tempted when you see them
  especially if they bring out one of the children
to pick them up.

These stories always bothered me, a lot. "But what if they really *were* children?" I asked her. I pictured my Shana, small, helpless, chocolate-y brown Shana, for some reason lost in a snowstorm and walking along Highway 666 near Shiprock, with no one driving by who would pick her up.

Sally shook her head, but she was patient. "But they aren't

real," she said. "They're witches. Dead people. They're not really there. You just think they are. And you will die out there in the cold if you stop to help."

I guess I should have learned not to interrupt. "What if it was me?" I asked her. "Wouldn't you stop for me and Shana if it was us?"

That made her angry. "But it wouldn't *be* you!" she said. "Can't you see that?" She closed her eyes. "The wise ones know the difference between a witch and the people. Witches are evil spirits. They are the dead who trick us into helping, because they look like us."

* * * * *

But even if the stories sometimes bothered me, or scared me even, I wanted her to know she was lucky she had them.

So one day, right after we'd finished eating our lunch by the duck pond, I made the mistake of telling her I admired her for knowing exactly where she was from. "I have Shana," I said. "But I don't know where I come from, not like you."

I remember we were standing under the piñon trees by the library before going back. Her brown eyes narrowed, and I could see she was going to close them, and that she wasn't going to let me continue.

"No, I mean it," I said. I should have known not to keep on going, but I went on. "You have your geography," I said. "The kind I read about back in the fourth grade in one of the five different schools I went to in Detroit." I waved my hands at the landscape so she'd understand. "You have the desert, the brown earth that's been yours forever. You know the place in the world you belong to. You have your spot."

When I looked up, Sally Spotted Pony's eyes were focused on a place off in the distance, in the mountains, behind my head. I turned around and looked up there, but whatever it was, I couldn't see it yet. As far as I was concerned, I was standing there, talking to her. I was as real right then as I would ever be.

"Nope," I said. "I don't even know if I'm German, or English, or Irish. Or maybe I've got a little French thrown in there. Or maybe I glommed onto Leonard like I did in the first place because I'm not white. I don't have the tie right now to Detroit, that you have, right this minute, to your town up north. I'm not from somewhere, like you are. My geography's been the inside of a bus. I'm not anything, I guess, Sally. Not like you."

I knew I was raising my voice, but when she got like that, when she closed her face away from me, I had the idea she'd hear me if I yelled.

"I've got to get back to work now," Sally said. She began to back away from me.

"What's wrong?" I said.

But she turned on her high heels with a click on the yellow pavement and ran away.

I didn't see Sally for a long time after that. I called over there, to Native American Studies, but someone else always seemed to answer, and I had the feeling Sally had told everyone there to tell me she was out.

* * * * *

All this had happened between Sally and me by November. I'd moved out to Albuquerque in June and had met her for the first time around mid-July. After a few months at the Morgans', Shana and I were living in a little rental place with a screened-in porch off Central Avenue I'd found.

Shana and I each had us a bedroom. I decorated hers with a Mickey Mouse bedspread and white organdy tie-backs from K-Mart, and I hung two piñatas from Old Town down from her ceiling, and it looked pretty smart. I didn't do much in my room besides sleep in it, but I spent a lot of time in our little living room, which had a great fireplace with a *banco*, a kind of wall-length hearth. There was a niche in the chimney where you could put your saint, whoever your saint was. I bought a pull-out sofa at the Salvation Army and put it facing the banco, and I found a

St. Francis doll at a garage sale and stuck it up there in my niche. I wasn't raised Catholic, or anything else for that matter, but I liked birds and all kinds of flowers, and I'd heard St. Francis did, too, so he seemed a decent choice.

I still drove Shana out to the Morgans' every day in a pick-up I'd bought out of the newspaper for three hundred bucks. Mrs. Morgan told me how grateful she and Pete were to have me and Shana. We were like family, she told me. She said that whenever Pete went out on one of his trips, it was nice to have Shana, if only during the daytime, in her house.

I'd pick Shana up at the Morgans' after work, and then the two of us would have our supper together in front of the fireplace, Shana there throwing her spaghetti around and trying to say her few words like *Mama* and *Mizmogan*. Then I'd put her in bed in her room with the piñatas, and I'd go back and sit in front of the fireplace by myself.

One night I sat there clear until the wood was all burned up. I stared into the chunks of burned wood till I could see the ancient cliff dwellings Sally had told me about. I could see a million lights shimmering there in the windows of the cliff dwellings, there among the embers and exploding sparks. And then I could see, standing in front of these cliff dwellings, along the ridge that Sally said these dwellings had like a great long porch, a long line of very old women, one long-haired, brown-eyed, shrunken-faced Indian woman after another, all of them linked to Sally by holding hands.

When I finally raised my eyes to my St. Francis, watching high above them from his little niche, I noticed that he was melting. He'd become too hot while I wasn't paying attention, and now his bald head was flowing down smooth, no ears, no eyes, no mouth, onto the wide place that had been his shoulders once.

* * * * *

In the middle of December, I called Sally again, and for some reason they let me talk to her this time. I asked her could she meet me for lunch.

Even though it was maybe forty-five degrees, we could still eat our lunch by the duck pond. I had my coat on, but in New Mexico the sun is almost always shining, and if you sit with your back to a wall to keep the wind off, you're almost always warm.

We'd been talking for a few minutes about something not too important, and then there was a little silence while the two of us nibbled at our sandwiches. I looked at the gold glint of the sun on the duck pond, and it reminded me of my first day down by the river. Beyond the pond, I could see the rounded corners of the adobe buildings there on campus that I loved, and beyond them the Sandias, pale and brownish-gray in the distance, and if you just knew those mountains were in the east, then you could never really lose your direction, no matter where in the world you were coming from.

That's when I decided to ask her. "Sally?" I said. "You know those people out on the highway?"

She looked at me, a little puzzled, but she just said, "Yes?"

"You said you'd once seen one of them yourself?"

Sally nodded slowly. She was still only a bit fidgety at that point. "Yes, I have."

"Well," I said. "Can you tell me something about that one who got in with the truck-driver? Who she was."

Sally looked down at her slender fingers in her lap. "She was a young woman with a baby. I told you that. The time I saw her, it was the middle of August, and she was holding the baby and standing next to the highway, beside an old white truck that had broken down."

Now, Highway 666 is a god-forsaken road. I know that. And if you're standing out there on that desert, in all that heat, and nobody wants to stop to help you, you just may die. "And so," I said to Sally. "Did you stop?"

Sally's eyes snapped up from her fingers to my face. She took a long time traveling the full length of the mountain that was my scar. "Of course I didn't stop. I've already explained to you about those witches. She wasn't real."

But I didn't want her to think it was quite that simple. I didn't want her to take just one look at this woman and her baby and go driving by. "Listen," I said. "I want to understand this. But I don't. I keep seeing myself out there on the desert with Shana, and it's hot. That woman could be a real woman there, in real trouble. She could be *me*. Couldn't you maybe stop there for a moment, just stop long enough to at least find out?"

What happened next, I can never tell. Maybe Sally was trying to explain to me about those witches one more time. But she lifted her hands from her lap, one at each side of her body, as if she were raising them in prayer, and she began to chant.

We the Navajo know that witches aren't truly real.
They are the phenomena of our evil imaginations.
Someday, the witches will be erased from the face of
*   the earth.*
Then the world will belong only to the Navajo.
The white men and their black spirits, and all their
witches, too, will disappear.

A chill like an icy stream ran down my spine. "Sally," I said. "Am I included in the white people, to your point of view?"

She looked at me with a kind of sadness. "Yes," she said quietly. "You are."

I squeezed her fingers. "Sally," I said. "Does that mean that I'm a witch, and that I'm not real?"

She hesitated. "Please don't take things so personally, Eileen."

I put my hand on her arm, but her eyes grew as big as the piñon nuts on the sticky broken branches on the ground, and for one awful moment I thought she was going to scream. "Please, Sally," I said.

But she stood up.

"Please don't leave me, Sally," I begged her. "And don't look at me the way that boy looked at me in your office. I know now why it felt as if he was looking straight through me. He didn't believe that I was real."

Sally began to walk away.

"Please," I said. I got up and pursued her. I reached forward as far as I could and grabbed her hand and held it, so she couldn't go. I stood there, kneading her fingers. "Sally!" I said. "You're my friend. And you started this. You're the one who asked me about my scar. Tell me I'm really a person. Tell me I'm not a witch and that my brown baby that I've held at my own breast and given milk to isn't a witch, either. Tell me you haven't been sitting with someone who's dead here by this pond. Tell me, Sally Spotted Pony, that you don't believe that I'm a ghost."

But Sally was staring at the connection of our flesh, as though she knew that if I didn't let her hand go she was going to die.

"I'm asking you a question, Sally Spotted Pony," I said. "If witches aren't really people, who made us up?"

And with one horrible cry, she pulled away from me, and began to run.

"What was it that got your attention?" I shouted after her. "See, I'm waving my arms here at you, Sally Spotted Pony! I'm saying, stop and listen to me, Sally Spotted Pony, stop and help! "

But I could already feel myself dissolving. A hole was beginning to form in my chest where I'd had a heart. I started walking as fast as I could towards the mountains. I had to go find my baby. I had to phone Mrs. Morgan and ask her if she was sure, was she absolutely sure, Pete was still alive.

I walked faster and faster. I had things yet to finish. It wouldn't be long now before I'd be a mirage out on a road in the desert, a wet puddle in the middle of asphalt, an illusion where once I'd been foolish enough to believe I was flesh and blood. I would be a cloud-shape people would watch as they approached in the air-conditioned comfort of their car, eager to know what I was till they reached me. Then they would see for themselves I was nothing, and they would drive on by.

THE STURBRIDGE TALE

Amelia's mother, age twelve, stands on the sidewalk in front of the rented house in Sturbridge, Massachusetts, on a cold November day in 1930, wearing the second-hand coat *her* mother has cut down. Amelia's mother's mother has managed a nice fur collar out of a moth-eaten seal cape she found in the charity barrel at First Congregational, and when she finished the collar, she still had enough fur left to fashion two soft, coiled roses for a black velvet cloche. The fur roses cling to the hat at cheek-level, almost concealing the overt panic that until this moment the girl on the sidewalk has been able to keep inside. Home, as Amelia's mother has known it, is about to break up forever.

"The day after Thanksgiving and there I was," Amelia's mother is saying to her now. "Strangers, complete strangers coming to get me to go to work, and it was wet-raw cold. I'd met the mother before, of course—the woman who had hired me to take care of her daughter—but not the little girl herself, and not the man. And when I think of the things that could have happened! Well, there I was."

Amelia has heard this story many times. But this time, she is lying in a twin bed at the Maple Leaf Auto Court, a *family-style motel* on the Canadian side of Niagara Falls. She is driving with her mother, Jeannine Cotter Massey, from Michigan to Massachusetts, where her mother, after five decades of moving around the country as the wife of an airplane mechanic, still says she's *from*. Amelia's father has stayed behind to take care of Amelia's daughter, Julie, because Amelia's husband, Howard, is away for the Dexter Saw-Mill Company on a business trip. It is early summer, several weeks before Howard will let Amelia know that he is leaving her for a male dancer he will meet in a singles bar on this very trip, and a good six months before Amelia's mother and father will tell her that they can't take the Michigan winters anymore and that they have therefore decided to move down south. But at this point, all Amelia knows is that her mother has wanted to take a trip with her for a long, long time. This is the first trip Amelia remembers ever taking alone with her mother. She is thirty-one.

All day, she and Jeannine have taken turns driving across the flat stretches of rural Canada, after crossing the bridge into Windsor from Detroit. They have driven past silent farms with wheatfields that wave like blond-headed girls who have lost their barrettes, and they have stopped to use bathrooms in tiny, thoughtful towns that boast neat little red-brick houses and flower-bordered yards. Amelia has decided that Canada is what might have become of the entire continent of North America, if everyone had just been willing to leave well enough alone.

As they drove through town toward the Maple Leaf Auto Court, which Amelia's mother found in the Triple A book she brought along, Amelia read all the signs for the hotels. *Honeymoon suites. Heart-shaped waterbeds. Free in-room breakfast. Complimentary afternoon tickets for Maid-of-the-Mist trip behind the Falls!* She was relieved when her mother pulled into the Maple Leaf Auto Court, a no-nonsense string of one-story white frame buildings that didn't have in-room breakfasts nor even in-room phones. Whenever her mother pauses in the story she is telling, Amelia can hear the roar of the water, because the Falls, just as the motel marquee advertised, are only four blocks down.

Amelia already has a pretty good idea that something is wrong with her marriage, even though Howard hasn't told her so, and she wonders if things might have turned out differently for her and Howard if they'd had a honeymoon together here in Niagara

Falls. They got married right out of high school in Reno, where they both grew up, and moved north to Michigan when Howard, with nothing but a Nevada high school diploma behind him, got a job at the Dexter Saw-Mill Company as a fork-lift operator. Then Howard, who was always good with people, climbed up the rungs. Now he is head of something called Outside Operations. Anyway, Amelia doubts that back when she and Howard got married in Reno, she had ever even heard of Niagara Falls.

She wonders how her father and Julie are getting along during their first bachelor night together back at home. She imagines the two of them watching television in the living room of her parents' condo. It is too late for Julie to be up on a school night, almost one o'clock. The remains of two macaroni and cheese microwave dinners peek out from beneath a scattered Sunday paper, cartoons on top, as the television casts flickering pseudo-fireplace flames onto pure white walls. *Your mother*, Will Massey has often told her as he walks from one room to the next in a home in which he is forbidden to put his feet up on the coffee table, *has always had a decorator's touch*. Amelia pictures an enormous bowl of greasy popcorn between her father and daughter as they curl up together without taking their shoes off on her mother's white plush couch. They are two people who love each other unabashedly and without conditions—*minus*, as Julie said to her once, *all that other stuff*.

But even as Amelia makes this habitual attempt to deposit her invisible spirit inside her parents' living room back in Michigan so that she can watch, what she sees instead of her father and daughter is her mother's mother in the Sturbridge story, over fifty years ago. As a mother, what on earth can this woman be thinking as she surveys the shivering girl out on the sidewalk from inside the house? How can she go along with this? Doesn't she know that nothing in the world is worth this loss?

"I don't know," Jeannine says from the other bed, almost as if she has heard the unvoiced question in Amelia's thought.

Amelia turns on her side to look at her mother, whose features are softened by a lamp with a pink shade that the motel owners have put between the beds. Jeannine is wearing the red nylon Vanity Fair peignoir that Will gave her for their silver wedding anniversary some years ago. *Always get Vanity Fair,* she has told Amelia. *Because unlike sex in a marriage, a nightie by Vanity Fair will not wear out.* Her face glows back at Amelia with the translucence of Pond's Dry Skin Creme, which she has rubbed into her skin every night since the mid-Thirties when she moved away from New England forever, traveling first by train to Chicago, where she found a first-rate job, and after awhile on out to California, where her oldest brother, Victor, introduced her to his Army buddy, Will Massey. She became the first Cotter woman to have abandoned New England since 1695.

"I guess my mother thought she had to do it," Amelia's mother tells her from the other bed. "It was the Depression, you know, and we didn't have any money. I babysat, but Jackie was too young to do much more than have a paper route. And for some reason, Mother never could find anything permanent for herself. I guess that's why she felt she had to farm me out."

Jackie, short for Jacquelyn, was Amelia's aunt, who has been dead for fifteen years now by Amelia's count. Never a tall, thin, elegant French *Jacqueline*, Jackie was all Cotter at their most British—very big-boned, stout—while Jeannine became known as the *Indian Beauty*, not just because she was slim and fairly tall, with flawless olive skin and thick, straight hair that was jet-black dark, but because the Cotters had been in New England forever. *Or at least long enough to have an Indian in the woodshed,* Aunt Jackie had always added with a laugh.

Amelia pictures Jackie, two years Jeannine's junior, as the girl watches her older sister drive away with the wealthy family in one of the town's few cars. Jackie's large brown eyes as Amelia sees them through the frost the child's breath is creating on the window express the same fear and disbelief they will betray some forty years later when she dies of what has been wrongly diagnosed as a benign tumor out in Southern California, after a fifteen-year-old Amelia has hitch-hiked clear from Nevada with the intention of staying with her aunt for several months. But two nights after Amelia arrives on Jackie's doorstep, her aunt says to her in a voice that is sweet and calm with the defeat of a woman whose three children have been awarded to her dissolute husband in a custody battle after a cruel divorce, *Well, thank you for coming anyway, honey*. Right before daybreak, Amelia wakes up on the sleep-sofa to hear her aunt call out. *Sis?!* When she goes into Jackie's bedroom to see what is the matter, her aunt has died.

Now Amelia wonders, as she lies awake in Niagara Falls, listening to her mother tell the Sturbridge story one more time, if Jackie was still watching her older sister drive away in the car with the wealthy family on the night she died.

"But still," Jeannine is saying. "How could my mother do that?" Then she adds, "The boys were still up with the aunts, you remember, at my father's house."

At this point in the story, Jeannine's two brothers, Victor and Broadmoor, have been living down county with some of their dead father's people, the Littlefields, two spinster aunts. The Littlefield sisters believe with all their hearts that their nephew's philandering and infidelity remain insufficient reasons to warrant Amelia's mother's mother's filing for Cotter Neighborhood's first divorce.

"I hated my father," Amelia's mother says without reservation in a strictured voice. "My mother was hard to live with, and I know that. I was always scared to death of her myself. But he still shouldn't have gone off and left her with four children. At school, on the morning they told me he'd died of pneumonia while he was off with some pretty cousin in upstate New York, I said to the girl who'd told me she was sorry to hear about my father, there in the cloak-room of that one-room school, *But I don't care, don't you see? I hated my father. So you need not feel the least bit sorry for me. I am glad he died.*"

Until Jeannine's mother has to sell the farm, Victor and Broadmoor keep up with Jeannine and Jackie by means of an ingenious Paul Revere-type message system that makes use of the entire dark valley of abandoned farmland between them, and of one thin, strong light. Every night, the two boys swing a lantern from the upstairs window of the Littlefield spinster sisters' three-story house, signaling to Jeannine and Jackie, from whom they have been wrongly separated, and whom they deeply love. In return, the girls, who can find no surplus oil or lanterns in that virgin-headed house, wave back at their brothers invisibly through the moonless dark.

But once Jeannine's mother has lost the farm, the boys keep running away from the spinster aunts. Over and over, they show up at the door of the rented house in Sturbridge. And over and over, a social worker comes to the door of the house in Sturbridge, and, after apologizing to the boys' mother, she takes them back.

"Clear until Victor joined the army and Broadmoor went to work at the shoe factory down county," Amelia's mother tells her through a reluctant yawn. "What time is it, Amelia? This has been such fun! It just seems to me we never get to talk like this, honey. I don't know, really. I know I couldn't have done it, as a mother. Can you imagine me ever doing that to you, Amelia? Abandoning you to strangers? Sending you out to work when you were twelve years old?"

Amelia lies on her back and looks up at the motel ceiling in the dark. "They say that's always the question," she says, more to show her mother that she is still listening to the now-familiar story than as a thought-out remark. "Even now, you know, with all these child abuse and incest cases that keep coming up, that's what always triggers the argument. Everybody wants to know where the mother was."

Amelia hears her mother clear her throat. "Incest?" she says in what sounds very much to Amelia like a cautious voice. The word is foreign enough coming out of her Cotter mouth. But under the crispness of the bleached white sheets of the Canadian motel, Amelia feels a shiver go down her spine. That is the trouble with all these stories. Just when she thinks she has heard one of them a million times, something new comes into it, something dark and grotesque that will not go down. No matter what the subject, her parents never seem to be able to tell their stories the same way twice. Their stories always end up dark at the bottom, even when they start out nice and light.

"It's funny you should mention incest," Amelia's mother says.

But I know this story, Amelia reassures herself. And sad as this story is, there is no incest in it. The Sturbridge story even has a reasonably happy ending. Jeannine goes to work for the wealthy family for about a year, during which time Jeannine's mother, Gertrude Stone Cotter, gives up the rented house in Sturbridge, and packs Jackie off to live with a doting aunt. Then Gertrude herself gets work as a governess in an equally wealthy home, near the one where Jeannine is taking care of the little girl.

And then something wonderful happens. Gertrude lands a really good job as a hot entrée worker in an uptown cafeteria in Hartford, and everyone—Gertrude, Jeannine, Jackie, even Victor and Broadmoor—all move in together and live happily ever after for a little while. Victor is just back from the army, where he has already met the dashing airplane mechanic who will become Jeannine's husband when she comes out to California to take care of her brother's dying wife, and Broadmoor has taken a job packing frankfurters at Armour's, so that even though there is still a recession in New England, and times are hard, Jeannine and her mother and sister and brothers have fruit gelatin salads and a bit of potatoes *au gratin* left over from the steam trays in the cafeteria every night, to go along with the ham or bacon or Vienna sausages that Broadmoor has managed to smuggle out of the meat-packing plant. The place they have rented in Hartford is only a very small apartment, but no matter, they are all of them happy, because at last they are all together, one big happy family— the eccentric mother and her four children, all of whom are now, in turn, adults.

Gertrude fills the new little apartment in Hartford with the stray pieces of *eclectic* furniture she's found. She places a rollaway under the bay window and covers it with throw pillows and the mismatched quilts and afghans that she inherited from the various anonymous women of her disbanded house, and that she managed miraculously to save from the auction of the family farm, and she calls this area *the window seat,* where they can all sit and watch the outside world as it wanders by. *Our own little La Bohème,* Gertrude keeps saying, though by her own admission she knows next to nothing about opera, and, in any case, she tells her grown children, she thinks Puccini's tragic ending is something everyone might have been better off without.

But, "*Incest,*" Jeannine is still saying thoughtfully. She has tried the word on several times now, as though it is a garment, with shape and size. "Funny, isn't it, Amelia? I realize I haven't thought of that girl in all this time."

Amelia doesn't remember any *girls* at this end of the Sturbridge story other than her mother and Aunt Jackie. What is going on?

"Oh God!" Amelia's mother says. "She could have died!" Her eyes are open wide, two white pools fixed on a portrait of someone Amelia can't quite make out on the motel wall.

"What girl, Mother?" Amelia whispers.

"Margaret Mulrooney," Jeannine replies. "Oh, Amelia! You know how you can just go on when something like that happens to someone, and you can just go on when you don't know what becomes of them, and you just go on as though nothing has happened in your life?"

Even before Jeannine begins to insert the story of Margaret Mulrooney into the Sturbridge tale, Amelia knows this is a story she would like to stop. But she is helpless. Like a spirit called up at a séance, Margaret Mulrooney's story starts drifting forth.

"She lived there with her grandmother and stepfather in our apartment building in Hartford," Amelia's mother tells her. "They lived across the court. Her father had died, and her mother had remarried. Then somewhere along the way, her mother died. I don't know that part of the story, because that was before we met her, so I don't know what happened, how her mother died. But I do know that this grandmother, the one who lived with her and her stepfather, was her mother's mother. So that makes you wonder if the grandmother knew what was going on. And if she did, how she could have allowed it. Maybe she was just grateful to have a place to live in those days and so she didn't ask any questions. This grandmother may have just thought it was the Depression and so she'd better not disturb a good thing, you know, when she saw it."

Amelia listens as Margaret Mulrooney knocks on the door of the Cotter apartment one afternoon to introduce herself. "Hello," she says. "I'm Margaret Mulrooney." She seems a little too eager, though her smile is shy. "I live across the court from you," she tells Jeannine and Jackie. Margaret Mulrooney gestures behind her with her arm. "Over there," she says.

With a name like Margaret Mulrooney, she is an Irish redhead standing in front of two English Cotters. She would have freckles and green eyes, and the arm with which she is pointing off behind her must be an *alabaster* arm. Amelia wonders what she must think of the overweight Jackie as she stands there talking, or of Jeannine Cotter herself, for that matter, *the Indian Beauty* who has been taught well enough to be aloof from someone with a name like Mulrooney, and so does not speak back.

"I really never paid her much attention," Amelia's mother says. "I can hardly even describe her to you, Amelia."

Amelia listens as Margaret expresses her joy at finding two girls close to her own age living so nearby. "She was somewhere between us in age," Amelia's mother says. "She was, oh, fourteen, maybe, though she was probably more like fifteen when this all came out."

Soon, Margaret starts going to Sunday School with Jeannine and Jackie every week. Sunday School was in the morning. Then, on Sunday afternoons, all day until dinner, Margaret Mulrooney would go with her stepfather to his downtown store.

"He managed a nice store," Amelia's mother tells her. "We never thought anything of it. We'd sit in our window seat with the pillows and afghans, and we'd watch from upstairs as Margaret and her stepfather made their way to the trolley, Margaret still in the Sunday School clothes she'd worn to go with us, and him in a nice suit, and a nice coat and hat. Everyone thought it was so nice, how he took an interest in his stepdaughter even after his wife had died. How he let her go with him every Sunday to that shop."

Then one Friday, Margaret told Jeannine and Jackie that she wasn't going to go with them to church the following Sunday.

"She told us she and her stepfather were going down to New York for the weekend to visit an old friend of her mother's," Amelia's mother says. "Margaret's mother's friend wanted to get to know her friend's daughter, was what the paper said. Anyway, apparently, the friend had fixed up two rooms for Margaret and her stepfather—and they were *separate* rooms."

Amelia's mother takes a deep and audible breath in the darkness of the Maple Leaf Motel. "The stepfather apparently threw a holy fit. The paper said he told Margaret's mother's friend that he and Margaret would be perfectly fine in a single room."

Amelia watches as this Margaret, an intruder into her family history, follows her stepfather into a room at the end of a long, dark hall.

"You've got to understand that for us," her mother tells her, "Margaret was just another kid who liked to come to our apartment. Lots of people did. The boys brought home their friends. We had a player piano. Lots of people came over on Sunday nights. We would dance and sing."

Amelia knows that the dancing and singing part of the story is really true, because usually, when her mother gets to the Hartford place in the story, she breaks into one of the tunes she and the other young people used to dance to in the Cotter apartment in their little *La Bohème*. She will sing to Amelia, *I'm only a bird in a gilded cage*. Or, *Let me call you sweetheart, I'm in love with you*. Always a little off-key in her high-pitched voice. But this is the first time there has ever been any Margaret Mulrooney among the happy guests. Why has her mother left Margaret out of the story for all these years?

"It wasn't like you would think," her mother says. "You know, that there were signs, or something an outsider might notice, so that we might have become suspicious of her stepfather and tried to help. Before this thing came out in the paper, I'd never thought much about Margaret Mulrooney. She was just someone who walked to Sunday School with us, and someone who hung around with the others on Sunday nights."

But during the visit from her dead friend's husband and daughter, the woman down in New York began to suspect that something was very wrong. "The paper said that she walked up and down the hall outside their room all night long," says Amelia's mother. "It could have been the wee hours of the morning before she knew for sure."

Amelia pictures Margaret's mother's friend in the hall of the comfortable house down in New York. She is a big woman, with a big heart. Though she loves children, she hasn't had any children of her own. She is wearing a blue cotton dress, with white collar and cuffs, and she is very tall—a hefty, Swedish-looking woman who winds her thick blond braids around her head in a kind of crown. Amelia sees the woman stop in front of the guest-room. It is late at night. The woman inclines her head, heavy with the braids, toward the door. Pressing her hand against her chest, she holds her breath, and listens.

Amelia's mother says, "The woman in New York told the paper she knew her old friend's spirit would not let her rest until she did something about the sounds that she heard coming from behind that door."

Amelia sees now that another figure has stepped up out of the sepia darkness to stand behind the friend of Margaret's dead mother in the hall. Amelia can barely make out the second figure, which is dark on the bottom and light on top, but it, too, has the shape of a woman. For one moment, Amelia feels as if she is seeing double, because the dark/light figure behind the friend of Margaret's mother stands so close. Margaret's mother's friend seems blurred at the edges, like an old and badly focused photograph that a child might keep of a mother who has long since died. Slowly, the second shape melds onto the body of the woman who is standing there listening to the sounds from behind the door. The woman hears Margaret Mulrooney inside the bedroom as she cries out softly, "Oh, no, please don't!"

The next morning, the woman in New York tells her

husband, "Think of an excuse, any excuse you can, to take that man out of my house. Tell him you want to show him where you work. Tell him you want to take him out for coffee. I don't care how you do it, but get him out of here so that I can talk to Margaret by myself.'"

As soon as the men leave, the woman goes directly to Margaret's room. "Listen to me, Margaret Mulrooney," the woman says. She takes Margaret's thin, pale hands inside her own. "I heard what was going on inside this room, and I'm going to help you."

An absolute terror fills Margaret's eyes. "He told me he'd kill me," she whispers. Her *alabaster* Irish skin is ghastly white. "He said he would kill me if I ever told."

"He won't kill you," says the friend of Margaret's dead mother. "I'm going to help you. Now sit down and tell me everything you know."

It had been going on for years, ever since Margaret Mulrooney's mother died.

"All those Sundays Margaret was going with her stepfather down to his shop," Jeannine says to Amelia. "He kept a cot in the back. No one was there, you know, because it was Sunday. We'd see the two of them from our window seat, the one with the afghans and the cushions, every Sunday after church when they went downtown together, and then every Sunday evening we'd see the two of them as they were coming back."

Margaret's mother's friend set up a plan. She gave Margaret a name and a phone number in Hartford. "You wait until a time when he would normally think you're out," she told Margaret. "Then you go to a phone somewhere and you call this friend of mine in Hartford who's a social worker, and you tell her everything that you've told me. Don't leave one detail out."

On the following Sunday morning, when Margaret didn't come to their apartment to walk to Sunday School with them, Jeannine and Jackie Cotter were hopping mad. "Well, she hadn't said she wouldn't be coming," Amelia's mother tells her in her own defense. "She'd told us the week before that she wouldn't be coming, when she went with her stepfather to visit her mother's friend there in New York. But this time she hadn't said anything, and we were waiting. And finally, we had waited so long that we were late for Sunday School. We had to walk past all the little kids sitting in those baby chairs in the front of the assembly during silent prayer."

Amelia presses her hand to her left breast as she lies there listening to her mother in the Maple Leaf Motel. In the place of her left breast are all mothers and children—herself and her mother, herself and Julie, Margaret Mulrooney and her dead mother, Aunt Jackie and each of the three children she battled her husband in the courts to keep, but finally lost. There are no spinster aunts inside this place in Amelia's heart. *Oh God, if only I had my mother*, she can hear Margaret Mulrooney praying. She hears Margaret saying softly, *Oh please don't!*

"You told him," Amelia says as the horrible truth dawns on her mind. She realizes what her own mother has done to another woman's daughter, if many years ago. "You told Margaret's stepfather." She sits up in bed and begins to shake. "Margaret was out calling the number her mother's friend had given her in New York, and you went across the court to tell her stepfather you had been waiting, and that she'd made you late. He thought she was with you, but that was to give her the time to make the phone call the way the woman in New York had told her, and then you went over there to tell her stepfather because you were mad. And it was because of you that he found out."

Amelia's mother raises her hand up to her mouth. "You have to understand we had no idea. We went to her apartment. We were late to Sunday School. She hadn't said she wouldn't be coming. We were mad."

A few hours later, after Jeannine and Jackie get back from church, Margaret Mulrooney runs into their apartment, looking wild-eyed and frantic. "Hide me!" she cries. "Hide me!"

But Jeannine and Jackie stand there, arms crossed, nodding and nodding, their lips set in that *now you're gonna get it* look Amelia knows so well. The look comes from the Cotter side of the family. It has not left New England since 1695. "So where were *you*?" Amelia's dead Aunt Jackie keeps asking. She sneers at the terrified Margaret Mulrooney. "We waited and we waited, but you didn't come."

"Hide me!" Margaret is sobbing. But as she stares into their stupid, satisfied, unyielding faces, she begins to scream.

"Durn right we told him," says Jackie. Amelia can see her aunt—big-hipped, slouchy-bosomed, acne-pocked—the beloved aunt who sang and tap-danced at all family functions to everyone else's embarrassment even after her ex-husband stole the children and took them to live with his mother in Vermont. The sad, beloved, pitiable aunt who never refined the *bad side of the tracks* accent she picked up from the mill workers at the public school in Sturbridge after her blue-blood Cotter Neighborhood mother had to sell the farm. Jackie Cotter says to this inferior Irish girl, "And that's the last time we're ever inviting you anywhere, Margaret Mulrooney, so there you are!"

Margaret runs out of the happily-ever-after apartment in Hartford with its *Bohemian* pillows, its colorful magpie afghans and its roll-away couch, and she runs down the corridor, out into the courtyard, and on into the winter evening, where she disappears among the trolley tracks, a wisp of a girl wearing only the thinnest of sweaters, and no hat or scarf. "He's going to kill me!" she screams until they can no longer hear her. "Where can I go? He's going to kill me now, and I have to hide!"

That is the last time Amelia's mother or her aunt ever see Margaret Mulrooney. She leaves Jeannine's and Jackie's lives forever, until she surfaces again, some fifty years later, churning up like a corpse in the roar of the waters of Niagara Falls.

Amelia's mother is lying on her side, propped up on one elbow. "The next day, we saw an ambulance drive up," she says. "At first, we thought it was the grandmother, you know, because she was old. We still had no idea what had happened. We just saw them wheeling someone out on a stretcher. And then it was all over the paper. *Prominent shop-owner, accused of molesting step-daughter, denies charges, attempts to take own life.* The social worker, the friend of the woman in New York, must have moved quite fast."

The room in the Maple Leaf Auto Motel is silent as two women breathe. True to the motel's marquee, Amelia can hear the roar, that *noise of many waters*, four blocks down. She realizes that she is surprised that the roar is still going. It must be the middle of the night, perhaps almost morning. Something in her had actually believed that the roar would stop at some point or other, like water from a kitchen faucet that can be turned off. Her mind begins to swim at the thought of all the water in the world she cannot control.

Amelia looks at her mother from her twin bed in the motel room in Canada that seemed so cozy and home-like only hours ago. Where has Margaret Mulrooney been all these years, this Margaret Mulrooney who lived across the court from Jeannine and Jackie Cotter in Hartford? Did she grow up and get married? Does she have a daughter now, who in turn may have had another daughter of her own, who may then someday have another? Perhaps Margaret Mulrooney is lying right this moment on her back in some motel, during a trip she has taken with her grown daughter, to whom she is finally revealing this secret about herself.

Margaret Mulrooney has been a watery roar in the distance that has not turned off. Amelia envisions a long line of women stretching from Sturbridge to Hartford, then on out to California, then up to Detroit, then circling back. They have come *home* to Massachusetts, where they are *from*. And like the infinite paper dolls she used to cut out of the funny papers with Julie, the women in the long line that has become a circle are holding hands.

Neither Amelia nor her mother say, *Good night*. After awhile, Jeannine reaches up quietly and turns off the light. In the darkness, Amelia sees her Aunt Jackie peering from the window of the Sturbridge house. Jeannine stands on the sidewalk on the day after Thanksgiving in 1930. It is very cold. She is wearing her made-over coat with the little fur collar and the fur-trimmed hat, and she is still carrying the familiar straw suitcase, still waiting for the wealthy family that is going to come.

But it isn't the same story. Amelia knows she will never get it back.

After what seems like hours, Amelia hears her mother begin to snore. It is a noise her mother often makes when she is sleeping on her back, an offensive noise so completely unlike Jeannine Cotter Massey, so coarse and unfeminine, a noise that has frightened Amelia ever since she was a child, when she would hear it coming from behind the closed doors of her parents' bedroom late at night. Sometimes, Amelia would get up in the darkness and walk down the hall. She would stand outside the closed door of her parents' bedroom, listening to the awful sound as her mother snored. The noise made Amelia think of a fat man pulling his pants down in public. He would be pink and fat and ugly, all soft and round.

As Amelia lies awake, listening to the unstoppable roar in the distance of Niagara Falls, she wakes her mother up every now and then, to tell her softly, "Mama, please don't do that. Mama, roll over, Mama, please don't snore."

Each time Amelia says this, her mother wakes up long enough to apologize. "I'm sorry, Amelia," Jeannine Cotter Massey says before she turns over on her stomach to go back to sleep. "I'm really sorry, Amelia. I didn't know."

BERKELEY

People always ask me how it was. They romanticize it, talking about the assassinations, saying so-and-so is a Sixties Person—always in regard to someone who is way too young—or holding forth about the Beatles' Apple albums, or about the Rolling Stones. I want to step up and ask one of them, *What do you think a Sixties Person is, Sonny?* But I know I won't.

We're historic, like flappers. I used to feel that way about the Roaring Twenties as a child. My father had an elderly relative, a woman who was his second cousin, who often came to visit while I was growing up, and who, although she had once been both beautiful and wealthy, was neither now. She traveled around the country by Greyhound Bus, and whenever she stopped at our house, I used to corner her and make her tell me about the Twenties. She said fashionable women bound their breasts to make them flatter. She said they dieted until they almost died of starvation. She said she and her girlfriends danced in skinny, silvery dresses, their skirts up above their knees, hemlines riding up and down like caresses on their kicking thighs.

So maybe someday my great-nephews and nieces will ask me, *What was it like in Berkeley back in the Sixties, Auntie Lisa? Did they really beat students with black-jacks? Is it true you still won't let people take your picture, because back then they took pictures of students on the Sproul Hall Steps for the FBI? Did you really walk away from those noon rallies to go to your cancelled classes, as you wiped away the pain of the tear-gas from your eyes?*

I won't be telling my own children and grandchildren about Berkeley, because I'm almost fifty now, and it has recently *ceased to be with me after the manner of women*, to put in Biblical terms the physical detail of menopause. I received a letter from my mother last week, telling me she and my father had resigned themselves to the fact that my sister's son Mikey was going to be their only grandchild. *So Lisa*, said my mother, *never mind.*

I know I don't look old enough. But then, haven't you noticed? No one from this generation ever does. It's not the same as it was for our parents. The men don't necessarily have a paunch around their middle. The women's faces don't always exhibit the cosmetic ads' proverbial *little tell-tale lines*. Nowadays, when someone is forty-eight, fifty-two, maybe even sixty, you can't always tell. And it can't just be all the exercise, either. Or the vegetarian cooking, all those stir-fried veggies in the Chinese woks. I am beginning to believe that something occurred to keep us from aging. It's as if the whole damn Baby Boom Generation has fallen victim to some sort of spell. We are like that woman who was written up in the nineteenth century medical journal, *The Lancet*, whose case I have always intended to research in the library, who never grew any older, because she went crazy on her wedding day when her fiancé, who was apparently her very last prospect, stood her up.

* * * * *

I transferred to Berkeley my junior year from a community college down the Peninsula in Mountain View, and I got an apartment on Shattuck with a girl I'd met at the college in English Comp. Sarah and I had both decided we were ready for a change of pace. She put down Latin American Studies as her intended major when she applied to UC, and I put down European Studies, thinking it was a possibility that I might do something in international relations later on.

It was the first time either one of us had lived away from home. We sat in our little window seat on the eighth floor of the apartment building, looking out over Berkeley and, in the distance, the Golden Gate Bridge and Alcatraz. We took turns discussing our reasons for being, in deep, soft voices. We ironed our hair between sheets of waxed paper to make it straight, and we took the bus over to San Francisco and had our ears pierced, so we could wear the long gold dangling earrings we both had bought. We put on our black stockings and black turtleneck sweaters and our gray A-line minis and we walked up Telegraph Avenue to Sather Gate, careful to wear only a whitish-pink lipstick, but with a lot of heavy black Indian kohl around our eyes.

It was just one big costume party after another for both of us. We dressed up and became part of the scenery. We went to the Rathskeller for coffee and their special green salad with the secret dressing. We ignored the street people who slept on the sidewalk, and kicked them away if they grabbed at our ankles. We were always laughing. It never occurred to me that Berkeley had anything at all to do with life.

For the first few weeks, because neither of us had as yet made other friends, Sarah and I met at noon in the Student Union and then walked outside to Sproul Plaza to eat our lunch. Bettina Aptheker or Mario Savio would be speaking. I didn't care much about what they were saying, about the need to screen student organizations before we let them set up tables on the Plaza because they might be CIA fronts, or about The Weather Underground's plans for revenge on the ROTC building, or about Vietnam.

My parents were Republicans, and my father had a pretty important defense job in San Jose. He warned me I was going to have to be careful—that I would have to keep watching my thinking for signs of perversion, because the Communists were very, very convincing, and very crafty. They knew exactly what they were doing, even if the rest of us did not.

Sarah said her parents were the same way. We took the train down the Peninsula every Friday together—her to San Mateo, me on to San Jose—and then we swapped our family stories laughing uproariously, every Sunday night. We told our parents Berkeley wasn't the least bit like what they saw on Walter Cronkite. We said you could just go to classes if you wanted, and so long as you just minded your own business and stayed out of trouble, you'd be all right.

I got into a routine with my classes. And though I listened to the speakers at noontime and jeered with the crowd at the FBI men who were wearing sunglasses and taking photographs, I didn't get involved. I wasn't that great a student, for one thing, and I didn't see how anyone could join the protests and still get the grades to stay there, how they found the time. I was just barely getting C's, and I'd had all A's and B's at my community college. But I liked people to know I was up at Berkeley now. And I liked the way my parents always worried about me, how they phoned me nights.

During my second semester, I met Sonya. She kept showing up at the meetings of the religious group my mother had made me promise I would join. The religious group was supposed to be for college students from Cal-Berkeley, and Sonya only went to a secretarial school over in Oakland, but they let her in anyway because some kind soul had said they thought that we could help.

The first thing I noticed about her was her hair. It was short and pitch black, with the plastic shine of an LP record, and it stood straight up in stiff little curls around her head. Her eyes were flecked with gold and brown, like cat's-eye marbles, glass within the glass, and they never seemed to focus on any one person in the circle when she talked.

And she did talk. Constantly. She always wanted to sit by me at these meetings of the religious group I belonged to, but I could never remember afterwards what she said. All I knew was that there was something about her that scared me.

One day my roommate and I agreed ahead of time to meet in one of our favorite haunts, a donut shop on Telegraph. This donut shop had obviously been there since before Berkeley *went political*, as the locals had it, and so, a little like the community college Sarah and I had gone to, it was behind the times. A long string of sleighbells hung by a leather strap against the door, and whenever a customer came in, the bells would ring. Other than the two of us, no students ever went in there, just old ladies wearing thick pink make-up and little dusty hats. They all looked like Mamie Eisenhower, whose picture I remembered seeing often in the newspapers when I was a child. My parents had given me and my little brother a big red, white and blue bumper sticker with General Eisenhower's and his wife's picture on it for our red Radio Flyer, and for several years my brother and I pulled our wagon around town, proclaiming in our innocence, *I like Ike.*

Sarah and I enjoyed the donut shop, because we could sit there in our black stockings and turtleneck sweaters and giggle quietly about the little old ladies who all looked like alcoholic Mamie, while we ate one fantastic powdered-sugar, jelly-filled donut after another, all warm and fat. On this one day, Sarah was telling me about a guy from Chile who was in one of her classes. He had told her she spoke Spanish like a native of Mexico City, and that she turned him on. We were both still virgins— the only virgins we knew from among our high school friends— but Sarah had learned to do the mambo and the samba during a trip to Guadalajara she'd taken with her parents the previous Christmas, and she loved to dance.

"You wouldn't believe this guy, Lisa," she was saying. "What a gentleman he is. He is just *so nice.*"

Sonya walked into our donut store at about that point. Sarah didn't know who Sonya was, of course, not ever having gone with me to the religious group, but Sonya was enough to attract anybody's attention. I tried to continue as we were, just eating my donut and talking with my mouth full, but Sarah shoved me in the ribs with her elbow and said, "Get a load of *that.*"

I glanced over at Sonya, who was standing in front of the glass door. The sleighbells at the top of the door were still ringing because she'd pulled the door just a bit too hard. She was wearing the holey long brown cardigan that she always wore, V-necked, with leather buttons and baggy pockets, way down on her hips like a weird old man's, and some sort of filmy, old-fashioned white blouse that looked like it belonged on one of the donut shop ladies, and an ankle-length brown plaid Pendleton skirt that had lost its folds. Thick white nurse's stockings, and three-inch black pointy-toe heels topped the outfit off.

Sarah was always a little suspicious of my going to that religious group, so it was embarrassing, when most of those people were quite normal, to have to introduce her now to one like that. I was hoping that Sonya wouldn't see me, because of the way her eyes were always out of focus, one of them always directed slightly heavenward, a little off. But she did see me. She waved happily. Then, just so Sarah wouldn't think she was a friend of mine, I groaned and shook my head and said, "Here she comes."

Sonya walked over and sat down on the empty stool next to Sarah. She reached across Sarah's lap to grab my arm. "It's so good to see you, Lisa!" she cried, her voice far too loud. She sounded breathless and eager, as if she had been reading books on how to appear enthusiastic in social situations. As though, if she hadn't read a book on how to be normal, she would never know.

Sarah drew back as far as she could, so that Sonya's dirty brown sweater wouldn't touch her arm. She looked over at me and rolled her eyes.

"Sarah," I said, "I'd like you to meet Sonya." I was very careful not to add, *my friend*. "Sonya's in that religious group I told you about that I attend sometimes."

"Oh, I *see*," Sarah said. She made a big point of reaching for her jelly donut, and then she sat there slowly chewing it, looking out the window at the people passing by on Telegraph, clearly letting me know she didn't want to be involved. I could see that she was already contemplating the moment of her escape.

Meanwhile, Sonya kept talking as if she couldn't stop. "Oh yes Lisa and I are great friends, aren't we Lisa, and I've been looking for a friend, you know, someone I can talk to, for so very long, you'll have to come over to my house, you'll *both* have to come over, and then maybe we can play Scrabble or something, or Monopoly, would you like that? And you can meet my grandmother, would you like that, I *live* with my grandmother, my mother is always traveling so my grandparents have raised me, and sometimes I think I'd like to have an apartment like you two and not live at home, but then I can't do that, either, because I think they need me, and this man at my secretarial school loves to play Scrabble, but I've never really played it, you know, myself, but I thought I'd try, I try to get into these things that other people are doing, are you like that, you try to learn their games and be like they are but it's really hard, I dropped out of high school, didn't finish my, you know, just hung around, was into, the, further down on Telegraph, you get, but I can show you if you want, and now I'm just in, secretary school, because I'm not too smart, but you are, aren't you, Lisa, going to school, but it's not like what you think you're seeing, all this in Berkeley, you're really not, because I have lived, in Berkeley, like my mother, like her parents, all my life, and you think it's all love and freedom I know, don't you, but you'll see, I know these people on the sidewalk, I pretend that I don't know them, but I do, and when I walk along, I'm hoping they won't notice, but there was one they called the Angel, who was surely not an angel, he was a devil, and you just think it's on the surface, but it's not, I know them, all these people, every one, and I wish that you'd come over, if you come over, I could tell you, what they're like."

By now, Sarah had dropped all pretension of looking out the window. "Jesus," she said. She grabbed her backpack and jumped off the green plastic-covered metal swivel stool at the counter and said, "So long."

I was furious with her for abandoning me like that. I whirled on my stool before Sonya could start up again, and I said, "Well, gee, Sonya, it was real nice running into you, it really was. But I've got a class I have to go to. Sorry I couldn't stay a little longer so we could talk."

By the time I caught up with Sarah, she had almost made it to Sather Gate. "Wait a minute, will you?" I called out.

"You better watch it," she said, turning around to face me. "That woman is really a weirdo."

We laughed about Sonya as we continued on to Dwinelle, me for my French class, and her for Spanish. But I had already seen something in Sarah's eyes.

* * * * *

A few days later, Sonya phoned me late at night. "You've got to come over," she said. "I can't stand this any more. I don't know what's wrong. I think I'm going crazy. I went crazy, once, just before I knew you, and now I know again there's something wrong."

"Now, Sonya," I said in my best, slow voice. "What's bothering you? You know there's nothing to be afraid of." I took a gamble. "At least, not *now*."

An audible sigh of relief ran through the phone. "How did you know about that?" she said. "Can you come over tomorrow? Tomorrow would be okay, if not tonight. You can meet my grandmother. She's old and everything, you know, but she's very nice."

Sarah was staring at me darkly from between her sheets. "For God's sake," she hissed. "It must be four o'clock in the morning. Could you tell that psycho, please, not to wake us up?"

I told Sonya I'd be over tomorrow, to get her off the phone.

After I hung up, Sarah rolled over, her back to me. "You are *really* in for it now, Lisa," she said.

The next day, after Intro to Poli Sci, I walked to Sonya's house. It was in an old neighborhood that had gone over to students, just past the campus part of Telegraph where it widens out. I looked at the address I'd written down on an envelope and stopped in front of a dilapidated brown shingle Victorian, its only remaining splendor from the big-family, middle-class era in which it had been built the blood-red, leaded-glass window in its huge front door. I walked up four rotting steps and knocked.

It seemed to me as if I stood at that front door for a long, long time. I could hear someone inside, running up and down stairs, in and out of rooms, scurrying quietly, like a mouse scratching its way on tiny toenails inside a wall.

I wanted to believe that no one had heard me. Then, all of a sudden, I didn't want to stay there anymore. I turned around and started down the steps, catching my toe in one of the rotten places, almost falling down. Just as I reached the sidewalk, Sonya unlocked the door.

"*Hi*, Lisa!" she shouted. "Where are you going? Here I am now, Lisa, did I take too long?"

And indeed there she was, a little breathless, but with a shy, sweet smile. Her hair looked stranger than usual, though I did not know why. And then it hit me. Her hair was turned around. The curly black layers of what should have been the back of a bubble hairstyle from a few years before hung down in lopsided bangs along her brow.

"I'm really sorry I took so long," she said. "I was trying to find my wig." She tucked a few stray pale hairs beneath the black fringe, thick as yarn, that tumbled to her eyes. "I don't like people to see me without my wig. I get very self-conscious. I'm trying to improve my image. Look more mature or something. That's what I think will happen when I get a job."

She moved quickly down the steps toward me, and, placing her hands on my hips from behind, she pushed me up. "Come on in and meet my grandmother. She's really looking forward to meeting you. She's really happy for me, that I've found a friend."

Sonya ushered me in across a worn, speckled-linoleum floor. I could see rough wooden planks through the ragged holes. The first room, entirely empty except for a fireplace that was boarded up, must have been a parlor at one time. We came into a small, dark room with crowded walls. Clothes hung from hooks someone had hammered in at different levels. I recognized Sonya's old brown sweater and the pleated Pendleton skirt that had lost its folds.

"Here she is!" she announced. We were standing in what I thought was a closet. I could see the light from the kitchen windows about ten feet beyond. I had the feeling that I was seeing the light at the end of a tunnel but that I would never be allowed again to go outside.

In the dark, Sonya's long, cool fingers pinched my arm. I looked down at a very old woman, who gazed back at me benignly with a toothless smile, from the little cot where she lay beneath a filthy quilt. "This is my grandmother," Sonya said. "You can say hello to Lisa can't you, Gram!" she shouted. "Say hello!"

The old lady struggled up onto her elbows, and put out a wizened hand. "I'm so glad to meet you," she said in a tiny voice. "Sonya has told me so much about you." She glanced at Sonya shyly, then back at me. A thin braid of yellowed white hair lay across cheeks that were curiously unlined beneath a wrinkled brow. "There are cookies in the cupboard, Sonya," she said. "Ginger snaps, they are, the ones you like. Gramps made sure he asked for those when he called the store."

The old woman hadn't let go of my hand. "You're certainly nice and warm, aren't you," she said.

Sonya smoothed the quilt and tucked the edges in around the cot. "Gram takes a nap after lunch everyday, don't you, Gram?" I heard unmistakable tenderness in her voice.

"It's really very nice of you to come," the old lady said. She let go of my hand as she lay back down. "We've been quite worried about Sonya. It's been hard on her, growing up with just us old folks. Not enough young people around."

"Oh, *Gram*," Sonya laughed, an explosive puff of trapped and knotted air.

She turned to me. "Come on, Lisa. I'll fix us a plate of cookies, and, lemonade, would you like that, Lisa? And we'll take it all up into my room at the top of the stairs so we can talk."

Out in the kitchen, she took the ginger snaps from a red and yellow cookie jar, a ceramic replica of a big-skirted, black-faced slave from the ante-bellum South. Sonya removed the cookies one by one, as though she might be counting them. "These are my favorites," she said. "Gram always had them when I was growing up. Then my mother would come for awhile, and eat them, and so I always thought about her when I ate them after she was gone."

She touched my arm. "I lied about my mother in front of your girlfriend, Lisa. It's true she used to visit us every now and then when I was little, but now she lives in a place where she can't come out. Are you comfortable here, Lisa? Do you like us? Can I get you coffee maybe instead of lemonade, or is this enough?"

"Lemonade will be fine, thank you," I said, watching the slow progression of ginger snaps from the belly of the slave onto the chipped white plate Sonya was holding in her pale right hand.

"I don't know if you can tell," she said, "but I don't have people over here very often. For a long time I just dressed up and met people down on Telegraph, you know, but then that Angel I told you about, you know the one?"

It took me a moment, but then I remembered the run-on monologue she'd delivered in the donut shop. "Yes," I said. "I remember."

"He raped me." She didn't change her fixed expression, didn't stop taking the cookies from the jar.

I began to shiver, as though I had to go to the bathroom or was very cold. I tried to concentrate on the growing mound of cookies on Sonya's plate. There were more there now than we could ever eat. They were about to topple over. *Did it hurt*, I wanted to ask. *Of course it hurt you ninny.* There were shattered pieces of cookie on the dull red floor. The room began to turn around the cookies. *And what did you expect, what sort of answer, with a thing so small. Don't be frightened, will you, Lisa. They're just cookies, only cookies, that's all they are.*

"There now," Sonya said, brushing crumbs from her fingers. "That should be enough. Let's go up to my room, why don't we." And she led me up some stairs and down a hall.

I thought of my nice, safe apartment back on Shattuck, with its blue and green studio couches, its warped Maurice Utrillo view of Montmartre on the dull white wall. I summoned up Sarah, normal, giggling Sarah, the nonchalant familiarity of her long gold earrings and black stockings, all of it just a costume, after all. I found myself praying to her. *Please, Sarah.* I wasn't sure I wasn't actually saying her name out loud.

"This is my room," Sonya said. "We'll be in here, that is, if you want to be in here, Lisa, for a little while."

She put the cookies and lemonade down on a scuffed nightstand that was covered with a frayed and dirty embroidered cloth. "My grandmother used to do a lot of needlework," she said. "I'll show you something she made for my mother. A Spanish shawl."

I watched, fascinated, as she pulled a large piece of white fringed silk from a series of accordion-like coat racks on the flowered wall. *Cat got your tongue? Are you fearful? Because she told you, and you can't begin to imagine, can you, and you'd like to ask her, wouldn't you, how it felt.*

Sonya was standing in front of the door, wrapped in the white silk, its red embroidered camellias blooming across her chest like exploded hearts. "If you like it, I'll give it to you," she said. "Lisa, why are you staring at me like that? Is something wrong?"

She started dancing slow motion in front of the door of her bedroom. I wanted that door to open so I could run out.

"Why don't you say something?" she said, turning and turning. "Aren't you having a good time here?" She twirled across her room to the closet. "Wait a minute. I know. I know what I'll show you. A picture I found in a book. A beautiful man with beautiful lips. And he's smiling. He's the man I love."

I sat down on her bed and carefully, deliberately, folded my hands and counted, one, two, three. *Sarah*, I said. *Please Sarah.*

Sonya brought out a mildewed book and sat down beside me, the Spanish shawl trailing dejectedly along her arms. She was rifling through the book so roughly that I was afraid she would tear the brittle pages. As her fingers grabbed at the ragged edges, I could smell the mold.

"Here he is!" she cried. She pointed, triumphant, then tossed the book on my lap, and jumped back up. "Just look at him!" she said. "Don't touch." She paced the floor, wringing her hands.

I glanced down at a pink-skinned young man from the eighteenth century. He was wearing silk breeches, a powdered wig, a flowered coat. His thin, colorless hands emerged from white lace cuffs. "Sonya," I said, "this is a painting. A portrait by Gainsborough, maybe, or a Joshua Reynolds. We look at paintings like this on slides in my art history class three times a week. You can't fall in love with a painting, Sonya. It isn't right."

At the word *right*, she looked frightened. She grabbed the book away from me and slammed it shut. "But what if he were alive?" she said, kneeling down on the floor in front of me, so that her chin hovered just above my knees. "What if he just walked right out of the painting? What if I saw him someplace, walking, like on Telegraph? Would that be enough?"

I looked at her drained face under its lopsided black wig, her cat's-eye-marble eyes glowing, unfocused, and I went along. "That would be very nice," I said. Carefully, slowly, I went on eating the ginger snaps, aware that I was avoiding the probably perfectly safe lemonade in its cloudy glass. I knew as I sat there, shaking badly now, that she was beyond my help.

As soon as I thought it was possible to leave, I excused myself. "I really have to go now, Sonya," I said. "I have to study." I thought I heard it echo, that word *study*. It sounded small and powerless, like a hollow shell.

Sonya seemed neither disappointed nor surprised that I was going to leave. She walked me back down the stairs, back the way we had come, past her grandmother, still lying in the darkened room on the little cot.

"You're leaving already," her grandmother said as I walked by. "Nice to have met you." She sounded much less enthusiastic than when I'd come.

When I got back to the apartment on Shattuck, I ran into Sarah's and my white ceramic tile bathroom and I threw up. Light-headed and feverish, I made my way to the convertible day-bed and climbed between the blue cornflower sheets my mother had bought for me, announcing as she gave them to me that they were for *your first new house,* and I stayed there until three hours later when Sarah, home with books and a bag of groceries, woke me up.

She was shaking me by the shoulders. "Lisa! Are you dreaming?

What are you saying? What's the matter with you? Jesus, why in
God's name are you so hot? What's your parents' number down
there, Lisa? *Lisa!* Oh Jesus. *Jesus!* I'll call them up."

*   *   *   *   *

I was bed-ridden with mononucleosis for the next two
months. Mononucleosis was what the doctor told my parents I
had anyway, what he diagnosed. He said it was only a coincidence
that the crisis had begun the day I visited Sonya, and that I
must have been carrying the virus, ignoring the symptoms, for
quite some time. He said that my illness couldn't possibly have
come just as a result of my visit to Sonya's rotting house. But I
knew better.

It wasn't until spring term, in April, that I was well enough
to go back up to Berkeley, and even then I didn't really want to
go. I talked to my parents about the possibility of going over to
Europe for a year, using the money they would have spent on
college for a year abroad. I said Sarah could get another roommate easily enough for the apartment on Shattuck. I didn't know
how to tell them that she already had. She had phoned to say
that she'd been letting the student from Chile stay there while I
was gone.

"He's been sleeping on your studio couch, Lisa," she told
me. "Just till you got better, of course. But as soon as you come
back up here, he'll move out."

My mother said they couldn't possibly let me go off and travel
around Europe till I finished school. "Someday you'll thank us,
Lisa," she told me. "I know you think we're being harsh, but
believe me. You'll never amount to anything if you drop out now."

I told my parents I wanted to stay down on the Peninsula with
them if they wouldn't pay for Europe, and that I would get a job.

"If you will just wait, Lisa," my mother said. "If you will just
finish up there at Berkeley. After that, if you still want to go to
Europe, maybe we can help. A graduation present, Lisa, would
you like that?" In the end, they offered me the trip as my reward.

When I got back up to Berkeley, everything looked strange,

including the apartment. Sarah had tacked up *Viva la Revolucion!* posters everywhere, even on the back of the bathroom door. A poster had taken the place of Utrillo's *Rue de Montmartre* above my studio couch. Sarah said she'd take the posters down if they bothered me, but she looked defensive when she said it, so I told her it didn't matter.

I also said it didn't matter when she told me she'd started *having sex*, as she put it, with the student from Chile. She hugged me and said it was wonderful, just wonderful, that I couldn't imagine how wonderful it was. She promised that she would only bring him over on weekends. The Chilean would only be there when I went home.

I told all my professors I would get to work on making good on my incompletes. While I was away, the Weather Underground had bombed the ROTC building. FBI men, wearing suits and dark glasses, were taking pictures of anyone who happened to join the crowd on the Sproul Hall Steps. "Excuse me, Miss," one of the FBI men said to me one day as I walked in my continuing stupor through Sather Gate. When I stopped to see what he wanted, he pointed a Nikon at me and shot my face. Somewhere, deep within the student activist archives in Washington, D.C., a puzzled young woman smiles tentatively into the future, her mouth a little open, her eyebrows raised. *Yes?* she will ask the world forever. *Were you looking for some sort of direction? Were you asking me?*

I walked to classes like a somnambulist, my ears ringing with loud speakers, people picketing all the buildings, sign carriers asking me just what I thought I might be doing as I went to class, all of them tight-lipped and patient, all of them superior and forgiving, if I said I had to go into the building because I had a test.

Towards the end of May, at about two o'clock on a Sunday morning, Sonya called. Sarah and the student from Chile were in the other bed.

I stumbled into the closet where we kept the phone. "Hello?" I said as quietly as I could. I half expected to hear music on the other end, because we'd had a lot of those kinds of phone calls lately, with music in the background, and a lot of rapid breathing, and other muffled sounds.

But the minute I answered this time, I heard Sonya's voice. I could hardly understand her non-stop monologue: "Hello Lisa this is Sonya I'm so sorry I'm so sorry did I wake you up and where have you been I've been calling and I've been calling and did I say something wrong last time you were over because it's been three months."

At that point, Sarah and the Chilean sat up in bed. "Tell her to get the fuck off the *telephone!*" Sarah shouted.

I hadn't ever heard her use that word before. Fuck. *Fuck.* Fuck you, Lisa. I'd heard others use it, but only in anger. In those days not everyone said *fuck* every other word, as they do now. And not Sarah. Not with that voice.

"You and your fucking religious fanatics!" she shouted. "I can *tell* it's her. She's been calling ever since the day they took you home."

I put my tongue on the black plastic face of the mouthpiece and closed my eyes. "Listen," I said to Sonya. "I can't help you. I don't have it in me to help you, Sonya. I don't know how. You'll have to get some outside help, someone professional, you know? Because right now I don't really even know how to help myself."

DOG STORIES

Amelia's daughter Julie wants a dog. Amelia's ex-husband, Howard, who always used to wear neat slacks with creases he pressed into them down the front, and who insisted on doing all his own perma-press dress shirts in Amelia's Whirlpool by himself, would never have let her or Julie have a dog. But now Howard has moved to Florida to live with a man he met last year in New Jersey at a singles bar, and Amelia thinks maybe it wouldn't be so bad to have a dog.

For one thing, she remembers always wanting to have a dog herself. Her father told her lots of dog stories while she was growing up, either about the dogs he'd had when he was a boy, or about the dogs Amelia's dead older sister Carolyn owned when she was young, but Amelia herself, for all the stories about them, had never had a dog.

"A dog means a lot of responsibility," her father told her every time she brought it up. "You can't just go out and buy a dog and bring it home. After it gets here, you have to feed it, take it for walks, make sure it's warm. And I'm not sure how long you could do that, Amelia. I'm afraid it would be your mother and me who would be responsible for the dog before too long." Then he always added, "We just don't want to have to go through all that again at this point in time."

Amelia's parents were well into their forties when she was born, *the surprise to end all surprises*, as she was called. Amelia's older sister Carolyn was killed when Amelia was three, in a Jeep accident in the Philippines, where she was serving as a volunteer in the Peace Corps that President Kennedy had formed two years before. Carolyn was born the same year the United States entered World War II, while Amelia wasn't born until fifteen years after the whole thing was over. That meant that Amelia and her dead older sister came from two different generations in history, even though they had come from the same parents. Amelia, statistically included among the Baby Boomers, was one upon whom the importance of flickering black and white newsreels about the Kennedy years, or documentaries like *Berkeley in the Sixties*, was forever lost, while the rebellious and beautiful, blonde and waif-like Carolyn, dead at only twenty-three the year before Freedom Summer, was excluded from the very era that she reflected, and that took her life.

Amelia thought she might remember her older sister, in one of those dream-like visions of early childhood, as a tall, thin, unhappy woman who ignored her in front of their parents when she came to visit, but who pinched her and told her scary stories when they were alone. Based on this blurred memory and the details her parents have provided about her sister's life, Amelia thinks of Carolyn as being a little like the dogs in her father's stories—an out-of-place creature with a cruel ending, a being with the potential to be warm and intelligent, but one who was so abused by conditions entirely beyond its own control that in spite of the love someone might have poured out upon it, it eventually either became vicious or lost its life.

Amelia's father's dog stories have been floating into her mind at odd moments ever since she and Howard got divorced. It's as though these stories contain some truth she knows she needs but cannot quite find. They come to her out of context, like the sentence her best friend's mother is said to have uttered only moments before the entire family was involved in the car accident that killed Amelia's best friend's mother and maimed Amelia's friend, Evelyn, for what has turned out to be Evelyn's entire life.

Once, while Evelyn was doing up Amelia's hair from her

wheel-chair in the beauty-shop that she bought years later with her money from the trust the insurance company set up for her, Evelyn told Amelia that just before the accident, she and her mother had been arguing about something Evelyn couldn't even remember anymore. *I will not be intimidated!* Evelyn told Amelia her mother was shouting at her as they approached the other car. Everyone was laughing at Evelyn's mother for her choice of words. *Intimidated! What kind of a word is that, Mother? Who do you think you are, some sort of czar?* All in regard to the minor argument that Evelyn and her mother were having at the time.

Amelia cannot lose her impression that if people could just unravel the truths in these kinds of things, they wouldn't hurt each other, or fail at business, or go off to some exotic far place in the world and not come back.

One of Amelia's father's dog stories was about an Airedale that somehow managed, out of sheer love and loyalty, to come limping home on two broken legs to the boy he loved, after being run over by a car on the dirt road that ran in front of the ranch where Amelia's father grew up in Ventura County, some seventy years ago. In that story, people from the city who had no business driving cars without any training, and least of all driving them too fast past all the horse-drawn wagons and farm equipment that were still likely to lumber by in rural Southern California back in those times, roared by Amelia's father's ranch at forty miles an hour and ran over the dog's legs and never even knew it. It never seemed right to Amelia that the people in the car got away with this, as though as long as you weren't aware that you had hurt something in your path, it was not your fault.

Amelia's father also told a story about a collie he had to leave with a farmer when his family lost the ranch in Ventura County during the Depression and he had to enlist in the Army Air Corps because back then going into the Army was the only way a decent, God-fearing man could stay honest and still have enough regular meals to stay alive. Two years after he left the dog with the farmer, Amelia's father was furloughed from the Army Air Corps, because his mother died. He hitch-hiked out to the farm where he'd left the dog, and, standing outside the farmer's fence, he cupped his hands around his mouth for his special whistle, and called the dog.

"That collie was clear across the pasture," Amelia's father told her. "But she put up her ears, like this." Amelia's father became the collie, head cocked to one side, brown eyes liquid with recognition, sharp nose pointed toward the scent of the young man who had been her companion in better times.

"So I could see she knew me, see," Amelia's father told her. "Well, for a moment the collie just stood there, absolutely motionless, like this." Amelia's father's tan, muscular arms tensed to become the dog's long, graceful forepaws, all cream and brown. "Then, suddenly, she jumped into the air, like this!" Amelia's father leapt straight up into the air, knees together, toes pointed, pivoting halfway round in a demi-pirouette that was better than the ones the boys in Amelia's ballet class had ever done. When her father landed, he pulled his arms in close to his chest and, squatting upon his knees, he folded down.

"Well, after storing up all her strength, the dog bounded across that pasture toward me." As Amelia's father said this, he shifted from the shape of the dog to his younger self. Crouching low on the floor of the kitchen in front of Amelia, he opened his arms up wide to catch his dog. The collie ran with all her being into his arms.

"Your sister used to love that story," Amelia's father told her. "When she was little, before you were born, she always liked to pretend she was the collie. She would run as fast as she could into my arms."

At this point Amelia's father became sad and wouldn't talk. Amelia watched him walk away slowly with her long-dead sister and the long-dead dog.

Often, when he told the dog stories that had Carolyn in them, Amelia's father, who was a registered Republican, and so had not voted for President Kennedy in the first place and did not like the man, would tell Amelia that he thought it was a national shame that anyone could shoot the President of the United States that easily and throw the entire country into a state of shock. Then he would add, "But I'll be damned if I'm ever going to forgive John Kennedy for taking your sister's life."

Sometimes, Amelia wonders if Carolyn said something equally as profound as Evelyn's mother before she died. *I will not be intimidated!* she imagines Carolyn shouting proudly as her Jeep rolls over and over in the foreign mud. *I will be immortal! My father is going to mourn for me all his life!*

One of Amelia's father's dog stories was about the stray dogs that used to follow Carolyn home from school. At that time, Amelia's father and mother lived in a little tract house in the San Fernando Valley, in a subdivision that had been newly built after World War II. The subdivision was called Citrus Hills, because the contractors who had built the houses had plowed under a fifteen-mile stretch of orange groves to make quarter-acre lots. Although the houses might have been built with less than what Amelia's father called Before-the-War Quality, they had style and charm, each with its one and three-quarter bathrooms—which meant one bathroom had a tub and the other a shower—a family room, three bedrooms, and two genuine orange trees left over from the citrus groves.

Of course, most of the people who were moving to Southern California from Oklahoma or Texas or someplace in the Midwest to get in on the big post-war boom in employment could not afford these homes. These people moved into white stucco apartment buildings in downtown Los Angeles that glistened with hard white light when they caught the sun. The apartments were on either side of streets lined with thirty-foot palm trees that had been brought into Southern California on enormous trucks almost overnight. When these people moved into their shiny new apartment buildings from wherever it was they came from, they discovered that their landlords wouldn't allow them to keep their dogs. And so they would drive out over the weekend to the new tracts that were being built in the San Fernando Valley in the ex-orange groves, and they would let their dogs loose, these dogs they loved. Amelia's father would see these people pull up in their cars right around the corner from the house. They would open their car doors and put their dogs out on the street and drive away.

Amelia's father told her, "And maybe the kids would be screaming, *Daddy! No, Daddy! We'll take care of the dog, Daddy, we promise, oh please don't!* And the wife would be saying, *How can you do this, Roger?* And I'd hear the husband saying back to her, *Shut up will ya, Wilma? We have to do this. The landlord don't accept pets now, does he, Wilma? So we don't got a choice.*"

Amelia's father would shake his head and look thoughtful. "People shouldn't take on a dog like that they're just going to dump." Then he always added, "Anyway, your sister would find one of these dogs, and she'd say, *Here doggie, here doggie,* all the way home from school. And when she got home, she would look your mother and me straight in the eye and she'd tell us, *Poor doggie. I couldn't help it. He followed me. Can't we keep the poor dog? He doesn't have a home.* And we'd have to keep these dogs, see, because of your sister, till they either ran away, or got hit by a car, or till some Mexican who worked in the few orange groves that were still left out there among the houses would decide he wanted a dog for company and would pick him up."

Amelia's father always sighed at the end of the story. "You see, Amelia," he told her, "your sister always had an enormous heart."

* * * * *

Up until now, Amelia has been keeping Julie's request for a dog on some kind of hold. But one night in February as she is tucking Julie into bed, she glances through the Pricilla curtains in her daughter's window and notices that the light from the next door neighbor's living room is shining on the snow to make a clean, yellow shape of its own on the ground outside. The next door neighbors are the kind of family she would like to have—a father, a mother, and a boy and a girl all living in a single house—and the pale yellow of the light from their window looks soft and warm. Amelia almost says out loud, *How could you do this to us?* Even though the remark is meant for nobody in particular, she stops herself.

"Mommy," Julie says as Amelia sits on the edge of the bed, watching her own hands as though from a distance. It does not seem to Amelia that the hands are hers, that they belong to any part of her that is herself. She watches, astonished, as the hands carefully smooth the flannel sheets. Her daughter's sheets are faded now from two winters of washing, but if Amelia looks closely she can still see the repeated pattern of a blue basset hound walking across them on a tight blue leash. "Mommy," Julie says. "Can I have a dog?"

Amelia has a flashback of all the dog stories her father told her when she was growing up, and of all the times she asked her parents for a dog and they turned her down. Her parents, who moved from Nevada to be near their granddaughter up here in Michigan when they retired, decided to leave Amelia and Julie and move to West Virginia three months ago. On the day they left, Amelia's mother said to her, *You and Julie don't really need us anymore, Amelia. You'll be fine without us. You two are tough.*

Amelia kisses Julie's forehead. The skin of her daughter's forehead feels as soft and fragile as rose petals against her mouth. *Sure we're tough*, she thinks. But she means, *We're not.* To Julie, she says, "Maybe this weekend you and I can visit the Humane Society, just to look around."

* * * * *

The best of all of Amelia's father's dog stories was about a German Shepherd named Duchess who came to live with Amelia's parents and her dead older sister after World War II.

For a very long time while Amelia was growing up, the fact that Carolyn had been born so long before she was mainly meant to her that her dead older sister had been privileged to witness the stories about Duchess, whereas she had not. By the time Amelia's father started telling her his dog stories, Amelia had moved with her parents from the increasingly over-populated and polluted Southern California, to Nevada, where they lived in a small house on a quiet street in Reno, among new neighbors who didn't know about her dead older sister and so always thought of Amelia as an only child.

The Shepherd story was the one Amelia most wanted to hear at the dinner table, while her mother was taking away the dishes and was cleaning up. Amelia would say to her father, "Tell me the one about Duchess."

Duchess had been in the Canine Corps out in the Pacific during World War II. After the war, her trainer couldn't keep her anymore. "He became a drifter, poor guy," Amelia's father told her as he shook his head sadly and clucked his tongue. "It happened to a lot of those people. You know, they'd been important, they'd had these important top-secret positions in the war. And then there was nothing important or top-secret for them to do when they got home."

The Shepherd had been the man's constant companion as he carried out his secret assignments in the jungles on the Pacific front. "Maybe the poor guy couldn't get over all he'd seen out there," Amelia's father told her. "But anyway, he started drinking. And I guess the poor guy had enough of a conscience left after all he and this dog had been through together out in the Pacific to know he couldn't just leave her sitting outside in his truck while he went to bars."

At this point in the story, Amelia's father took a deep breath and stared a little sheepishly at her mother's back. Amelia's mother continued to wash the dishes without a word. Amelia knew that in order to be given Duchess in the first place, her father had to have frequented that bar. And that was a bone of contention between them, because they had been very hard up for money at the time. Amelia's father and mother had sold the picturesque little tract house in what had once been the orange groves of the San Fernando Valley, and had moved with Carolyn to a tiny, run-down cottage out in Ojai, because a friend of Amelia's father who had been losing his shirt in an automotive shop he owned had convinced him to move out to Ojai and to buy this automotive shop from him and to go into business for himself. Now the friend was out of debt, and Amelia's father was into it. To make matters worse, he had already quit his other, well-paying job.

Amelia knew, from her mother's point of view in the story, that right from the start of that automotive business, things had gone all wrong. Amelia's dead sister had to go into the fifth grade out in Ojai with the unkempt, dirty children of migrant workers who couldn't read or write. She came home one day in October with a case of lice. Amelia's mother had to rub kerosene into Carolyn's scalp after cutting off all her hair, which was very beautiful—blond and thick and long.

"It must have hurt like the dickens," Amelia's mother would tell her when it came her turn to tell the story. "Kerosene wasn't exactly invented to be poured onto tender scalps. But your sister clamped her mouth shut in that way she had whenever she didn't want something to beat her." Amelia's mother would catch the sob that was about to escape, then say through the tight stretch of her lips, "Oh, that girl was strong!"

Carolyn didn't own a bicycle of her own. It broke Amelia's mother's heart to have to sit with her little girl that Christmas as she thumbed through the Sears and Roebuck Christmas Wishbook over and over to pick one out. "Do you like this one, Mommy?" she would ask her mother. Amelia's mother would have to look at her blonde, lost daughter, who was her one beautiful, sweet, only daughter at the time, and know that the child wouldn't be getting anything at all for Christmas, let alone a bike.

Eventually, Amelia's father had to sell the automotive business at a loss and go back to his old job at lower pay. But for Amelia, all these facts were only the necessary, minor details in the greater story about the dog. "So now, get to the point where you tell how it was you got Duchess," she would beg her father, daring her mother to interrupt him, glaring at her mother's silent, retreating back.

"Well, sir," her father said. "The Shepherd's owner came into the bar one day while I was there inside." Amelia's father glanced quickly at her mother. "Of course, you have to understand, Amelia, that I didn't spend too many afternoons in places like that, in I mean, that bar. Not that I want to judge the guy, you understand. It's just that I had a family to feed, while this guy did not. It was, shall we say, Amelia, unusual, yes, highly unusual, that I just happened to be in this bar this one afternoon when this guy started talking about his dog. And he said to me, he said he didn't have a place to keep her anymore, because he couldn't get enough together to rent an apartment, and so here he was with this Shepherd named Duchess, the two of them just living in his truck. And then, well, I guess you know this part of the story well enough."

Amelia's imagination moved outside the bar to the parking lot. She could see the Shepherd sitting there on the passenger side of the World War II veteran's ratty pick-up truck. The dog's coat was a warm beige. She had dark forepaws, ears, and belly, and a nice black saddle marking across her back. Nothing could distract the dog's attention. The Shepherd's eyes, lined round with a black that was almost like the Maybelline that Amelia borrowed from her mother's bureau when she played at dressing up, had been riveted for the last hour and a half on the brass tacks and faded blue leather padding of the door of the bar through which she'd seen her trainer disappear. If another customer drove up and parked beside her truck, Duchess closed her mouth with a renewed but momentary alertness, glancing only long enough in the direction of the stranger to check him out. If spoken to, she growled once in warning, as she had been taught, but then turned away, her attention going back to the door of the lounge, as if she were annoyed at the interruption from this well-meaning stranger, who was only trying to be friendly after all.

"The dog would have waited there all day for her master if need be," Amelia's father told her. "Even when her trainer left the windows wide open for air, she would not jump out. And of course when the guy finally did come out of the bar with me, he was drunk as a skunk and not fit to be driving. And probably it was well past the dog's feeding time, too, and it was getting dark."

Amelia's father became quiet and watched his hands. Never in his life, he often told Amelia, had he allowed himself to weep, with the sole exception of his complete and total despair when his father died. But he had come very close two other times. "Once, when we lost Duchess," he told her. "And then again, all those years later, when your sister died."

In the story, Amelia followed her father and the man who owned the German Shepherd to the truck. Her father moved slow-motion, his boots kicking up the Southern California dust as he crossed the parking lot. The dog's head was cocked a little to one side as she watched her master coming toward her, the other man behind. Amelia knew the Shepherd was listening to the men as they talked about her, but so far the dog didn't understand her master's plan. She opened her mouth in an expectant smile, her fine, leathery black lips and strong white teeth forming a neatly ridged trough for her clean pink tongue.

"Now *that* was loyalty," Amelia's father said. "That's how a man wishes everyone in his family would feel about him when he comes home." He glanced over at Amelia's mother, who rolled her eyes. Then he looked off into that place behind Amelia's head where she knew he kept everything that was uncompromisingly good and final. It was the place where her dead sister Carolyn had gone. Though she could never quite follow her father's eyes when they went there, Amelia knew that everything that mattered to him was tucked up neatly together there, like the envelopes full of rare coins and photographs and yellow documents that he had once shown her in the oblong metal safety-deposit box he kept in the vault at the local bank.

"We were standing there in the parking lot," her father said. "And Duchess was, you know, careful. She kept looking back and forth from him to me. But she didn't bark. Then her trainer whispered, *It's all right now, girl, it's all right.* She knew the command to charge could only come from her trainer. And then, of course, you have to remember that in the work they had done together during the war, the man's life could have been endangered if the dog had decided to bark at the wrong time. But her trainer was there, telling her I was all right, and so she was letting me pet her. She was letting me touch her. And then the guy says to me, he says to me so quietly I can barely hear him, Amelia, and I know he's so upset he can hardly talk, he says, *Will,* calling me by my first name, even though this is the first time I've ever met him in my life, *Will,* he says, *I can't keep her. Can you take her home to your family, give her a kid to love and a decent home?*

Amelia watched her father and the dog's trainer as they talked about the dog in the parking lot. Like Duchess, she couldn't make out everything the two men were saying, but she saw the trainer pull the dog out of the truck with a heavy tug on her leash. *Heel, Duchess!* the trainer said. Then she heard him say to the dog, *Okay, girl, this is it. Duchess, this is your owner now, do you understand me? Duchess! Sit!*

The trainer handed Amelia's father the Shepherd's leash and ran around to the driver's side of the pick-up and jumped inside. Amelia started crying. The man sped off down the gravel street away from the dog, who didn't know why her owner was driving away and leaving her with a stranger. The man's truck disappeared around a corner of the little town, his exit from the dog's life and from his place in Amelia's father's story, forever a soundless explosion of dust and forgotten longing in the yellow light.

Occasionally, Amelia has read about some Army veteran who has died in a homeless shelter, and left a dog. The newspapers pick up the story, because the veteran has usually done something brave for his country, and earned a Purple Heart. His mother and father and ex-wife and all the adult children he hasn't seen for years are surprised to find out he was homeless when he died. *I hadn't heard from him in ages, of course,* the ex-wife tells a reporter. She has been married for some time now to someone else, and she only feels slightly puzzled about her former husband's life. Whenever Amelia reads one of these stories, she thinks of the man who left Duchess with her father at that bar. She thinks of him driving out of the Shepherd's and everybody else's lives in his pick-up truck. *And it seems to me,* the homeless vet's wife tells the reporter as she squinches up her eyes and looks way off, *it seems to me that, yes, I think when he came home from the Army, he had this dog....*

In the part of the story that went on for Amelia, though, it was still a good long time before the dog moved in with Carolyn and her parents in the shabby house. There was a long, slow middle section to the story, a part in which Amelia's father took Duchess to his automotive shop to be a watchdog, which she didn't like.

"You have to understand she was pretty confused, and that made her vicious," Amelia's father told her. "I took her to the shop there, and I chained her up. And she went on mourning for her trainer, weeks, maybe even months, after he had gone. She got hungry enough that she would let me feed her, but every time I reached out to touch her, she always growled."

For awhile, the Shepherd stayed at the automotive shop. She watched in the night and kept thieves from taking Amelia's father's tools when he closed the shop for the day and went home. Amelia could imagine the dog alone in the dark—fearsome and lonely and proud as she patrolled the grounds.

"But she still wouldn't let me get close to her when I'd come back," Amelia's father said. "She wouldn't let me touch her. And then one day, I don't know what happened, I guess I just got tired of her growling at me like that, and here I was taking care of her, and feeding her, and she didn't even seem to appreciate it, she wasn't grateful, she would not respond. And so one day I just kept walking toward her, and I knew when I started walking I wasn't going to stop."

Here, Amelia's father paused and looked at her mother sideways, and Amelia knew that this was the other part of the story they did not agree upon. "Well, you can't put up with that kind of abuse from some creature that's sharing all that you have to offer, can you?" Amelia's father asked. He swallowed hard and added just a little too loudly, "That goes for everything, too, whether that something is a woman, or a child, or just a dog."

Amelia's father got up from the table. Amelia's mother, whose back had been turned as she washed the dishes, let out one breath of disallowed anguish and cried out loud, "Stop it, Will! Don't tell it! Why can't you just let the whole thing die in peace, and just sit down!"

But Amelia begged her father to go on.

"And it was right then," he said as he started walking toward the imagined dog, "that Duchess lunged."

Amelia's heart stopped as she watched the Shepherd tear with all her strength against the rope. The chair in which her father had been sitting rocked back on its haunches, then tumbled down.

"She was that ready to attack me," her father said, throwing his hands up. His face clouded over. "So now I'm asking you, Amelia." He turned to his one remaining daughter, the only relic he would leave behind after a troubled life. "I'm asking you. What else could I have done to the dog but that thing I tried?"

Amelia looked over at her mother, standing in front of the sink, her mouth covered over with a soapy hand.

"So I hit her," Amelia's father whispered. "I had to. I picked up a two-by-four that was lying there in the shop-yard, and I threw it at her, really hard."

Amelia watched as the huge beam hurled above her through the air. At the other end of the trajectory described by her father's hand was the lovely dog. Amelia attempted, and failed, to picture her father enacting this cruelty on anything in the world, anything at all, let alone a dog. How could he do this? How could the trainer have left the dog in the first place? What was wrong?

"Right or wrong," said her father, shaking his head sadly, "it knocked her out." He righted the chair on the floor and sat down in it, then added, "After that, Duchess never growled at me again."

Then one day, for a reason no one seems to remember anymore, Amelia's father decided to take the Shepherd home. "It was just supposed to be for the weekend," he told her. "You know, a visit. I told your mother and your sister, who was maybe ten years old, to stay out of the dog's way, to leave the dog alone."

Recently, whenever she is thinking about this part of the story, Amelia thinks of some of the horror stories about dogs and children she has come to know. One of these is a story the mother of Julie's best friend, Derrick, told her a year or so before she died.

A teen-age girl who lived alone in a one-room hovel in Harlem with a part-German Shepherd, part-wolf dog, had just had a baby as a result of rape. The girl, who had been adopted as a baby herself, had run away from her adoptive parents in Indiana when she was fourteen years old, and was living on welfare in East Harlem under someone else's name. Her adoptive parents, who had loved her and cared for her and brought her up, knew nothing about the rape, or the baby, or even where she was, but for the last two years they had been placing ads that said, *Come home, please, Maryellen, we love you*, in papers all over the country, including *The New York Times*. The girl didn't want to have anything to do with these people anymore. They were religious fanatics. They wouldn't let her go to rock concerts or dances. They told her she had a demon living inside her because she smoked and drank. They were out of touch with the world, living as they did in the Bible Belt. She just wanted to be left alone, that was all, and to have something that belonged to her, like this little baby she was having, and like this dog.

The public hospital where she had the baby told her they were going to take the money she had in her purse to keep it safe when she went in there, and after the baby came they told her she would have to come back on Monday morning to get her money, because the office that was keeping it for her was closed over the weekend, and the girl's baby hadn't been born till late Friday night. There was no food for the dog in the room in Harlem, and none for the teen-age mother either. And the girl couldn't nurse the baby if she didn't eat.

So on Monday, she took the bus back to the public hospital to get her purse. She was still weak from having the baby, and she didn't think she should take a newborn on a public bus, so she left her baby in a laundry basket, in the room back in Harlem, with the dog in charge.

When she got back some four hours later, with a few groceries and a bottle of milk and some dog food and the rest of the money, her dog was asleep in the corner, and the baby, gone.

At first, she would not believe it. Those sorts of things do not happen. Everyone deserves to have some little break in life. But finally she called the police, and an ambulance, and by the time the horrible day was over, she had been charged with involuntary manslaughter, and her dog had been put to sleep. The girl still did not want to see her adoptive parents from the Bible Belt, whose answer to this, as it had been to every other crisis of her life, would just be one more quote from the Scriptures. *O deliver my darling from the power of the dog!*

Amelia thinks it was Derrick's mother's terminal illness that caused her to repeat this story, a story that, after all, did no good for anybody when it was retold. But Derrick's mother had insisted she'd actually read the story back in the Seventies in *The New York Times*. Amelia thinks Derrick's mother's insistence on telling this story probably had something to do with the darkness that overcomes people who already know they are doomed to die.

But for a long time, for Amelia, who learned the twenty-third Psalm in the Vacation Bible School she had to go to the summer between fifth and sixth grade in Reno while her mother worked, God was a German Shepherd, a benign and protective entity that was far more powerful and single-minded and loyal than any man.

The Lord is my Shepherd. Duchess could guide you through long, wet tunnels in the dark.

Yea though I walk through the valley of death. Duchess could walk with you from your bed to the bathroom if you got up at night.

Surely goodness and mercy! You didn't have to be afraid of anything, anything at all, as long as you had the Shepherd with you when you got up to walk.

"Well, anyway, the dog really took to your sister," Amelia's father said. "But I wasn't sure I should trust her. After all, she had been trained during the war to protect one man only, her trainer. And she hadn't been around children very much."

When it came time for Will to go back to his shop, Duchess

didn't want to go with him. "She had fallen in love with your sister," Amelia's father told her. "I could see that the dog had made her decision and that she wasn't going back."

Amelia watched her father in the story as he finished off his cup of coffee and then loped with his long, special stride towards his waiting truck. "Without looking behind me," he said to Amelia, "I called the dog to follow, but she didn't come."

Amelia's father turned around to face Duchess, who remained sitting next to Amelia's dead sister on the sloping porch. Carolyn had her arms around the dog, and was crying. *Please don't take her, Daddy*, she pleaded. Amelia could see right through the two of them, the dog and her dead sister, like shapes she sometimes made in the sky out of clouds and smoke.

Amelia's father spoke directly to the dog. *Are you coming with me, girl?* he said. Duchess whined, a sort of answer, but she didn't budge. She went right on leaning into Carolyn's knees on the family's porch.

From then on, the Shepherd belonged to Carolyn and to no one else. The two of them were inseparable, a lone girl and her black-and-tan shadow, a mis-matched pair of playmates, unlikely twins. Duchess could do anything. She walked Carolyn out to the school bus every morning, and she was there waiting for the bus at the white picket fence that marked their front yard when her girl came home. When the bus stopped, Duchess climbed up the steps to get on board. She was polite to all the children who reached out to pet her along the aisle, but her liquid brown eyes were fastened on Amelia's dead sister, sitting in the very back row of the yellow bus, wearing a red plaid cotton dress and red faille ribbons on her ash-blond pigtails, just as she did in the fifth-grade school picture that Amelia's father still kept of her on his bedroom shelf. Carolyn grinned out at Amelia through the black-and-white time between them, an innocent wraith suspended in the march of history, forever missing two front teeth from her pretty mouth.

Duchess watched over Carolyn whenever she played in the ditch-banks, the deep irrigation systems that criss-crossed the flat, brown fields behind the run-down house. "Your mother could look out there from the kitchen where she was working and see exactly where your sister was," Amelia's father told her.

Duchess was infinitely patient, infinitely tender. "Your sister could put her hand right into the dog's mouth, like this." Amelia's father opened one of his big, long-fingered hands, the way he did whenever he was making a dog's head as a shadow-puppet on Amelia's wall. He placed his other hand inside Duchess' imagined jaws. "Your sister could put her tiny hand inside that dog's mouth, right between her teeth, and that wonderful dog would not bear down."

But if something sad had brought the Shepherd into the story in the first place, then something sad eventually had to take her out.

One day, shortly after she'd had her first and only litter of puppies, Duchess went out to the bus to greet Amelia's dead sister for what would turn out to be the final time. It was very clear to Amelia's father and mother that there was something wrong.

"We'd wanted her to have a set of puppies," Amelia's father told her. "And you have to understand she was already pretty old when we got her. They were wonderful puppies, and she was a terrific mother. She stayed with them clear until they were weaned, in a big straw basket in your sister's closet, inside the house. I guess we shouldn't have done it, let her have them, but that's the way it was."

Amelia's father was always close to tears as he told her the rest of the story. "That day, when your sister came home from school, the dog's tail was barely wagging." He moved his pointer finger slowly, back and forth. "We could see that the poor dog could hardly make it out there to the bus. But she felt it was her duty, that she had to go. She wanted to greet your sister coming home from school that one last time."

Amelia's father bowed his head with its thick black wavy hair and covered his face with the long, big-veined hands that Amelia loved. "She died that night."

The Shepherd left the story to go somewhere with Amelia's

dead sister, of whom Amelia remembers next to nothing, really, only perhaps some hissing and pinching, that scary time, and then maybe, she thinks, maybe also the pale, thin man that her parents have told her came to the door one day to tell them about the Jeep accident in the Philippines where Carolyn died. *I will not be intimidated!* Amelia's dead sister cries forever into the lush jungle as the Shepherd watches over her beside the road. The dog has come back to the place where she began her journey. She walks along, marking the mud where Amelia's sister lies dying. The prints of the dog's paws wash away in the torrential rain with the woman's blood.

But suddenly, Amelia's dead sister is sitting up. The dog's eyes are soft, her ears pointed and alert with her watching. *Heel, Duchess*, says Amelia's dead sister. And side by side, their paces measured precisely to the sound of a muffled drum, the dog and the tall, slim, beautiful young blond woman begin to walk.

Amelia's father and mother gave away all of the puppies as guide dogs before Duchess died. "Seeing-eye dogs, they used to call them," said Amelia's father. "The one real regret I always had was that your mother and I didn't keep one of those puppies for ourselves."

* * * * *

When Saturday rolls around, Amelia gets Julie up early, and the two of them drive over to the Dexter pound.

But when they get to the pound, there is no one in the Humane Society office to talk to them. They find themselves alone in a foyer that smells of antiseptic and ether. As they stand there on the brown linoleum, surrounded by dark fake-wood paneled walls, they can hear hundreds of dogs barking in earnest confusion down the darkened hall.

"Poor dogs," says Julie. "Do you suppose they know what's going to happen to them if they're not picked out?"

Amelia imagines a parade of dogs marching toward a gas chamber—is it a chamber?—where they are put to sleep, their lives and deaths all accomplished in one quick jumble of all the dog stories she has ever heard or told. She has a flash vision of Howard, her ex-husband, the way he looked as he stood in their kitchen several months ago. It is late at night. *I would be sorry to have to do this to Julie, of course*, Howard is saying, as though *this* is only a possibility at this point, but Amelia later realizes that Howard was giving her his first and only warning. In the note he leaves Amelia a few days later, Howard writes: *You'll see, you'll have somebody new in no time, Amelia. For one thing, you tell a good story. And you're really sort of pretty, too, in a funny way. I wouldn't be surprised if some guy right there where you work already has you all picked out.*

When Amelia finally looks up from the large curious dark spot she has been staring at on the Humane Society's brown linoleum floor, she sees that Julie has found a bulletin board and is reading. No one has come from the back of the pound yet to answer their questions, so Amelia walks over to the bulletin board where Julie is standing. She thinks she hears the sudden cessation of a particular dog's barking. Is it possible to distinguish one dog's voice from another? What have they done with this one dog that it no longer barks?

"What have you found there, honey?" she asks her daughter. She tries to make her own voice sound very sure of itself. *I will not be intimidated!* Who do you think I am, anyway? Mine is not a voice you can just snuff out.

"Oh Mommy, look at this," Julie says, tears clearly audible in her slender throat. "Who could do something this awful to a defenseless dog?"

Amelia steps up to the bulletin board, and presses her head close to her daughter's. Julie is tall for her age, and Amelia has always been thought of as a little short, so from behind, the two female bodies could be those of two sisters, born to the same set of parents many years apart, one of them *the surprise to end all surprises*, the other not. Since her divorce, food hasn't really interested Amelia very much, and the unexpected benefit of her grief is that for the first time since she was a teenager, Amelia has a figure, with firm, small breasts and tiny hips. Meanwhile, her daughter, at twelve already an avid reader of *Seventeen*, has taken an unabashedly admiring interest in Amelia's clothes. They are dressed similarly today, in outfits of Julie's choosing—tight, brightly flowered leggings and solid-color shirts.

Amelia has forgotten the bifocals that her optometrist has prescribed, so she squints at the bulletin board that has startled Julie, as she tries to make out what appears to be a wide, white, wrinkled pyramid, with two enormous black circles at the very top. "What is it?" she asks her daughter, giving up.

"Oh, this is so sad!" Julie says. "Listen to this. I'll read it to you. They've even got a warrant out for the guy's arrest."

Julie reads out loud to Amelia in her cracking voice:

"Meet Monty, a mixed beagle retriever collie about two years old. Last December, one of our volunteers arrived at work at six a.m. to find Monty lying on a blood-soaked towel inside a cardboard computer box, on the steps of the Humane Society's back porch. Monty had been shaved down to his skin, his toenails partially removed with a blunt instrument. He had cigarette burns around his nose and mouth. Someone had drawn circles around Monty's eyes with black shoe polish.

"The inhumane treatment or abandonment of an animal is a heinous crime. Anyone with information leading to the arrest of the individual who inflicted this cruelty on one of the creatures we as human beings are meant to protect should call this office immediately to report the crime. In the meantime, Monty is available for adoption. He has a sunny disposition, in spite of the cruel treatment he has received, and he is good with children. Like all the pets made available for adoption at the Huron Valley Humane Society, Monty has been neutered, and has all his shots."

Amelia's eyes focus and then blur again on the deformed dog. Is it really part beagle? Could she also be seeing part pit-bull? She doesn't know.

"Isn't that terrible?" Julie says. "How could anybody go off and leave a dog like that?"

Amelia feels sick to her stomach. A thin, foul, foreign liquid fills her mouth as every dog story she knows floods through her mind. The dogs come all at once—Midwestern strays, faded blue basset hounds, broken-legged California Airedales, long-haired, graceful collies, all of them parading before her, and then Duchess, making her final, painful trip past all the reaching children as she walks down the center aisle toward Amelia's dead sister, who is forever smiling from the very back bench of the yellow bus.

"Julie," Amelia says. "I don't want to get a dog. Can we go home?"

Julie turns around and stares at her mother in disbelief. "But you promised," she says. "You've always told me you wanted to have a dog and that your father wouldn't let you have one. And now here we are."

Amelia touches Julie's shoulder, and as she does, her heart lunges forward towards the place she has never been able to understand before. It is the Place of the Shepherd, the place where her dead older sister Carolyn has gone, and the place her father has always looked whenever he is straining to see someone or something he has loved too much. Julie's brown, shoulder-length hair, still soft and wispy like a child's, brushes up against Amelia's arm.

"A dog is a big responsibility," Amelia hears herself saying. She opens her mouth to say more, but it does not come out. She wants to tell Julie how wrong all this is, how we only hurt the creatures we say we will take care of, how in the end we always go off and leave the beings we say we love.

"But we could take this one," Julie is saying. "We could help this one." Amelia is already walking toward the door.

Then she feels it. Something is walking beside her, a kind of shadow about a third as tall as she is, and rather dark—at least, dark down towards her feet, but light on top. The Shepherd is heeling. Amelia can feel its hot, bright breath against her thigh.

"Mom!" Julie is sobbing as she tugs at Amelia's right elbow. Amelia keeps walking. If she reaches her left hand out only slightly, she will touch the dog. She stops at the door, the invisible

Shepherd her only guide. She can see her twelve-year-old Chevy across the parking lot, the sea of gray cement she must cross with Julie before they reach the car. *Heel, Duchess!*

Amelia holds her breath. *I will not be intimidated!* The shadow nudges her gently toward the door.

PERMANENCE

I got in touch with Peter MacKinnon for the last time during that famous Massachusetts blizzard some years ago. Bumper stickers on a few old cars in downtown Boston still bear me witness. *I survived.*

Three feet of snow had fallen overnight, and the Green Line wasn't running beyond West Newton, so I couldn't have gotten all the way in from Riverside if I'd tried. I propped myself up on the sofa, under an afghan my mother had knitted for me for Christmas with a note that said, *Daddy and I are hoping this will keep you warm,* and I was reading Hortense Calisher's story, "Il Plœ:r Dā Mō Kœ:r," laughing and laughing there on the sofa all by myself, and trying to decide if I could do anything with it for my Honors Freshmen, who were taking their first linguistics class with me at B.U., because the story is written in fundamental French phonetics, just like the ones Peter had taught me way back in high school in northern California my senior year—when all of a sudden it occurred to me that what I really wanted was to send this story off to the man himself.

At that point, Peter MacKinnon hadn't heard from me in about ten years. Since the day I'd called him just as I was leaving for Paris and the graduate program I'd been accepted to at the Sorbonne. I had thought I was going to live in Europe forever, but as it turned out Paris was only the one place after another that would never stop.

"I figured it would be all right now," I told Peter over the telephone that day. "I figured you couldn't think I wanted you to marry me or something, if I just called up to say good-bye on my way to France." *Let bygones be bygones*, my mother had said about Peter during our second try.

By then I'd learned that revenge could be empty. You can't punish people who are unaware that they're guilty. I think I've actually read that somewhere, in regard to capital punishment—that if the defense can prove the accused doesn't understand the punishment, that he doesn't know he's going to be executed for what he's done—then he can't be legally done away with, and he doesn't die. I'm sure Peter went on after me pretty much as though nothing had really happened in his life. And I still don't know, with Peter himself probably dead now, because of what he always told me about his heart—whether he ever understood what I was doing that second summer we dated, or whether, like the last night I saw him, when I left him out on the driveway in front of my parents' house, he just went on thinking forever, *She was crazy, that's all. Interesting girl maybe, but crazy. I shouldn't have spent all that money on her and stuck around.*

* * * * *

Peter and I are driving to my father's boat. It is a three-hour drive from my parents' house in Los Amitos down on the San Francisco Peninsula up to the berth on the San Joaquin River where my father keeps his boat, and it says something for my parents' hopes for Peter that they have agreed to let me drive alone with him three hours in his racy little silver Corvair convertible on these country roads.

I have only been out of high school for about a month, and I have had next to no experience with boys. At twenty-five, Peter MacKinnon qualifies as an older man. He has been a student teacher from Stanford in my high school, teaching my fourth-year French, and I will only find out many years later in a best-selling book about the Baby Boom Generation, that mine was the last innocent Sixties senior class.

Peter called me for a date the very weekend I graduated. "I wasn't sure if you noticed me looking at you during class," he said. "But I've wanted to ask you out all year, and now I can."

The fields along the San Joaquin smell like Witch Hazel from all the artichokes, and the sun burns pale through the pearly iridescence of the not-quite smog. We are meeting my parents and my brother up at the slip—*we want to get to know your young man a little better, Jenny Alice*, is what my father said—and we are going to have a picnic and take a ride on the San Joaquin in my father's boat.

Peter has the red leatherette top down on his Corvair, as he often will all this first summer, till he has his wreck, and I stretch my legs out straight under the dashboard, admiring the deep bronze of my *California girl* suntan, my legs all shiny and smooth since I stopped shaving them with my father's electric razor and started using Nair.

"Shall I turn the radio on?" Peter asks, and as soon as he does, he starts singing. He was in a men's quartet during his undergraduate days at Occidental, and now he sings along with the radio, adding another bass to the Brothers Four:
Someday, when I'm awfully low,
I will feel a glow just thinking of you
And the way you look tonight.

* * * * *

Sometimes, when I'm awfully low, I think to myself, *Maybe it's because of your ancestors, Jenny Alice, that you move so much.*

My father always said that I was from California, not just because we lived in northern California for the four years I was in high school, but because I was born down near Santa Barbara—even though that was only because my parents happened to stop there on their way to someplace else—and that made me fourth generation California by my father's count, since on his mother's side *that* great-grandfather had helped found a goldminers' bank in San Francisco, leaving New England and sailing in one of the last of the commercial Great Ships around Cape Horn, and bringing with him the heavy cherrywood dresser and nightstand that are mine now for his shy new bride.

My father's other great-grandfather, on his father's side, was a law-man, a kind of vigilante sheriff, a secretive, tall man who deposited his seed in his young wife in Texas, then went off to end corruption in the gold camps north of San Francisco, where he might very well have met the other great-grandfather, the banker-lawyer, though of course did not, and returned three years later to the wife in Texas, only to find that she had remarried, this time to a local rancher, and that his own three-year-old son didn't know him.

And then one day while the law-man was visiting the small son who didn't know him, and his no-longer wife, a cardsharp with whom the law-man had argued in some bar in San Francisco, caught him in this little town in Texas, but without his guns, and shot him in the back, and left him to crawl back to the ranch to die in his ex-wife's arms.

The small son who had witnessed all this in the ranchyard in Texas moved with his mother and stepfather—a man whose name, appropriately enough, was Pinchback, *because,* my father always added, *he was a coward, Jenny Alice, who hid himself in the barn when the law-man came home and would not come out*—clear to Southern California, first to Bardsdale and then to Ventura, where my father still could remember planting a row of palm trees as a small boy with his father, himself the son of the Texas law-man, after all, the two of them walking along and planting palm trees, as if nothing extraordinary had ever happened in their lives.

And with that kind of background, Jenny Alice, my father always told me, *you have to be from California, a native. You were born in California before we left there, and you went back there to go to high school, after all.*

But I know that background in itself counts for nothing. For one thing, family trees being the tangled, storm-broken branches that they are, there must be hundreds of little girls hearing that story about the law-man hero in Texas while they're growing up. And anyway, my mother's family was *from* Massachusetts, from a distant branch of the Bellwethers, who fathered the famous nineteenth century inventor Arasmus Bellwether, *you know, of course*, and the Bellwethers went clear back to the Mayflower, she always said in her stories. But once, during a day I took off from teaching just to be alone, I visited the monument they have for the Mayflower Pilgrims at Plymouth Rock, and I couldn't find any Bellwethers listed. Instead, I happened upon a name that was the same as that of my father's ancestors, the ones who were supposed to have made me a native of California when they came around Cape Horn. There they were that January day in Plymouth, just like me, uprooted, hands in pockets, probably just as cold, longing for some sense of permanence, their journey from one place to the next nothing but recorded history on a small gray rock.

And I saw that, just like my father, who had moved his family all over the country, including a stint in Marietta, Georgia before integration, so that I can always say to people whenever they get too nosey at academic conferences that I *grew up down South*, and just like my mother also, who married my father during what was supposed to be a short vacation in California, I am possessed by a demon that prods me to wander. Pilgrimage, not permanence, is in my blood.

And with that kind of background, Jenny Alice, my father might just as well have added, *perhaps you can see why the courtship with Peter MacKinnon would not work out.*

* * * * *

Peter seemed genuinely happy to hear from me when I called him as I was leaving for Paris. He said that was fine, no problem, no worry. "Gee, it's good to hear from you, Jenny Alice," he said. "Just to hear your voice."

He asked me how I'd been, and what I was up to. He said it sounded pretty exciting, that I would head off like that on my own and go to France. He said he had often wondered what had become of me, after that night he'd waited for me out in front of my folks' garage, during that second summer he'd been hoping we could get back together. Then he paused.

He said he'd married someone and started a family, though of course his wife could not possibly be anyone I'd know. "But keep in touch now, won't you, Jenny Alice?" he asked when I said that I had to be going. He sounded as if he meant it. He sounded as solid as an anchor, like the one we'd dropped that day into the San Joaquin River from my father's boat.

And I remember, once again, trying to convince myself. *He made a mistake, that's all, Jenny Alice. And you were so young, Jenny Alice. You were fresh out of high school, barely formed. So how could Peter have known there was anything more to you? How could he know that by the way he treated you after you left for college, he would somehow help to shape you into the person you would become?*

But I know that is only intellectual reasoning. I'm trained to be good at intellectual reasoning. I went on to take my doctorate in French linguistic theory at the Sorbonne, and since then I've taught linguistics at any number of universities—at many here in the United States, and, just last year again in fact, at some abroad. So I know how to weed out the extraneous. How to take passion and feeling out of words and gestures, how to see them as nothing more than *signs and signifiers,* as they are called. In short, I am an expert on taking words for nothing more than for what they are.

* * * * *

Peter is water-skiing in the wake of my father's boat. His slim, tan body looks robust and healthy despite his heart, which he has already told me could quit any day after he turns forty. But that still gives him fifteen more years by my teen-age count, and to me, fresh out of high school, that seems enough. One time he laughed and said his heart had come in very handy. He had qualified 4-F for the draft, so at least he knew he wouldn't be sent to Vietnam.

Peter's whole body strains as he waves with one hand at me and my brother, while with the other he's holding on for dear life to a thin silk rope. My brother, two years younger than I, and a football player in our Bay Area high school, is big enough to be Varsity, though second string, and as the two of us wave back at Peter from our canvas chairs on the clean white Plexiglas deck of our father's boat, my brother says to me over the roar of the Chrysler inboard, "Jesus, Jenny Alice. I wish you'd pick a *man* for once. I mean, a French teacher, for God's sake? Will you just look at him out there, J.A.? He's got nipples just like a girl's!"

And as I continue to smile and wave at Peter, I see he *has*.

That was thirty-five years ago. Thirty-five, plus what Peter was that summer, would make him sixty now. That means he may have been dead now for twenty years.

* * * * *

After the famous Massachusetts blizzard had at last blown out, I made a copy of the Hortense Calisher story with the French phonetics, and I put the story in a manila envelope and addressed it in care of my old high school in Los Amitos—a high school that was built essentially out of wallboard in order to house the short-lived Baby Boom Generation, and that was soon defunct—and the next time I walked by a post office I mailed it. I figured the school district could always find Peter. I had learned years earlier that Peter MacKinnon was someone who could not be lost. On top of the story I attached a note, saying, *I'm living and teaching in Boston these days, but I don't know anyone here who would see the humor in French phonetics, so I'll send this off.*

Two weeks later, I received a ten-page letter from Peter, telling me everything he'd been doing since the last time he'd heard from me, all about his life. "I don't write many letters, Jenny Alice," he said in his letter as he started out. "But lately, I've been feeling the need to sit back and look at the last ten years of my life. So I guess you're the one I'm going to tell this to."

He wrote, "And next time, Jenny Alice, don't wait ten years, will you, before you get in touch."

* * * * *

Peter makes a handsome first impression with my high school crowd. He is tall and slim, with black hair and blue eyes, and the thin, strong nose of a Spanish aristocrat. I learn that first summer that his parents died within a year of each other while he was still in high school—his mother of cancer, his father of the hereditary heart condition to which he has already told me he is also prone—and that he has helped his grandmother to raise his two younger sisters.

In the eyes of all my friends, Peter's good looks are enhanced by this tragic note. *God, Jenny Alice*, the girls I graduated with say when they meet him. *What a hunk! And, How groovy to be dating your teacher! I sure wish I could meet some cute older guy like that, Jenny Alice.* And then, since Peter and I spend a lot of time on the beach at Aptos, driving down on the Santa Cruz Highway in his snappy car, my friends always add a comment about his terrific tan.

One night, Peter and I run into a girl who was in the French class with me when he did his student teaching. She is a short-haired, skinny, unattractive girl with acne who tried out for cheerleader and pom-pom girl and class officer and pep squad all through high school, who ran and ran, and never won anything. I am on my way with Peter in his silver Corvair convertible to see a movie in downtown Palo Alto when she spots us. Peter slows the car down and cruises along on Main Street to find a place to park. The girl from the French class waves at me wildly from the sidewalk. She leans way out into the road, and she calls and calls. *Yoo-hoo! Jenny Alice! Hello hello!*

As Peter pulls into a parking place two doors down from the theater, the girl from my French class runs over and folds herself into the window on my side, even while the Corvair is still moving, her terrible, acne-pocked face pressed close to mine. *Is he your boyfriend, Jenny Alice? Is he?*

I watch envy bloom on her cavernous face like a purple cloud. And I want her to go on asking me this forever and ever, just so I can keep my distance from her, just so I can go on saying to her forever, *Yes yes yes I have a boyfriend, yes he's mine.*

* * * * *

In one place in the letter Peter wrote after I sent him the story with the French phonetics, he asked if I remembered the piece of land he'd shown me up in the hills behind Los Amitos, that ran alongside the property of his grandmother's house. He'd shown it to me during the summer after my sophomore year in college, the second time we were dating. When he showed me his grandmother's property, he told me, "Someday, Jenny Alice, when I get married, I'm going to build my wife and kids a permanent, beautiful, custom house here on this family property. And we are going to live on it, happily ever after, all our lives."

I kept on walking. So far, he was still only hinting. I wanted him to spend all summer at it if he had to. And when he actually came out and said it, when he actually said, *I want you to marry me, Jenny Alice,* I was going to get back at him for what he did to me when I went off to college. I was going to tell him, *So what makes you think that's what I ever wanted, Peter MacKinnon? What makes you think I ever had any intention of settling down?*

I was wearing a shift made out of faded blue denim, and white toe-between Quali-Craft sandals I'd bought at the Stanford Mall, because my smallish feet had been something about me he had always liked. *All the better to hurt you with, my pretty,* was what I thought.

The denim shift came four or five inches above my knees, because minis were very much in fashion then, as they are now, and it had huge yellow elbow-length sleeves with blue dots on them. The sleeves opened up like bat-wings and flapped straight out onto the Bay Area breeze when I raised my arms, and while we were walking across the piece of property Peter was showing me, he rested his arm lightly across my shoulders to keep my bat-wings down. Furrowing his forehead above fine Spanish brows, he said to me, "You know now, don't you, Jenny Alice, that mine is an old and settled California family? And so it is important, before I say what I have to say to you, Jenny Alice, that you realize that in my family there could never be any question of a lack of permanence, or of, say, divorce."

When I didn't respond, Peter pretended to change the subject. He wanted me to see that he could be patient. He joked about my outfit. "The trouble with liking someone like you, Jenny Alice," he told me, "comes down to those blue and yellow wings that you're wearing. I'm afraid if I don't hold you firmly down to the earth, you're going to fly!"

I remember that the earth of his grandmother's land smelled of eucalyptus and of stiff, dry pine, and that the eucalyptus leaves and pine needles poked through my open Quali-Craft sandals to scratch my tan, bare feet as I walked along.

* * * * *

Well, anyway, Jenny Alice, Peter said in the letter he wrote after the blizzard, *I built that house.* His wife and his daughters loved it. And did I remember his sisters, either of them, very well? Both of them were married now, and all three of the married couples in the family went to plays up in San Francisco together. This was the way he had always hoped it would be with his family, he said in the letter, that they would all stay close to each other, and would live nearby. And the sister who had been such a hippie? The one he had said he thought I might someday be friends with? The younger one with the long straight black hair she parted right down the middle and wore in two braids like an Indian maiden, and who had dropped out of school to live in Haight-Ashbury for a little while? The one, if I could remember, with the wild, loud laugh? The one for whom his grandmother had bought the yellow Mustang convertible when she learned to drive? Well, that one had started a chain of

day-care centers there in the Bay Area that had turned out to be
very successful. After she had two children of her own, she sold
the business. She still went in every now and then to visit the
present owners, to see how they were doing, if she had the time.

Peter himself worked for a personnel firm now. And though
personnel work might not seem very interesting to someone like
me, he said, since he knew how much I loved to travel and that
I'd moved around, and even though it might not have been what
he'd thought he was headed for, either, back then when he'd met
me, teaching Fourth Year French in that high school—which, he
wondered if I knew already, they had taken down—still, he said,
he was happy. He enjoyed using the counseling skills he'd learned
in his teaching for this later job. But now that he'd heard from
me, he thought he might see if he could still read Corneille, Racine,
Baudelaire, and Verlaine in the original. So my few words about
the French phonetics in the Hortense Calisher story had certainly
been very amusing, reminding him, as they had, that he should
keep his language up.

Peter also said he had taken up jogging, not just because it
was the thing to do now, but because his doctor had told him he
should start running, for his health. "Maybe you'll remember,
Jenny Alice," he added, "that I have always had a problem with
my heart."

* * * * *

Peter took a lot of photographs the first summer we were
dating, with a custom Nikon he asked the Camera Shop at Los
Amitos Rancho Shopping Center to special-order for him, and
when I left for my college in Oregon at the end of the summer,
he gave me copies of all the pictures. In one, taken that day on
the San Joaquin River on my father's boat, I was sitting on the
deck in my light blue two-piece Lanz bathing suit with the little
button hearts, and I was leaning heavily towards my brother, who
two years later would get engaged right out of high school, then
enlist in the Navy so he wouldn't get drafted and be sent to Viet-

nam, and who would think through his whole life during basic training in a swamp in Georgia, and then apply to be a conscientious objector, and be excused from service through special decree by President Nixon and Admiral Zumwall, only to learn that his tiny brunette fiancée back home in California would call him a coward for not being willing to serve his country, and so would cancel the engagement, after my parents had moved away from Los Amitos forever, and after my brother had already made the announcement that even though they were leaving he was going to live in Los Amitos permanently, married to his tiny brunette fiancée all his life.

It all comes now right into focus. But in that picture, taken the first summer with Peter on my father's boat, long before the United States finally gave up trying to make a permanent peace in Asia and just pulled out, I'm looking straight into a future I don't even know. I haven't asked any questions. I don't even know I'm supposed to ask. I'm just sitting there next to my football-playing brother, that high school jock, each of us the other's best and oldest friend. Our cheeks, just a little bit sunburned, look soft and warm.

* * * * *

Two weeks after the trip on my father's boat, I get a job working as a keypunch operator for a girlfriend's father at Stanford. "They're working on a textbook in the math department," my friend tells me. "And I thought maybe, I mean, I know you're spending a lot of time with Peter this summer, Jenny Alice, but I thought maybe you'd like to earn a little money with this extra job."

One day at lunch, I walk out to the parking lot with my friend to eat my sandwich, and Peter's there, waiting for me. He isn't driving the silver Corvair convertible with the bright red top. Instead, he's sitting in a dull-colored '57 Plymouth that is rusted out. "Jenny Alice?" he calls out to me softly.

He is wearing dark glasses. When I go over to the driver's

side of the car to see him, I see that he has a bandage up high on his forehead, and that his face is scratched.

"I've been in a wreck, Jenny Alice," he tells me. "I totaled the Corvair going around a curve up at Tahoe. A bunch of us drove up there to do some water-skiing, and now my best friend is in the hospital with a broken back."

I look at Peter MacKinnon and think that I see a miracle, a modern Lazarus. I envision the Corvair rolling over and over down the mountain at Tahoe, and Peter not even wearing a seatbelt, and then I see him stepping out of the silver car that is totaled, and just brushing himself off before slowly, steadily making his way back up the mountain to call for help. *How did you do that?* I want to ask him. And as I look at his scratched, handsome face, a dark, closed place below my belly begins to soften and yield all by itself, and I feel an unfamiliar creaminess as it flowers out.

"Come with me for a ride, Jenny Alice?" Peter asks.

I get into the old Plymouth with Peter, and I ask my girl-friend to explain to her father that I appreciate his hiring me, but that I am leaving now with my boyfriend and that I will not be back.

Peter and I drive up to Buena Vista Road in the hills behind Palo Alto, and after awhile we get out of the rusty car and walk along together, not saying anything at all to each other, just walking along and holding hands in the tall, white grass.

* * * * *

But after I went away to college up in Oregon at the end of the summer, Peter didn't call and he didn't write. He didn't give me a reason. He hadn't even hinted that there was something wrong.

Don't worry about that dude, my brother wrote me in a rare letter. *I told you that day up at the boat he was a wimp, didn't I, Jenny Alice? Maybe now you will believe me after all.*

I couldn't understand what had happened. Maybe there'd been another wreck up at Tahoe. But then, Peter, I knew, would have lived through it. Peter had proved he was permanent. He'd told me a little at a time, all that summer, about his old California family, the Scottish ranchers, the MacKinnons, who had mingled over two hundred years earlier with the *conquistadors*. He couldn't be killed off so easily. Peter was one on whom the second death would have no power.

So it had to be something I'd done. Something I'd said on one of our last trips to Aptos, as I'd been sitting next to him in the borrowed Plymouth, playing games with the letters of the license plates in front of us in the Sunday traffic jam. *CGD* on a car meant *come get dinner*, I told him, and he laughed and laughed.

I bought Peter a card at the college gift shop. It showed a Dalmatian wearing a hat and a little red sweater. The dog was peering sadly into an empty bowl. *I miss the fun we had last summer*, I wrote inside. Before I sealed the envelope, I added, *Will you please write back?*

But Peter chose to remain silent. Meanwhile, everyone else in my dorm was going to mixers, meeting boys. They kept knocking on my door, calling, *Come on, Jenny Alice, you ready? Lots of frat men at this one, Jen, so you better come.*

I said I already had a boyfriend. I said I didn't want to answer the same old questions over and over, either. *So what's your major, Jenny Alice? What kind of name is that, anyway, Jenny Alice? Are you southern or something? Is your name like Mary Ellen, or Ida May, or Lulu Belle? Ha ha, Jenny Alice! Where you from?*

"That's rough, what he did," said my roommate, a happy Home Ec. major from Klamath Falls. "But you've got to get up and get going." Still, she stayed home from a fraternity party with me one Friday night, and held me in her arms while I cried and cried.

By November I had a severe case of acne and had lost ten pounds. I flew home to San Francisco for Thanksgiving vacation and watched Ben Cartwright and Hoss and Adam and Little Joe on *Bonanza* with my father in our playroom on the stuffed tweed couch. My brother, coming home late one afternoon from football practice, said, "I tried to tell you that day what he was,

Jenny Alice. He's a fairy or something, J.A. I hate to say it, Sis, but I told you so."

My father added, from his gold-toned vinyl recliner chair, "He is a coward, Jenny Alice. Just like that man Pinchback who raised my father. The one who hid in the barn because he was afraid of what was going to happen to him if he came on out."

Meanwhile, my mother kept saying, "It's actually better if he doesn't call you right away, anyway, Jenny Alice. This way, maybe we can clear your face up a little before he calls."

But Peter didn't call before I flew back up to Oregon on Sunday night. As I was buckling my seatbelt on the plane before taking off, I remembered a conversation I'd had with him, parked one night in his Corvair convertible by my parents' lawn. He'd told me all about the girlfriends he'd had before me, that they'd all been too anxious to marry, and that he'd managed to break up with each of the girlfriends without hurting their feelings, one by one. To me, those college girls had sounded like aggressive and desperate older women. They'd flirted with him and hinted too broadly. I thought they'd just wanted him for his family's money, and I told him so. "*I* won't ever be after you like that, Peter," I promised.

He hugged me, placing his clean, narrow brown hand just under my still tiny bosom, which my mother had quietly reminded me earlier that summer he should not yet touch. "I'm just glad there weren't any hassles," he said of these older women. "No big fights between us or tears, or anything emotional like that, you know, Jenny Alice. They just faded out."

I told Peter I was never going to get married, so at least he didn't need to worry about me. He could tell me anytime he wanted to stop going out. I told him I'd decided clear back in the sixth grade that I didn't want to get married, while I was growing up down South.

Peter laughed and rubbed my shoulders and kissed my cheek. "Of course you say you don't want to get married *now*, Jenny Alice," he told me. "But you're just saying that because you're young."

And as I flew back up to my college in Oregon after the Thanksgiving vacation during which Peter had never called, I looked at the acne-scarred face staring back at me in the mirror of my Corn Silk compact, and I knew something had been permanently settled. *Ah, Jenny Alice, you pilgrim*, was what I thought.

I began to revel in my own aloneness after that. I decided I was my own best company. If I went to the Peter, Paul, and Mary concert, or to hear Ferrante and Teicher or the Montevani Strings when they came to town, or if I went to see Audrey Hepburn in *Breakfast at Tiffany's* one more time, or if I walked up into the wet green hills behind campus, which were so different from the dry, yellow hills behind Palo Alto that I'd walked through with Peter that afternoon after he'd rolled his car, or if I took a picnic down by the Willamette River, then I went alone.

Don't be too standoffish, will you now, honey, my mother warned me. *I know you're having a rough time sorting all this out about Peter, but it doesn't sound like you, what you're doing. From your letters, it sounds as if you've become some sort of bookworm, a hermit, honey, whereas you were always so popular and well-liked in high school, always talking and laughing, always having fun. So just be yourself!*

I backed away from people in Oregon I thought were too normal, too middle-class. I ignored my roommate, the Home Ec. major from Klamath Falls, whenever she offered to find me a blind date for the weekend. *What do you say, Jenny Alice, maybe just this once?* I shook my head and said I wanted to study. And as she went off Friday or Saturday evening, and sometimes both, with her dark-rinsed hair teased up and sprayed into layers of bubbles, and her pink wool tweed A-line skirt and matching Garland sweater exactly so, I watched out the window till she and her date disappeared around the red brick corner of the dorm, their arms linked around an ever-present umbrella, because all that first fall I was up in Oregon it poured and poured.

I read every book I'd ever avoided, curled up at one end of my bed with the ruffly pink bedspread my roommate had insisted on buying, just reading and studying all evening, grateful for the rainy Oregon night outside the window, till I fell asleep to the sound of the rain that was steadily falling that was like my thoughts, long before my good and solid roommate was deposited by her well-behaved date exactly three minutes before curfew in front of the double-locked entrance to our women's dorm.

I started reading about the riots in Berkeley. What people were saying about Vietnam. When I'd applied to colleges my senior year, I hadn't even considered going to the University of California, so close to home. But now, from up in my dorm in Oregon, where every one of the other girls living on my floor had cried if they didn't get into the right sorority sometime that fall, I began to see Berkeley as the serious university experience, the *alma mater* I should have applied to, the one I *would* have applied to, if I hadn't been so wrapped up in a good-looking French student teacher from Stanford, who, I began to chant to myself in my dorm room, could go to hell.

I began to dress as I thought I would have if I had gone to Berkeley in the first place. I became the first, maybe even the only, freshman that year at my Oregon college to wear long dangly gold earrings, and to pair an un-ironed blue cotton Sears workshirt with thick black tights. Let Peter pull out if he wanted. He was far too meat-and-potatoes for the likes of me. I could stick it out in Oregon for the first two years if I had to. And when my grades were just a little bit better, I would transfer over to Berkeley, where I should have gone in the first place, if only I'd been thinking about what was most important, that is, myself.

But just before Christmas, during finals, I called him up.

"I thought we were friends," I told him. "I thought that you liked me. This is the sort of thing people do to each other when they've been in love. But how could you do this to someone you liked and were friends with, Peter? You could have told me. You could have written me a post card. All you had to do was call me up."

"I *do* care about you, Jenny Alice," said Peter. "And we *are* friends." Then he confided, "It's just that I've been seeing a lot of other girls, that's all. Oh, not any one in particular. Just going skiing with different girls every weekend at Tahoe. We were getting too serious, Jenny Alice, you and I. And I haven't made up my mind yet. I just don't think I'm ready to settle down."

After he hung up, I imagined him saying this, over and over, to all the older girls he had told me had wanted to marry him. I imagined him saying it, over and over again, to every one.

* * * * *

One evening in May, towards the end of my sophomore year in Oregon, someone in my dormitory shoved a letter beneath my door.

I was lying on my yellow chenille bedspread, propped up against the huge orange plush stuffed dog my brother had given me for Christmas the year before. Across from me was the unadorned striped mattress of the other bunk, where there would have been another girl, if I hadn't asked to pay extra for a single room so I could be alone.

As I walked over to the door to pick the letter up, I heard footsteps going away down the silence of the long bright hall. I found out later that a girl named Shelley had delivered the letter. She had come up from California to go to school in Oregon, as I had, and she was very quiet. She had told me once while we were brushing our teeth in the communal bathroom that she planned to marry an art history major she'd met through some friends in the Honors College. I used to see them together every now and then at the coffee house. I don't know how Shelley came to have Peter's letter, because it was just addressed in care of the college, but when I saw his name in the upper left-hand corner of the envelope, I went back to my bed and I sat down.

I'd just been accepted to transfer to Berkeley. I had a 3.8 average at my Oregon college. A professor in Romance Languages had told me that after I graduated from Berkeley he wanted to help me. He had connections in France, he said, and he would personally see to it that I got some sort of scholarship, even financial aid from the French government itself if need be, *a special dispensation*, as he put it, for the Sorbonne.

I opened Peter's letter and read it. He said he wanted to see me again that summer. He said he'd done a lot of thinking in the year and a half since we'd last talked. "I have something to say to you now, Jenny Alice," he said. Then, in French phonetics, he spelled it out. *I have found, my Jenny Alice*—and in French that's *ma*—*that you are different from all of the others.*

* * * * *

It is a beautiful July day during the summer after my graduation from high school, and Peter is driving me up the Bayshore Freeway to San Francisco in his grandmother's Cadillac, shortly after his Corvair convertible has been junked. His grandmother's Cadillac is a big silver-blue Fleetwood with double lights. I keep glancing over at Peter across the front seat. A few months later, when I leave for college, the image of Peter's profile will keep floating up, like a triangular motto in those Magic Eight-Balls kids used to bring out at birthday parties when they were growing up. In this image, a dark male head looks forward through expensive sunglasses. Beyond the handsome profile, the blue and white landscape of the San Francisco Bay Area whizzes by.

I will also have real photographs of that day to take along when I go off to college. In one of the pictures, Peter and I will be standing at a vista pull-out on the other side of the Bay from San Francisco, near Tiburon. I am wearing a new green suit I have bought for the occasion, because my mother has said it will make me look older, but I have ruined the look in the picture by clutching my coat to my sides with my elbows, forgetting to adjust my collar, so that I am all undone, my thick, curly hair blowing up into spirals. Meanwhile, Peter, well-dressed, well-groomed, smiles nonchalantly into the Nikon on its tripod, just ten seconds after he jumps into the picture he himself tripped off, forever looking as if he has always been there, tall and tan, in shirt-sleeves, standing there smiling into the wind and the fog above

San Francisco, permanently settled and happy, not even cold.

* * * * *

I wanted so badly to hurt him. I wanted him to know how it had felt.

I agreed to go on a picnic in Santa Cruz with Peter and his sisters when I got home. But I wouldn't hold Peter's hand at the picnic, and when he told me again he had something important to tell me, I wouldn't let him talk. My plan was to be pleasant but silent. After a few weeks, when he brought up the *something important, Jenny Alice* in earnest, I would tell him off.

For six weeks he took me to expensive places. A French restaurant in Atherton that served escargots and shitake mushrooms stuffed with lobster under a white wine sauce. The Orpheum Theatre up in the City, for a Molière play presented in French by the Comédie Française. The outdoor amphitheater at Stanford, where we heard Mozart's *Nachtmusik*, performed on period instruments by the light of gold candelabrae, in a rare California appearance by the *Orchestre de la Suisse Romande*, the orchestra members all dressed in red velvet tunics with gold épaulettes on their shoulders and in tight white pants.

"Do you realize how much money he's spending on you this summer?" my mother asked. "You should give him a second chance, Jenny Alice. A man has respect for a woman if he spends a lot on her, so now you be nice!"

One day I ran into Peter while I was on my way to an interview at Stanford for a free-lance typing job for a professor in the French department. Peter happened to be looking out the window of the office where he was doing some research, and when he saw me coming, he came on out.

"How did you know where to find me?" he asked.

"I didn't even know you worked here," I told him. "I'm looking for a summer job, as it happens. I wasn't really looking for you at all."

"Well," he said, "now that you *are* here, Jenny Alice, why

don't the two of us go on over to the Union and get some lunch?"

"I can't," I said. "I'm busy. My brother's got a job pumping gas down on El Camino so he can save up enough to buy an engagement ring at the end of the summer for his fiancée, and as soon as I get done here I have to pick him up."

Peter leaned into the terra cotta curve of the building. "Your brother," he said. He smiled, his white teeth small and perfect against his summer tan. "Remember the time we all went up to your father's boat for that picnic? Your brother was just a little bit sullen. I've decided he was probably just into phys ed and wheat germ like most kids his age, and that he might be more tolerant of me now. Anyway, when I wrote to you up at your college I couldn't help but think of that Chris-Craft. I was hoping we might all go up there again this summer. But so far you haven't even mentioned your father's boat."

A bright green lizard with a yellow stripe moved up the wall behind Peter like an electric flash. My father liked to tell his friends that his boat had gone to college. It had paid for my whole first year up in Oregon. *Your ancestors may have been pilgrims and wayfarers, Jenny Alice,* I could hear my father saying. *But they did what they could for their children. And if you just make a success of your life, Jenny Alice, we will be very proud.*

"My father sold his boat," I said to Peter. "Anyway, I've got this appointment, so I have to go."

"Sure," he said. "Jenny Alice," he said, coming closer. I could see he was going to kiss me. I felt a panic close to nausea, imagining that long pink tongue taking its old sweet liberties as it sought my throat.

"Listen," I said, backing away. "I have to get on with this interview thing so I can help my brother out."

Peter raised his perfect dark eyebrows, two question marks. "Okay," he said. "Go ahead then." He cocked his head to one side and crossed his arms. "But a gas station, Jenny Alice? Times must be tough all over. Did your brother honestly make an effort to find something else?"

I set my jaw. No use doling it out in small doses. I was

waiting for the one perfect moment to let him have it, the *something important to say to you, Jenny Alice*, when I would be ready and waiting, when it could all come out.

"So long," I said, and set off running.

"Bye, Jenny Alice!" Peter called after me. "I'll give you a call tomorrow. After lunch?"

* * * * *

Peter did go on calling me, for about a month. My mother said that was a miracle, considering the way I was behaving. "Why can't you just let bygones be bygones?" she asked one morning while I was helping her put the breakfast dishes into the pink enamel dishwasher she and my father had added as one of the extras when they bought our house. It was a tract house, four bedrooms, a bath and three-quarters, built on a cement slab in the new part of Los Amitos, and it hadn't even been finished yet when they signed the papers. My father planted pampas grass and redwood saplings in the bulldozed quarter-acre of the flat backyard, and a lemon tree in the front where the two fences met. The lemon tree never stopped bearing fat, juicy lemons, as big as grapefruit, and my mother made lemon meringue pies and fresh, sweet lemonade the year around.

"He must be really interested in you, Jenny Alice," my mother said as she poured Cascade into the plastic dispenser of the dishwasher. "Maybe he just had to think it all through before he formed a permanent attachment."

One night in mid-July, Peter took me to a movie in downtown Palo Alto, a film that starred, I think, Cary Grant or somebody like that as leading man, with maybe Audrey Hepburn playing his romantic interest, in some sort of comedy-mystery thing involving millionaires and thieves and charter boats. The film was showing in the same theater we'd been approaching two summers before when the acne-faced girl from my high school French class stopped us. The theme-song of the movie won an Oscar, I believe—*The Second Time Around*.

After the movie, Peter took the long way back to my house from Palo Alto, driving up Atascadero to Fremont, then heading south. He drove slowly, and he was very quiet. He parked the gray Cadillac Fleetwood in front of my parents' mailbox, then turned the engine off. By now, his grandmother had bought the Mustang convertible for his sister and given him her car. Peter said, "I liked that movie, Jenny Alice."

I noticed the hum of the lime-green lights of the built-in clock on the Fleetwood's dashboard. A California nightingale was singing in one of the redwoods my father had planted six years earlier in the stripped backyard. This was the longest my parents had ever lived anywhere, anywhere at all.

"I liked the theme," Peter said. "The idea that things can be better for two people the second time around."

I pressed my back into the silver-blue front seat of the Cadillac and tried not to look at him, the serious, eager set of his handsome jaw. Lately, I had begun to feel just a little bit guilty. Peter wasn't such a bad person. Maybe he understood now what he'd done, and was sorry. If he didn't matter to me, as I'd insisted whenever my mother asked if it was from her that I'd learned to be so blasé in regard to boys, then why was I going on with this? And here he was, so eager, so solid, all dressed up in a suit and shiny black pointed dress shoes, with a shirt and a tie and a haircut, all on my account. I didn't love him, and I didn't want to get married. I should apologize for the way I'd been acting before I called it off.

"Listen, Peter," I started.

He seemed pleased, almost surprised, that I'd spoken. I thought of all the times during the last six weeks that I'd sat across from him inside this car, refusing to talk to him, refusing to discuss anything that was halfway interesting at all. He hadn't even appeared to notice that the conversation was boring.

But as I opened my mouth to finish what I was going to tell him—that I'd been planning all summer to hurt him, to pay him back, and that I realized now I was wrong ever to have agreed to see him in the first place, with the way I felt—Peter interrupted, reaching across the seat to pull me toward him in the enormous car.

"Oh Jenny Alice!" he said, his voice so low it almost sounded like a growl. "I have something important to tell you, something I've been wanting to talk to you about now all summer, but each time I've tried—"

I added up the lime-green numbers on the clock on the dashboard. I was a hussy. A bitch. Maybe my mother was right and I did have some sort of problem in regard to *boys*. I picked at my nails and worked on the numbers. Let's see. Midnight, take away seven. That leaves us, five.

Peter cleared his throat. "What I have to say, Jenny Alice, concerns you, and me, and our families."

The green electric hum of the clock that said midnight jumped up from the dashboard, sprinted across my face, and tugged my arm. *I have something important to say to you, Jenny Alice.*

"That first summer," Peter continued, "after you graduated from high school, I wanted to ask you to marry me, right then. I wanted to give you a ring before you went off to college, but as it all turned out—"

"Peter," I said, "there's something here you have every right to—"

"No," he said, putting a hand up. "Let me finish, Jenny Alice."

I chewed on my lip and waited.

"Of course," he said, "I would have waited until you completed your education. In fact, I had already spoken to Grandmother about my plans."

He took a breath. I felt too horrible to stop him. *Here it comes.*

"But what happened, Jenny Alice," Peter continued, "is that I got to thinking about the social differences between our families. And it didn't seem a kindness, somehow, to you, to bring you into my family, with your lack of background, at the time."

My mouth fell open all by itself. "My lack of what?"

"Background," Peter repeated. There wasn't even a hint of humor in his voice. "But now, Jenny Alice," he went on, *sotto voce*, "I've decided it doesn't matter about your family, or their lack of permanence or breeding. It seems to me you've gone beyond your family, Jenny Alice, if I may say so. You've gone on to college, and you've found a sense of permanence and breeding all by yourself."

My head hit the back of the seat as I guffawed, part laugh, part sob. I'd been waiting all summer for Peter to propose so I could put him in his place, so that I could turn him down. Instead, here he was, my genteel *suitor*, explaining the subtle inequities between us, putting me down for all he was worth in this kindly voice. Once again, I'd been one-upped by an honest snob.

Now he was adding in French, *"Et il me semble que tu ne viens pas de tout de chez ces gens."* And it seems to me that you do not come from these people, my Jenny Alice, not at all.

I leaned over and hugged my rib cage, trying to contain my laughter against my thighs.

"Jenny Alice?" Peter said. "What on earth is so funny?"

But I couldn't stop. I went on giggling, then laughing. Sometimes they were outright hee-haws. Sometimes they slowed for a moment into a chortle, but then just as I thought I might be able to stop, they would start back up. Peter looked more puzzled than angry. I pictured the headlines in tomorrow's Palo Alto *Times*: *Stanford graduate kills co-ed from Berkeley!* Under a photograph of a perfectly respectable-looking, handsome young man being led away in hand-cuffs, there would be this caption: *Killer MacKinnon tells police, 'I couldn't stand her laughing at me anymore.'*

I knew I was going to have to get out of the car if I was ever going to stop. I told Peter in a strangled voice that I had forgotten my key *this evening*, and that while I ran in through my parents' garage he should wait out front.

And so I ran away from him then, who was calling and calling, *Jenny Alice, Jenny Alice*, and I opened the door of the double garage of my parents' house, and I slipped under the garage door without Peter, still laughing and all the while laughing, and at the same time starting to cry now, also, because

I knew there had been excess in my behavior all summer, and that I should have been big enough just to say, *No thank you*, and that instead I had been trying to punish a man who couldn't be punished, and now here I was.

Peter remained out on the dark driveway, calling again and again, "Can I help you, Jenny Alice? Please just let me help you!" Inside the dark garage, tears ran down my face as I laughed and cried, and Peter went on calling out to me, "Are you all right in there, Jenny Alice? Can you see your way in the dark there, Jenny Alice, all by yourself?"

When I finally went through the house to the front door and opened it, Peter gave me a fast, dry kiss, and, turning around smartly on his clean black shiny shoes, announced, "Good night!"

A week later, my mother leaned around the corner of the bedroom that had been mine during high school, but which she had since redecorated for guests, with white organdy curtains and a few antiques, including the cherrywood dresser and nightstand that had come all the way from New England around Cape Horn. My mother asked me, "What happened that night, Jenny Alice? Would you like to talk about it? Why haven't we seen your young man lately? Aren't you going to go out with Peter anymore?"

* * * * *

In the letter I received from Peter after the Massachusetts blizzard, he said that once, while he was traveling in Europe with his wife and two sisters, about a year before his sisters were married in a dual wedding ceremony, he had tried very hard to find me, starting with the address I'd given him over the phone when I left for France.

But everywhere he went, he said, I was apparently one step beyond him. He would find people who would say, yes, they had known me, and yes, I had lived there for a little while, or at least they thought, but they were quite sure I had left by now. So he was grateful, Peter said in his letter, to learn that I was living in Boston permanently now. "I always wondered, Jenny Alice," he wrote me, "where you would finally land, and what it was going to take before you would settle down."

And who, Peter asked in his letter, had I finally married? Whoever he was, he said, he'd certainly like to meet him, because any husband of mine must be quite a guy.

But the truth is, dear Reader, I didn't marry him. The truth is, I didn't marry anyone at all.

I tucked Peter's letter into "Il Plœ:r Dã Mõ Kœ:r," by Hortense Calisher, the story that was written in French phonetics like the ones he'd taught, and I placed the book that contained the story on my highest shelf. Come to think of it, the book, and Peter's letter, may still be there, right where I left it, because I sold that house completely furnished, as I often do, bookshelves and all.

I walked over to the big bay window and looked out at the bright sun shining upon the snow from that famous blizzard I had survived, and suddenly, I felt like singing. I burst into song in my solitary, cracked soprano, singing all alone in my house at the top of my lungs:

Ah but you're lovely
With your smile so warm
And your cheek so soft!
There is nothing for me but to love you
Just the way you look tonight.

ALL THEIR SECRETS

Occasionally, it would happen that customers would not come back for the shoes they'd left. If the customer was someone he knew, someone who had come into the shop regularly over the years, he'd give the family a call, and after they told him their sad news, he'd say, "Oh, well, I'm sorry to hear that." Then, when the necessities were finished—after all, he'd say to them, he and Tom had gone to school together years back, or Mrs. Kidd had raised three children all by herself, hadn't she, or, Chuck was a fine old guy, wasn't he, never heard an unkind word coming out of him—then he would tell them, "You know, I'm sorry to have to tell you this, but your Tom—or Mrs. Kidd, or Chuck, or Susan, as the case might be—left a pair of shoes in here to be fixed awhile back and I just wondered if you—"

But sometimes there were customers who only came into his shop to have some one simple little thing done to their shoes, people he didn't know. If one of these people left a pair of shoes too long in the shop, he was likely as not just to throw the shoes away.

It was different, though, with this pair of boots. They'd been here since last winter, almost a year now, with some name he didn't recognize, but he was still keeping them in the shop because they were such nice boots he couldn't bear to just chuck them out. They were ladies' boots, a size 7, the best, made in Italy of soft brown kidskin, and whenever he looked at them hanging there by the clothespins to the line he'd strung up over his head in the shop, he couldn't help but be grateful there was someone still left in the world who cared enough about nice things to buy a pair of boots like that. Most of what he saw in here was vinyl, or a cheap grade of cowhide at best, so that sometimes you'd wonder why they even bothered to have them fixed.

And you'd think, with these boots as nice as they were, he would have remembered more about the person who brought them in. That he would have looked up from the boots as she lay them on the see-through counter by his cash register, and that he would have taken better note of her face. What she was wearing. How long it took her to explain what she wanted him to do to the boots. Something about her, anyway. And that he might have made some light conversation with her at the very least. Say: "What beautiful boots! Hardly ever see them like this any-more." Then add: "Not in this town, anyways." And shrug: "Stay warm and dry, that's all these people think about nowadays. Wear those damn down parkas so's you don't know whether they're a boy or a girl!"

Perhaps she would have laughed with him at that one, since she herself must have been delicate and fine, so that he might have ventured on with: "You're not from around these parts, then, are you? You passing through?"

But he couldn't remember her. He couldn't even remember her coming in. The ticket said February. And that was about the time his second wife started acting queer.

"You don't care about me," Lillian started saying around then, and was saying still, almost a whole year later. "You don't know what it means to care about someone. You don't know anything about me. You've never tried. Any woman I know could be what you want from a woman. Do your dirty laundry, give you a little sex, clean up your house and cook your meals. Sometimes I don't think you even care if I'm alive!"

Every time she said that, he was alarmed. Of course he loved her. Of course he cared that she was alive. Her going on like that made him feel frightened and alone. "What are you talking about?" he would ask her. It pained him, the way she had changed, just from that first September, when he had married her, into this last February. "Didn't you want to marry me?" he'd asked her. "Didn't I take you down to Florida for two weeks this winter like you wanted?" How was he supposed to know, if she didn't tell him, that she'd changed her mind?

But she would purse her lips shut tight and not answer him. As if she had some sort of secret, and she was the only one who knew it, and she wouldn't tell.

His first wife, Ruthie, had died, cancer of the vagina, when he was 53. It was a good five years before he could get over that. He felt it had been his fault, something he'd done wrong, some hidden cruelty he'd inflicted on her without knowing, where it could not be seen. He couldn't tell what Ruthie really thought about anything, not in all the thirty-five years he'd been married to her. She'd told him, right before she said yes, all right, she would marry him, that she'd been in love with a sailor who'd gone off to serve in the Korean War and had never come back, no trace, not even a body, an MIA. And she'd told him she had to be honest, she would always be faithful to her sailor, because as long as nobody could tell her that he was dead, then for her, he might just as well have been alive.

And he'd said that was all right with him, it didn't matter at this point in his life, he just wanted to marry her, that's all. And so she agreed to marry him. She never spoke about that other guy again.

But when Ruthie's friends from the church she went to every Sunday came over to go through her things after she died so he wouldn't have to do it, they found a sepia-toned portrait of a young man in a Navy uniform. It was right on top of the things he knew she used frequently, even every day, as if she'd been taking the sailor's picture out for years and looking at it each morning, even before she looked at her rightful husband, which was him. The inscription on the portrait said: *To Ruthie, my sweetheart and future wife. Till death do us part. All my love forever, Your only Tom.*

Wouldn't you think the ladies in her church would have

something to say about that, that could comfort him? Say: *The poor thing. Have compassion.*

You'd have thought they would have said his wife was deluded, or that at the end there she couldn't have been thinking straight when she got so sick. They might have reassured him with that story in the Bible—Book of Matthew, he thought it was—the one where Jesus tells the woman at the well how many husbands she's had, and you can see for yourself that the Master's telling this woman she's not supposed to split her heart up like that into a bunch of little pieces, she's not supposed to have a lot of husbands, she's just supposed to focus on the one.

But then, that's what he meant about Ruthie. You just never could tell what she was thinking.

Anyway, after Ruthie died, he stuck pretty much to Knights of Columbus and the bingo games down at the town hall. Wasn't going to go out looking for another woman. It had been fine enough, all those years with Ruthie, even when he was wondering what she was thinking, why she would cry out and murmur, *Thank you,* whenever he made love to her. That was just Ruthie, that was all. You couldn't talk to her, couldn't get her to say what was on her mind, never knew if something was bothering her or not, and that was fine. But he didn't want that kind of thing again.

It was his old friend Sydney Weyanowski who said he should get married again. Sydney and his wife Pat introduced him to Lillian, who became his second wife. And it had been all they could do to get him to come over to their house when he found out what it was they were doing, that there was going to be a woman there for him to meet. Only after they made it sound like he would lose their friendship if he didn't come over did he agree to come.

He had to hand it to Lillian for how she went into the whole thing. Right from the start she was willing to talk. She asked him what his favorite foods were. What he liked to do in his spare moments. Whether he believed in hunting or animal rights, and what did he think about the expansion of NATO, or about capitalism in China, all that kind of stuff.

So he married her, and for a while she seemed to him to be happy, or happy enough. She'd ask him, when he got home from the shop, how his day had gone. If one of his old customers died, she sent flowers to the family for him. She cooked all his favorite foods, at times even ordered up a live lobster and boiled it in a big pot on the kitchen stove. She went through his house and cleaned and dusted and washed away all the vestiges of the five years of bachelorhood he'd had after his first wife died.

And that was why it was so hard to figure out what happened to her so soon. Because even by December, she was starting to complain about little things. Why didn't he work ordinary hours like other men? How could he expect her to cook and clean and be all happy when he got home? What about her? Did he expect her to be there all by herself, snowed in and alone all day and still be happy? What difference did it make if some old fool didn't get his stupid shoes till a day after he'd expected them, why should her husband stay way past working hours putting soles on an old man's smelly shoes when here she was waiting for him with a nice hot potroast that was getting overcooked?

Probably it was one of those nights he was working late, and worried about what Lillian would say about it, that the owner of those boots had come in. He couldn't say for sure. But that might be why he couldn't remember her. She could have been one of those annoying, one-time customers who drive up in their shiny, late-model cars about 5:15, and when they see your sign that says, *Closed*, they proceed to knock on the door anyways, like they're frantic, like their whole lives depend on your opening up and saying you'll fix their shoes.

And probably he had let the woman with the boots in late like that, and she had come in and shoved the boots at him in a brown paper sack, and he had taken the sack quickly without looking inside till a few days later, just so he could get it over with and close his shop and go home to Lillian, and by then he had forgotten who had given him the boots.

Probably he had given the customer a receipt without even looking at her face. Probably he was late and thinking about what Lillian had said about the trees outside his living room window, how after awhile, during a storm, and him not there, her alone and looking out at the bare winter trees, she would begin to think, and she would imagine herself a small child being lifted up, up, up in those stiff, cold arms to go to sleep.

Lillian said strange things like that, a lot. He didn't ever know whether he was supposed to answer them or just keep still. Mostly he just sat and listened. But if he did that, if he just listened to her talk, and didn't say anything, she'd get mad at that, too. No matter what they wanted you to do, it seemed, they kept it a secret.

But at least he knew his working late bothered her, so he really did try to leave earlier these days. Today, for instance, he was trying to close up right at the hour it said on the sign in his window. Tonight, at five o'clock sharp, he was going home. That should make Lillian happy—that he would drop everything, just like that, and head for home.

He turned out the lights of his shop and flipped the sign on the door to say, *Closed*, and then went out into the cold gray day that was almost evening now. It would be dark before he got home. A heavy wind was blowing, and a few snow flurries whirled on the air. The radio had been saying, right before he turned it off at the shop, that gale warnings were in effect along the coast.

As he approached his house, he saw that only one dim light was burning in the dining room. That was funny. Lillian always kept the lights on, every one. He opened the front door, and with a cold, lonely feeling in his stomach, afraid even as he called out cheerily, "I'm home!" that she wasn't there, that she had finally done what she had threatened and had left him, he walked in and threw his hat down on the chair.

"I've asked you not to do that many times," she said. She was standing in the corner, in the dark. Even though she sounded annoyed with him, he was glad she was there. He felt the empty pit in his stomach fill in a little, and he smiled and started to walk toward her in the dark.

But just as he was about to put his arms around her for a nice big hug, it hit home that there were no smells of cooking coming from the kitchen. She had never done this to him before.

"I'm sorry," he said, going back to the chair and picking up his hat. "I always forget." And then, trying to beat her to what he thought she might be thinking, since she obviously hadn't started dinner, he added, "You want to go out, Lillian, just the two of us, is that it, and get a bite to eat?"

But she didn't answer. She turned on a light in the living room and walked into the kitchen. He followed her. He saw newspapers spread out all over the kitchen table. She hadn't washed the breakfast dishes, or even put his cereal box away.

"They've found a woman," she said. "In the gorge, behind Petersen's Ridge. She was identified by the coroner through dental charts. She's been dead now, the paper said, for about a year."

He looked around the kitchen at the unwashed breakfast dishes and the newspapers on the table. She herself was neatly dressed, in a green sweater and skirt he'd never seen before. Her hair was freshly washed, and he thought he noticed a new kind of reddish tint to it. She looked nice.

"They know who it is?" he asked. What in the world was it she wanted? What was she getting at? If it wasn't to go out to dinner, then what was it? *What?*

"A woman from down on the Cape," she said. She had the air of someone who has been wronged and wants to show it. He wondered if he had left some big chore unfinished. He hadn't chopped up that big limb that had fallen off the apple tree in the last storm, and so she was retaliating by not doing the dishes, was that it? He wanted to tell her he didn't give one hoot in hell about the dishes, she could do them or not do them so far as he was concerned, he just wanted a little something hot to eat, was all, and then to go to bed, and he'd let her alone there, too, if that's what she wanted, he was glad she was there, was all, it didn't matter. He moved towards her, putting out his hand to touch her hand.

"The woman's been missing since last February," she said, drawing away from him, walking backwards at the same time as he advanced. "They hadn't even bothered to try to look for her way up here. She didn't know anybody in this part of the state. They can't find any connection, no family here, no friends. She was a schoolteacher."

He sat down carefully in the chair beside the table and untied his shoes, moving almost daintily, he thought, like an old man picking his way over black ice on pavement so as not to fall. He studied his shoes. He kept his shoes in good repair. He could afford to, since he did them himself. "What's for dinner then?" he asked without looking up.

But she sprung at him. "*You would!*" she cried, her face thrust now right into his. Her face was horrible. He tried to remember when he had seen such a horrible face, like a scare-baby maybe, like one of those jack-o-lanterns you hung out on the fence by the highway when you were a little kid. And she was making some sort of horrible, gurgling noise, too, inside her throat, half-strangled, it seemed to him, like she was trying to yell at him but nothing was coming out.

Until finally she said, "You *would* sit there asking about your dinner, worrying about yourself, wouldn't you, never bothering about me, or anyone else for that matter. You don't care, you don't take responsibility, and without responsibility there's nothing, and you don't care, one bit, about that poor woman, a stranger, a poor stranger, and you don't care for *me*, when it could've been *me* out there, all frozen, don't you see?"

She broke into tears and sat down at the table and put her hands over her face.

He looked at Lillian sitting across from him, and it seemed like she was miles away, and that he couldn't touch her now, no matter what he did, and he felt more alone and afraid than he ever had in his life. The trouble was, you just never knew what they wanted. What they were going to do next. You tried one thing and the other was what you should have tried. You never knew how you should act so they wouldn't do this.

He stood up and went over to her, walking clumsily in his untied shoes, and he patted her head as he might have patted a dog's. "Aw c'mon, Lillian, old girl," he urged her. "C'mon now, it's not so bad."

She looked up at him with that awful, fearsome, hate-filled face. Through her small, tight teeth, clenched in fear or anger, he could not say which, she said, "Get away from me." Slowly. Watching him like he was some kind of animal. Fixing him with her awful, scary eyes. "Get away from me," she said. "Don't touch me."

She rose. "If you want something to eat, you'll have to fix it yourself. I don't want to live another minute in your house. You don't feel anything, you don't care about anybody, you can't see past your shoes, your smelly shoes."

She sniffed. "The smell of that old, sweaty leather makes me sick. There's no way you can hide it. You come in here smelling like it every night. You smell like a tomb. You smell like that dead woman's body. You make me sick."

She turned and went up the back stairs to the bedroom and closed the door. He could hear her lock it after she went in.

The kitchen was gloomy with only the one light on. The light didn't reach into the corners of the enormous room. Familiar objects—the antique pie pantry she'd stripped and refinished, the shelves on the wall full of jams and pickles, even the little old round refrigerator that always hummed—all took on foreign and unwelcoming shapes. His friendly black-and-red plaid woolen wood-cutting jacket had turned into a headless ogre, its truncated torso hanging from a hook across from him on the darkened wall. What had he done in his life, he wanted to know, to deserve all this?

He sighed and picked up the front section of her newspaper. The articles were full of the details about this woman they'd found. Nothing big like this ever happened up here. The paper was using every inch it had.

The corpse was that of a Plymouth schoolteacher, a Miss Moira Shannon, the paper said. They showed a picture of the woman, and she was kind of pretty in a tight and controlled and careful sort of way. She was a blonde, her long hair done up in a bun atop her head, her eyes sharply focused on the camera, her lips half smiling, as if she had a secret. She was thirty-one, the paper said.

Next to the picture of the woman whose body they had found was a picture of the men in the volunteer fire squad, pulling a sheet-covered stretcher up a wooded slope. One young man in the picture was wearing a plaid lumberjack jacket just like his, and he was smiling. The paper said this young man had found the body while he was out checking his traps. The local authorities were quoted as saying the young man deserved some sort of reward.

He looked at the picture of the dead woman again, quickly, as if it might burn him if he stared at it too long. He remembered seeing her a year ago. He recognized her, was sure now, that she was the one who had come into his shop to bring the boots. The knowledge of it flooded over him like a hot liquid. He smelled the leather in his shop, the oils and polishes and waxes, the smoky, iron-rich smell of the belts and pulleys on his old machines. He squeezed his eyes shut and tried not to see her, but she kept pursuing him. He saw her face at the window of his shop even when he shut his eyes. She kept knocking and knocking and pleading at his door, even though he was closed, couldn't she see that, and he had already hung up his little sign and she had ignored it and she wanted in.

He sat there in the kitchen, wondering what he should do next. Outside, it was pitch-black. The house was so quiet he had to clear his throat to make sure he wasn't deaf. He couldn't just sit here in the kitchen, couldn't just stay here in the house with what he knew. Something awful would follow him. All their secrets. Hers too, now. They wouldn't tell you anything. They just kept knocking and knocking.

Till against your better judgment you let them in.

FREEDOM

I was taking the train south to Verona to visit Kristen
Cavalcanti and her husband. Kristen's mother, Olga Giersdottir,
was Icelandic, and she and my mother were pen pals when they
were girls. Olga had married an American serviceman stationed
in Keflavik, and when she got to the States she looked my
mother up.

As children, Kristen and I saw each other whenever our
mothers managed to meet, but she was six years older than I was,
so we didn't have much in common then. Kristen's father, Larry,
was an alcoholic, a thin, pale man with bloodshot eyes. He came
with Olga a few times to my parents' house.

When I was in high school, Olga told my mother in one of
her letters that Kristen was going to marry an Italian doctor she'd
met while the family was living in Florida. Carlo Cavalcanti had
been doing his internship in a state hospital outside Miami where
Larry was a patient for a little while, and apparently he had wooed
Kristen during visitation hours. Five years later, when I left for
Europe, my mother wrote Olga to tell her that the younger of her
two daughters had enrolled as a student of international relations
in Geneva. Olga wrote to Kristen, whose husband had just taken
a position as staff surgeon at the NATO base outside Verona, and
Kristen sent me a telegram in Geneva, where I had been renting
a room from a Swiss woman by the name of Berthe Prah.

Madame Prah had hoped I would be a good influence on her

sixteen-year-old son, Rémi, who had dropped out of the Swiss equivalent of high school, with—as she explained to me the day I arrived with my suitcases—*the very foolish impression of the young that he must paint*. I, on the other hand, she noted, had come to Switzerland to attend the university, to make my mark. Rémi was into hashish and street language. I, on the other hand, she said, might speak an English-accented French, but *comme il faut*. I was *someone*, she told her son right in front of me. *Elle est quelqu'une*.

But by the time Kristen sent her telegram, which was late fall, all that had changed. By then I had dropped out of the program in international relations at the University of Geneva, and I was no longer *quelqu'une* in anybody's opinion, not even mine. Instead, the sixteen-year-old Swiss artist and the twenty-two-year-old American ex-student—living in bedrooms that adjoined each other in a tiny *bourgeois* apartment, and chancing to bump into each other more and more frequently whenever Madame Prah was at work or gone to do the shopping, her *commissions*—had fallen deeply, irrevocably in love. It was clear now to Madame that I knew no more about living my life with a sense of purpose than did her son. She placed my two suitcases out on the sidewalk, announcing that if I was not going to be a student, then at least I could have the courtesy to allow her to use the room. Since then, I had been traveling around Europe second-class, staying in youth hostels and in cheap hotels, using what I could of my stipend before the student-loan service learned I was no longer a student and cut it off. I did not know what I was going to do, or where I would go after my visit with the Cavalcantis.

When I arrived at the train station in Verona, it was late at night. I put a *gettone* in the payphone and dialed Kristen's number, and when Kristen's husband answered, I did not know I had to push the button down before the telephone would swallow the *gettone* and let me talk.

"*Accidenti!*" I heard Kristen's husband say. "The poor girl doesn't even know how to work the stupid phones."

I put the phone back on the hook and waited. But the same thing happened again the second time.

There were only two other people in the second-class waiting room—an old wino, and a custodian. The old wino was vomiting. The custodian was reprimanding him for having had this *indiscrezione* on his floor.

I had just decided to spend the money to take a taxi to Kristen's house when Carlo came. "You!" he said, pulling me from the cab in spite of the driver's protest. "You must be Lisa, if I am not wrong." He paid the driver, and led me to his Fiat Sport in the parking lot, talking the whole while in a rich, only slightly Italianized American English. I could hear a certain rhythm in his voice.

"Kris has been so much looking forward to this visit," he said as he put his hand on the leather gear-shift of the Fiat Sport. He was very beautiful. But when I compared him to my memory of slender, fragile Rémi as he had stood there on the sidewalk waving good-bye, dressed in his loose white silk poet's shirt and his red velvet bell-bottoms, the perfection of this grown man's body put me off. I tried to imagine Olga's daughter making love with Carlo, but the thought of all those perfect curves and valleys made me ill.

To be truthful, my imagination had to work very hard, because it had no facts. I was not yet a girl of my generation. I was still a virgin, even after graduating from Berkeley, and though I had been slipping from jeans and hiking boots into a sleeping bag like all the others over the past few months, I slept alone.

"So you are traveling by yourself," Carlo said, lighting a Doral. "It seems to me the kids of your generation have got it made."

"Yes," I said politely. "I'm on my own."

"Doing just what you want to do." A flick of the Doral, a turn of eyes.

"Mm, yes, well, I guess we are."

"Meeting up with strangers, staying with them just long enough to. . . ." He shrugged, implying what it was that the kids of my generation stayed long enough to do.

When we got to the house, Kristen was so happy to see me that I wondered if she had any friends at all. The three of us ate a late dinner in the large, white-tiled kitchen. Kristen had prepared a veal roast and fresh vegetables. Even though she could get all their groceries at the PX on the base, she said, she went into Verona every three or four days to buy fresh vegetables at the outdoor stalls. She said she would take me there tomorrow, if I liked.

Kristen told me she envied me. "I never did what you're doing," she said. "Travel around in different countries by myself. It must take a lot of courage." She continued speaking to me, but looked over at Carlo, who was pouring himself another glass of wine. "We had another friend of mine here a couple of months ago," she said. "But she wasn't like you, I'm afraid."

Carlo was peering carefully into his glass. "As I told you earlier, my dear," he said, "I would venture to say that was the first trip that girl had ever made in her entire life. Men frightened her, that's all. I think she had never had any experience with men."

"Well," Kristen said, turning back to me, "she was from a very small Midwestern town, Lisa, and not as sophisticated as you."

The next morning Kristen and I left her two little boys at their nursery school on the base and she drove me into Verona.

It was early morning and a ground fog was rising from the fields. I could not see the separation between earth and air. Kristen drove through the fog soundlessly with her yellow parking lights on, her Ingrid Bergman face a perfect shroud. There was a stillness in the atmosphere I could only imagine punctured by medieval hooves. It would not have surprised me if I had seen Romeo himself riding along on his eternal way to Juliet, as in Zeffirelli's movie, which I had seen in a theater in Geneva with Rémi Prah.

When we got to the center of Verona, Kristen took me on a tour. We went up and down little alleys that smelled of olive oil and peppers and tomatoes. It was intoxicating, that smell, and it was exactly what I had expected. But when we reached the tiny edifice that Kristen said held Juliet's balcony, I was disappointed. I had pictured large flower gardens, a grand villa, a high wall with rambling, spiny branches all around—something like Sleeping Beauty's castle, I suppose. Instead, we stood before a crumbling plaster tenement that was pressed so close between two other decrepit dwellings that I could not see where the Capulets' house began and the others stopped.

"I'll show you their tombs, too, if you'd like to see them," Kristen offered. "Although of course Romeo and Juliet aren't in them. Grave robbers during the 1500's stole their bones."

"Why would they do that?" I asked, astonished.

"I don't know," she said. "Romantics, I guess."

It was mid-November, so we were wearing coats, but our heads were bare and the sun warmed our heads, and it warmed the stones of the streets and of the square. All the men turned to look at Kristen as we walked. She was striking, very blonde and tall. What's more, she did not seem to know she was beautiful, not as she had known it as a girl. Whenever she visited our house with Olga, she had always fished for compliments, imploring me and my older sister to reassure her that her hair was not too short, nor her lips too full, nor her nose too long. I used to catch her in front of our hall mirror mouthing words. *So you think I am beautiful, Frankie? Elvis? Ricky?* Her mouth would press closer and closer to the mirror, until at last it responded to her teen-age passion with its vapor-clouds.

But I don't think she would have believed me, that day in Verona, if I had told her how truly beautiful she was.

She spoke Italian with the men who ran the stalls, and she smiled at them, but not coyly, and she filled her bags with their fruits and vegetables and we walked on.

"You make me feel very old," she said.

"Don't be silly," I said. "You're not so old."

"But I've never done what you're doing. And I can't now. I'm married, and I have children. I've become a wife. Something dies in you when you get married. You stop looking for adventure in your life."

"My mother said Carlo fell head over heels in love with you the first time he ever saw you," I said.

She laughed. The tiny lines that had formed at the corners of her eyes now crinkled up. "That! Hardly. I was twenty years old and had just won a beauty contest, and I had no intention of going on to school. Carlo and I had already met while my father was in the hospital, and he turned my name in to be a hostess at a dance the Sons of Italy were putting on. The dashing *Dr. Cavalcanti* took it from there. He was very handsome." She laughed again, and shrugged, a gesture I had already noticed that she and her husband had in common. "Whenever I complain, my father says Carlo and I deserved each other."

"And how is your father?" I asked. The last time my mother had heard from Olga, Larry was a patient in another mental ward.

"He's drinking again," Kristen said. "And my mother, bless her heart, won't leave her man."

I bought a pair of sunglasses that day in Verona. I had grown accustomed to the cool, gray tones of northern Europe, and the bright Italian sun now hurt my eyes. Kristen took me into a small shop down a shady passageway and a man brought out an entire tray.

"Are they plastic?" I asked him.

"But no, signorina," he said in an offended voice. *"Sono veramente cristalli, questi."* Kristen translated. *They are pure as crystal, little woman, every one.*

I picked out a pair of glasses that resembled some I had seen in pictures of Jacqueline Onassis. I have photographs of myself wearing those sunglasses—snapshots clicked by helpful passersby, after I left the Cavalcantis and was alone in Rome. I kept those sunglasses for a long, long time, even after I ran out of money and couldn't find anymore short-term jobs and had to fly back home. One day, while I was visiting my parents, I dropped the sunglasses on the hardwood floor in front of their television and broke a lens. By then, my mother had lost touch with Olga Giersdottir. She said she had received a strange phone call from Olga while I was still traveling in Europe, and that soon after,

Olga had stopped writing. My mother said she was afraid something awful had happened. In fact, she confided, Olga had sounded so aloof and distant during that one phone conversation that now she was wondering, given Larry's history of instability, if her old Icelandic penpal were even still alive.

On the way back to her house from downtown Verona, Kristen insisted we must stop at her best friend's house to have some tea. She said her friend, an American woman whose husband was also a doctor on the base, was expecting us. They had discussed my having tea with them, and special cookies her friend would order at the PX.

Kristen's friend, Myra, was a small, spreading woman in her early thirties, with short, convenient hair. She had three children, all in school. She and her husband rented part of a large villa, owned by an Italian family who lived next door. Knickknacks from America lined the shelves.

Myra told us a story about her car. The car had not been working that morning, she said, and yet she knew that Kristen and I were coming in the afternoon for tea. And so she had wondered what she could possibly do about the cookies, when here she was alone with this broken car! And then, while she was telling her husband about this over the phone, she said, she began to cry, because it all seemed so hopeless, and her husband felt so sorry for her that he offered to buy the cookies himself there on the base and to send them over with one of the ambulance drivers if she wouldn't mind. And so could we possibly imagine, she asked us, the ambulance arriving with these cookies, lights flashing, siren going, and in any case, if the ambulance wasn't saving anyone else's life just then, it was saving hers!

Kristen and Myra laughed and laughed. I did not see what was funny about the story, but I smiled. The smile hurt my jaws. I must have been very quiet, sitting there with Kristen and her friend while they laughed about things that were funny for reasons I didn't understand, because suddenly Myra broke into the middle of the laughter and asked me, "You find us very boring, I suppose?"

Their smiles were fading as I looked from one to the other. "Of course not," I said. "That's a very funny story. Especially the part about the ambulance."

"You understand there is nothing to do here," Myra said. She had eaten her bright coral lipstick off with the cookies. "No place to go. We can't go running all over Europe like you are. We have husbands. And children. Responsibilities. We don't meet a lot of people, staying home." She brought her face very close to mine. In her eyes, I saw myself reflected as the girl on the travel poster. And I already knew very well that she was wrong.

"What Myra means," Kristen said, placing her pale, short-nailed hand over Myra's, "is that for us, the excitement, the way you must think of Europe, does not exist. If something doesn't suit you, you can get on a train that's bound for Paris and disappear. We envy you your freedom, that's all."

Kristen and I left shortly after that so she could pick up the boys at their nursery school. Myra gave her a box of the cookies to take along.

Carlo was late getting home that night. Kristen was angry with him, because dinner was overcooked, and because she'd wanted to take me to a nightclub outside town and Carlo hadn't made the reservation yet. "He's so selfish," she kept saying. "He's so goddamn selfish."

The boys were already in bed when Carlo walked in the front door. "I'm sorry," he said. "I had a lot of patients, and then an operation held me up. And when I got through with that at five, there were more patients waiting in line."

"All women, no doubt," Kristen said in a low, tight voice. Her round, full lips were drawn up small. She stirred the spaghetti sauce.

"Oh, come on, now," he said. He went over and put his arms around her from behind. He smiled at me and winked, as though we were in a conspiracy together to make her happy. His smile revealed his beautiful, straight, white teeth.

Kristen turned to me. "It's true," she said. "These women go in there and they stand in line to see him, and when they get in the room with him they have absolutely nothing on but these clean, white sheets. And they say to him, *Please, Dr. Cavalcanti, won't you examine me?*" She faced him, her pale arms crossed under lovely breasts. "Well, Carlo? Tell our little visitor it isn't true."

Carlo sighed and went over to the refrigerator to take out a bottle of Chianti. "One woman's body is like any other to a doctor, Kris." He walked back over to her and kissed her cheek. "But for your information, darling, it was Mrs. McKelvie who held me up at the very end."

"*That* woman!" Kristen said. "You'd think that with a husband and four children she'd stay at home. Well? Was she sick?"

"She's only thirty-two," Carlo said, dipping a wooden spoon into the spaghetti sauce. "And she should be in better shape than she is. She's very unhappy. I'm going to recommend that she have therapy with Dr. Meilberg." He tasted the spaghetti sauce. "This is very good."

Kristen sniffed. "Therapy! The only therapy she'd understand would be in his bed!"

Carlo looked at her sadly. "My dear, you are far too hard on other women," he said.

After dinner, when I went to my room, I heard Carlo telephoning a friend out in the hall. "Very pretty," he was saying. "And traveling around Europe on her own."

"Lisa!" Kristen called from the kitchen. "What are you going to wear to this club tonight?"

The friend who agreed to be my date for the evening was short and round and slightly balding. He did not really know how to dance. The band was American, and they played Motown with a good, strong beat. After awhile I could feel my body keeping time. Carlo's friend, Giuseppe, shook his head. I saw that it embarrassed him to have me sitting there next to him as I moved my hips.

"Come on," Carlo said, clasping my hand. "I'll dance with you." He was much more relaxed than he had been at dinner, and he was as taken by the good music as I was. He had been sitting with his arm around Kristen's shoulder, tapping his fingers against her skin.

"What about Kristen?" I said, turning back to her. "Don't you want to dance, Kristen?"

"No," she said, smiling. It was the happiest I would see her on my stay. "You two go on. I've never been able to dance to this kind of music."

Carlo led me out onto the floor and we danced through two Aretha Franklin take-offs before they started playing Henry Mancini tunes. When *Moon River* began, I moved toward the table where Kristen and Giuseppe were sitting, but Carlo caught my hand. "Dance this one with me," he said. He was almost pleading, like a child. Kristen waved at us from the table that we should stay.

As Carlo held me against him, I felt his hardness, and I did not know what to do. He pressed his head, smooth and cool as a Roman statue's, against my ear. After the music finally stopped, I could not look at him. I danced the rest of the evening with shy, careful Giuseppe.

On the way home from the nightclub, Kristen insisted that we stop to look at the lake. "It's such a lovely lake," she said, turning around from the front seat where she sat with Carlo. "And it's especially pretty, with the mist, this time of year. Carlo and I go there sometimes, just the two of us, and leave the boys at Myra's. Don't we, Carlo?"

Carlo nodded. He had spoken very little since we'd left the club, but Kristen hadn't noticed. She was happy and talkative. "Lisa," she said, "do you remember that lake that was near the house you lived in when I stayed with you and your family when we were kids?"

"I remember the lake," I said. I was nine or ten the first time Olga left Kristen in my parents' care so that she could look for Larry, who had taken off one afternoon for what turned out to be a three-month drunk.

"There was a raft out in that lake," Kristen said. "Maybe twenty feet out at the most. You were always afraid to swim out to it, as I recall."

"I couldn't swim," I said. "I still don't swim very well."

Carlo looked at me in the rearview mirror. "You, Lisa?" he said. "Afraid to swim? Why, I would have pictured you jumping in before any of the others. Wading in above your head. Daring all the others to follow suit."

Kristen laughed. "Ah, but back then she wasn't like that," she said. "She was very, very afraid to go out to that raft. She was just a child, even younger than I was, and she was afraid of water. Weren't you afraid of water, Lisa?"

"Yes," I said. "I was very afraid of water. I still am."

"Well," Carlo said. "Maybe we should give her another chance."

"Where, Carlo?" laughed Kristen. "In our lake? In the middle of November?"

"Why not?"

"Come on, Carlo," Giuseppe said. "Stop making jokes. You don't suggest that we all go swimming now in all this dark? We have not even bring the proper clothing. So now! Stop!"

"Who needs clothes?" Carlo said. He tossed a quick, angry glance at Giuseppe in the rearview mirror. "I thought you said you could speak English, you stupid fool!"

"I understand English perfect," Giuseppe said. "And still I do not prefer to go to swim without my clothes!" He slouched against the back seat, pouting, and crossed his arms.

Carlo turned the car abruptly onto an unpaved road and we bumped along until Carlo pulled up beside a small, wooden pier. "This is it," he said. "Everybody out."

A mist was rising from the lake. The water was dark blue, the air, and all the trees and reeds, all shades of blue. Our skin was the grainy, blue-gray color of night as it is depicted in movies. Kristen's soft, clingy dress, once pink, was also blue. Her legs and sandals, blue. Even her blonde-from-childhood hair was silver blue.

Carlo opened his door and came around and opened Kristen's and my doors. His voice was too loud as it went out over the motionless water. "Last one into the lake's a rotten egg!"

Kristen giggled and whispered for him to be quiet. "People

are sleeping, Carlo!" She was delighted. Still, I don't think she believed him, clear until he began to remove his clothes.

"Carlo!" she cried. "You're not really going in!"

"Oh yes, my dear," he said. "I am. And you?"

"You're drunk," she said. She pulled her woolen shawl around her shoulders. "It would be freezing in that water."

But by now Carlo was down to his shorts. "It'll be warmer in that water than it is out here." He took his shorts off.

Partially hidden in the shadows now, I took a breath. He was beautiful. The muscles of his arms and chest. His thin waist, and long legs. The soft, vulnerable little pouch that hung like a lovely velvet coin-purse between his hips. *Private parts*, my mother had always said. This was the first time I had ever seen a man without his clothes.

In the blue light, I could see the smile on Kristen's face as she looked at him. "You really mean it, don't you?" she said.

Carlo walked away from us and disappeared into the stippled night. In a few moments, we heard the smooth, quiet strokes of his arms as they cut the lake. "Come on!" he called, a bodiless voice beyond us in the dark. "It's wonderful!"

Giuseppe sat with his head against the window in the car, eyes closed, annoyed. Kristen peered in the direction of the lake and began to cry. She turned to me and touched my arm. "Go in with me," she said. "I know you think we're crazy. But please come in?"

I nodded. Kristen and I walked away, leaving Giuseppe in the car.

I had only been swimming in the nude once before in my life, when I was fourteen and had taken my clothes off with three other friends to jump into a vacationing neighbor's swimming pool in a fenced back yard. That pool was nothing like the lake outside Verona, with its blue water the color of veins between my thighs.

Carlo and Kristen and I did not swim together. Carlo could not have said to someone about that night that I was promiscuous, could not have thrown it back, *She went along.* I stayed off by myself, several yards away from them, as they joined up together in the secret dark. I did the breast stroke, imagining the indigo world below, the fish moving in their cobalt depths beneath my belly like little darts. I cut through the water with more pull than I needed. The dark water grasped at my naked breasts, forcing them up to the surface to spread and float.

After awhile, I dog-paddled over to the little dock and clung to the underside of it as I watched Kristen and Carlo in the water further out. They were like two pale swans, gliding together in perfect rhythm in all that blue. I remembered reading somewhere that swans mated for life. I got out of the lake, alone and shivering, and put my clothes back on haphazardly behind some trees.

No one said anything on the long drive back. When at last we reached Giuseppe's apartment, he jumped out of the car and slammed the door.

Carlo watched him make his way along the sidewalk in the dark. "He is a fool," he said between his teeth. "Joins up with a big American company and thinks he's God." His hands tightened around the steering wheel of the Fiat Sport. He drove too fast the rest of the way home.

He dropped us off at the house and drove over to Myra's to pick up the boys. Later, after he'd put them to bed, and Kristen was in the kitchen making tea, Carlo came into the room where I was staying and took my hand. He was very formal as he sat down beside me. He said he was sorry if he had embarrassed me at the lake.

"It's all right," I said. "You didn't embarrass me."

"Then you enjoyed it?"

"Sure I did," I said. "So did Kristen."

He moved closer to me on the couch that was my bed. "No," he said. "Kris did not enjoy it. Kris is sorry she went swimming in the nude. She thinks that you will think badly of her."

I tried to laugh. "Tell her not to be silly. I liked the spontaneity of it. It was fun."

He brushed his long, white hand along my leg. "That is because you are of an age," he said.

I sat there, barely breathing, trying to think how I could tell him, in the proper words for a friend of the family, that his gesture was too familiar. *I'm not so free!*

After a moment he said, "I have to go into Padova tomorrow, to the clinic. If you like, you could ride as far as Padova with me. Then you could take the train on into Venice while I work. Would that appeal to you?"

"That's very kind," I said. "I'd love to go to Venice. But wouldn't Kristen like to come along?"

He shook his head. "Kris has things that she must do tomorrow. Here."

So I thanked him for thinking of me and I said I'd go.

In a few minutes Kristen brought a tea tray and set it down. The three of us made polite, meaningless conversation as we drank the tea. I was grateful when they finally stood and said good night.

It was about one o'clock in the morning when Gianni, the younger of the two boys, started crying the first time. He was crying for his father. Each time he cried out after that, I heard Carlo tell him, "I'm here, Gianni," and then the crying would be over for awhile. The last time it happened, I was just awake enough to look out and see Kristen in her filmy nightgown, and Carlo in his shorts, turn out the lights.

The next morning, Kristen was already dressed and making breakfast when I went into the kitchen. Carlo was in the bathroom, shaving. "He's running a little late," Kristen said in a clipped voice as she turned the eggs. "Gianni kept us up most of the night. He's been having these terrible nightmares."

"I'm sorry," I said. "I hope Carlo doesn't feel he has to go to Padova because of me. If neither of you got any sleep, I would just as soon go to Venice by myself. I'm used to—"

She wouldn't let me finish. Turning to face me as if I must be getting something wrong, she said, "But he has to go to the clinic, don't you see? So you *will* be going to Venice alone. He's only going to be driving you part way."

Carlo entered the kitchen. He was wearing a tweed jacket

with leather patches on the sleeves. He looked very tired. I had not noticed his graying temples before, nor the sagging little pouches beneath his eyes. He ate his eggs without speaking, and then said, "It's getting late, Lisa. We should be on our way." He got up and walked out, leaving me with Kristen to say good-bye.

I took my dishes over to the sink and picked up my coat. "You're sure you won't come along?" I asked her. "Maybe leave the boys with Myra? She wouldn't mind."

But when she looked at me and shook her head, it was as if I still did not understand something that was very obvious to her.

"I have to take care of the boys," she repeated carefully, as though to a slow learner. "Now go on."

Carlo joked with me as he ushered me into the Fiat Sport. "Hasn't anyone ever taught you the polite way to enter a sports car? Here. Get out. You do it—so." He backed into the seat, then swung his legs around, toes pointed daintily and absurdly in his big men's shoes. "You see? It's more lady-like." He was smiling. "Come on. Let's go."

When we got to Padova, he told me that he was going on with me to Venice.

"But you had to go to the clinic," I said. "Please don't let me stop you, please don't think—"

Carlo shrugged. "I can go to the clinic later. After I've shown you Venice. I would like to show Venice now to you." The other cars on the autostrada lumbered by.

We stopped once for coffee at a Motta along the way. When I excused myself to go to the bathroom, Carlo said that, too, if it was often, was just my age. And after I got back from the bathroom he laughed and said my youth must be infectious, because now he had to go, too, and he left me to wait for him for a few minutes at the door.

By the time we arrived in Venice, it was time for lunch. He parked the car outside the railroad station and we had a pizza at a small café before we caught a taxi-vaporetto on the Grand Canal. Everyone treated us as if we were a married couple—an Italian businessman, here for a lovely day in Venice with his younger wife. Gondoliers offered Carlo a price to take the new signora for a ride. We laughed, knowing the truth—a not quite Italian doctor, and not at all his wife.

Although that slow blue lake outside Verona may not really exist, for all I know, I recorded Venice in photographs I took with my Kodak Instamatic on that day. In one, Carlo poses against the Ponte dei Sospiri. Behind him, a weighted vaporetto passes by. Two lovers in a gondola interrupt the edge of the frame, to look up at us from beneath the bridge. Carlo, seated on the railing with one knee up, bestows a smile.

Only once, on a tour through a medieval dungeon, did he touch me, and that was to keep me from falling through an old escape. "Ah, sparks!" he said as he caught me in his arms. Later, we threw peanuts to the pigeons on San Marco Square.

It was almost dusk before we arrived back at the car. "Now for a stop at the clinic in Padova," Carlo said. "It will be short."

He opened the door for me and I slid in properly, the way he had taught me, and he went over to his side of the car and folded in. "Well," he said. "That's that."

We drove to Padova in silence. Just beyond the square in the middle of the city, he pulled up at a trattoria. A small sign announced a pensione two floors above. "You can wait here and have a coffee while I'm at the clinic, if you like," he said.

I moved to get out of the car.

"Wait." Carlo leaned back on the seat, fingering the leather-wrapped racing wheel. "There's no need to tell Kris about our day."

"But why? We didn't do anything wrong."

He laughed and shook his head, wearing the same, disbelieving expression that Kristen had given me that morning. As if I were not quite intelligent, and didn't get the point. "But don't you see?" he said. "We *could* have done something wrong. And that, even without the fact, will make her mad. It's hardly worth the trouble, is it?"

His arm moved behind me, across the seat. "Let's imagine that we had a flat tire on the way home," he said. "We would

have to stop at a hotel. That could happen. It happens to nice
people all the time. We would telephone Kris to tell her. Nothing would have been intended. But it might occur."

"That's hypothetical," I said, pulling away from him.
"Nothing like that did happen."

"But it could," he said. "And Kris would never believe we
have done nothing. You heard her going on about my patients
the other night."

I pressed my back against the door. "But to be honest?" I
said. "To tell her exactly? That you changed your mind at the
last minute and came along?"

He considered me a moment, genuinely puzzled. "Tell me
something," he said. "No. On second thought, you don't have to
tell me. But surely, someone of your generation, and you say that
you are traveling around on your own like this, meeting people,
sleeping in hostels, surely, you have had experience with men?"

I felt as cold as I had upon stepping from that lake the night
before. "I wouldn't discuss that with you," I said. "Even if I *had*
done something, the experience would have been between me
and the other person, and it would not be right if I—"

He nodded. "Okay, okay. I said you didn't have to tell me.
But a girl like you. And all this traveling. Surely you can see
how these things happen. Even when they are not planned
sometimes they—"

"I'll wait for you here," I said, fumbling with the handle of
the door. "I'll go have a cup of coffee like you said."

Carlo inclined his head in a kind of bow. "Fine," he said.
Then his face went tight. "But I'm going to tell you something,
signorina. Someday some man is going to teach you not to flirt."

He reached across my lap to open the door and let me out.
"And it won't be as friendly as this, either," he said. "Someday,
some man is going to drop you where you are."

I watched from the sidewalk as the Fiat Sport sped off. At
the intersection, it almost hit a Giulia from behind. I wasn't even
sure Carlo would come back for me. *Teach you a lesson, Lisa.
Some man is going to drop you where you are. Lisa stayed in Padova,*

Kristen. Some stranger she met in Venice on the vaporetto took her home. That was how she was, you know. The daughter of your mother's pen-pal! You and your dear mother got her wrong.

Or else, and this would be worse, he would know the truth. I imagined the conversation over the dinner table, the two of them sitting in that white-tiled kitchen, the boys in bed, and Lisa, some two months later, somewhere, gone. Carlo was saying, *But there was something strange about her, darling. I am sure that she had never had experience with men.*

I went into the trattoria and ordered a double *macchiata* at the espresso bar and sat down to wait.

Three hours passed before the Fiat Sport returned, its yellow parking lights dull in the growing fog. I paid for the four cups of coffee I'd drunk and came out of the trattoria. Even though I'd just gone to the toilet, I knew I would have to ask Carlo to stop at a bathroom again on the long drive home. He opened the car door and I slid in and we started back. He was very cheerful as he drove along the autostrada. He said his visit to the clinic in Padova had been well-timed. Even though they hadn't known for certain he was coming, he said, they were glad he did.

I had never traveled that fast before in any car. Carlo pointed out the summer castle of the Capulets atop a hill outside Verona as we sped by. Even obscured by the fog and the distance, this site looked more like the one I had expected to see when I had visited Juliet's balcony with Kristen—a dark, solitary ruin, tall and insurmountable and proud. Here was a place that was worthy of any tragic, immortal love story that could be told.

But within seconds, the Capulets' palace had disappeared. "Look out your window, Lisa," Carlo said. "The speed at which we are moving is the one that airplanes must reach upon the ground before taking off."

THE TEXAS RANGER

This happened at the University of Oregon in '65, the year before Shelley transferred to Berkeley, because, as she told her father, the University of Oregon was behind the times.

The real reason Shelley transferred to Berkeley, of course, was that Giorgio was going to Padova for his junior year, and if he wasn't going to be in Oregon, Shelley couldn't see any reason to hang around.

For the most part, Shelley has stopped telling people about anything that might have happened to her in 1965, let alone something that happened between her and her father when she was a child. She knows that it is a sign of age, this desire to tell the same story over and over, maybe changing the details a little, yet each time insisting on place-names and people and on dates and times. Nevertheless, she does remember, vividly, a scene from her childhood. She is sitting with her father on the big brown and yellow flowered sofa that is From Before the War. Her father is telling her one of his many cowboy stories, which are better than any of the ones on television, because the heroes in Shelley's father's stories do not wear masks. She can see these heroes, what they look like and what they're doing, for herself. What's more, Shelley is reasonably sure that these stories are the truth. Her father's father really was a Law Man Back in the Old Days. And before that, his father really was a Texas Ranger.

"History is a connection of moments," her father is saying.

"You and I exist in the latest in a long series of moments. Why, soon, even the moment in which I am speaking will be gone."

Shelley's mother walks into the living room, and interrupts. "Don't overdo it," she warns Shelley's father. "You get so maudlin you depress the child."

Today's story is about the Texas Ranger. He's been out on assignment for the government for a long, long time, catching shanghai-ers on the wharf in San Francisco. When he comes home to his ranch in Texas, he finds that his wife has given him up for dead to marry another man. His wife was three months pregnant when he left her, and now his son is already four years old. The Texas Ranger can see that his wife did what she had to do in order to go on living, but his heart will ache forever with this loss. He rides out to the ranch, just to see her one more time, and to meet his son.

When his wife comes to the door, her mouth falls open in a small O of surprise and pain that is a little like the O that stayed for a week and a half on Shelley's mother's mouth when the baby brother that Shelley was supposed to be getting changed his mind.

The Texas Ranger tells his wife, "I don't want no trouble, Lottie. I just come to say good-bye to you, and to see the boy. Then I'll be on my way, real easy, no trouble. I won't make no trouble for you, Lottie, none at all."

The Texas Ranger's wife, who is now also this other man's wife, wipes her hands on her big white apron that covers her long calico dress, and she looks through the door at a spot way off in the distance above the Ranger's head. The clouds haven't gathered in the sky for weeks. If there is no rain soon, the crops will go dry in the southern forty, and the cows will die.

"They told me you was dead, Hal," she says. "That's why I gone and married. For the child."

The Texas Ranger says back to her, in what seems to Shelley to be a display of infinite kindness, "I understand. And I bear you no ill-will for that, Lottie. Just let me meet your husband, and see the boy, and then I'll ride."

Meanwhile, Lottie's new husband, having heard that the

Ranger was coming, has gone out to the barn behind the house to hide. Lottie tells the Texas Ranger she'll go and speak with him and see if he'll meet with the Ranger. Then she'll be back.

While the Ranger's wife goes out to the new husband, Shelley stays with the best man she will ever know in her entire life. What does the Texas Ranger look at while he's standing there, waiting for Lottie to come back to him, his big, blue-veined hands resting on his twin six-shooters, his twin six-shooters slung low and strapped around cream-colored pants that are snug as a ballerina's tights around his thighs?

The Texas Ranger is also wearing brown leather boots with mustard-colored scrolls, like the ones Shelley's father bought her when he took her and her mother on a trip to Oklahoma, or maybe it was Texas, but really far. Perspiration presses through the Ranger's beige, pearl-buttoned Western shirt. He reaches up to push back a ten-gallon Stetson. He has a head of hair like Shelley's father's, thick and black. The Texas Ranger is thinking. . . *What is he thinking?* That he still loves this woman. That he would like to kill that other man and have her back. But he is too good to harm anyone who doesn't deserve it, and he would never leave such dishonor and sorrow on his son.

The Ranger puts his hand up to his eyes, forming a shield from the hot white light of the Texas sun. He walks over to the edge of the big front porch to survey the land. Shelley knows that nowadays, men wear big black glasses to protect their eyes. In the summer, when she sits on her father's lap in the backyard and looks up at his face against the sky, she likes to think of herself there inside his glasses, and that she's cool inside.

The Texas Ranger hears a noise behind him and turns around.

"You my daddy?" The boy is a blonde, like Shelley. *So how is my platinum-haired beauty*, her father always says to her when he comes home. The Texas Ranger's son has cornflower-blue eyes that turn up a bit at the corners, again like hers, and like her father's, also. And probably like her father's father's and his father's, also, for all she knows.

"Yes, son, I am."

"They told me you was dead."

"I know."

"But you ain't."

"No, son, I'm not dead. I am your father and I am very much alive."

Shelley wants the boy to run into the Texas Ranger's arms and beg him to stay with him forever. But her father explains that the boy has never seen this man, and that by now he thinks of himself as the son of the man who is hiding in the barn. Shelley hurts for the Texas Ranger. She reaches for her father's arm and pulls it around her shoulders, and she cries.

After awhile, Lottie comes around the house from the barn, shielding her eyes with her hand, just as the Ranger did.

"My husband says you can stay, Hal," she says to the Ranger. She stops just short of his shadow when she sees her son. "He says you can visit with the boy and welcome." Lottie must already know in her heart that the coward out in the barn won't measure up.

And Shelley thinks, what Lottie really wants is to go to the Texas Ranger and kiss him. But she knows she's got this other husband, so she better not.

"I want you to know I wish you well, Lottie," the Texas Ranger tells her.

"I understand that, Hal," she says. And she tells him that her husband doesn't really have but one request.

"Anything you say, Lottie."

She asks the Texas Ranger will he take his guns off. She asks him will he hang them up on the wall in her front parlor, on the pinewood peg. "It's the only way my husband will allow you to stay here," she says.

The Texas Ranger bows his head. Then he looks back at Lottie. Shelley knows every detail of that expression on the Ranger's face. It is her father's expression, as when he is answering an important question, his head cocked sideways, his chin lowered, his eyes a little more narrow than usual as he glances up.

There is a long pause before the Texas Ranger speaks, and when he does, it is with softness, as to a child. "You understand I'll be defenseless without my guns, don't you, Lottie?"

Shelley has always imagined the Texas Ranger in the places where he stays when he's on assignments, the frontier hotels. There is always a kerosene lamp beside his bed in these hotels. He hooks his guns over the bedpost, so he can get the guns real quick if he has to, if someone draws.

Lottie raises her arms as if she is about to make a protest, but then she lets them drop. "I know what he's asking you," she says. "But now I'm asking you, too, Hal. Leave the guns with us while you're here in town."

"All right, Lottie," he says in resignation. Shelley knows that Lottie is taking the Ranger's life in her helpless hands.

Shelley's father isn't big on details about Lottie's new husband, but Shelley is almost sure that she can see him if she tries. He is a small man compared to the Texas Ranger, and, in contrast to the Ranger's dark good looks, this man is drab. His hair is the color of damp straw, his eyes an indefinite beige. Something about him isn't all that manly, just isn't right.

The Texas Ranger agrees to stay in a room at the back of the kitchen and to hang up his guns in the parlor for just as long as he's a guest in his old house. But one afternoon, when the Texas Ranger goes into town without his guns, a cattle rustler sees him and tells him he is going to get him for the time the Texas Ranger sent him up.

"If you wait till I get my gun," the Ranger says to the cattle rustler in a quiet voice that is Shelley's father's exactly, "then I'll give you my word you will have a fair fight. You can even have the first draw. At least let me die like a man."

But the cattle rustler is grinning. He knows he wouldn't have a chance against those guns. "Your word ain't good enough for me, Ranger," he says. "So I'm going to drop you in your tracks, right where you are."

The Texas Ranger turns around and starts walking away from the man. Shelley can't believe how unafraid he is, how awfully calm. "Then you're going to have to shoot me in the back, Mister," the Ranger says.

The cattle rustler shoots the Texas Ranger in the back and rides away. The Texas Ranger crawls back on his hands and knees to the ranch, to Lottie. The Texas Ranger dies out there on the ranch in Lottie's arms.

* * * * *

Shelley knows young professionals in her neighborhood who hadn't even been born yet in 1965. If she told these neighbors that the reason they had open campus when they were in high school, and could come and go as they pleased, and could take their second-hand cars to the McDonald's drive-through for their lunch, was that she and other people of her generation joined the Free Speech Movement at Berkeley during the Sixties, they would probably look at her with an expression of disbelief. Like, *What is this woman saying?* And she thinks, *Like Before the War for me.* And she thinks, *Wow.*

She was eighteen when she left home for the University of Oregon. It seems to her that Vietnam hadn't really got going yet, or maybe it was just because she was at the University of Oregon, which was behind the times. Sororities were still big in Oregon. And people from California. She was from California, but her hair had gradually darkened since childhood, and she never felt like lying in the sun. So when she met George Simonds in Accelerated Italian, he assumed she came from some small town in Oregon as he did, and it was a while before he asked.

Shelley hadn't rushed the sororities that fall—not because she didn't believe in them, but because she didn't even know they existed. Thus, by sheer luck, when she met *Giorgio*, as the Italian professor fondly called him, she was classified as an Independent. And in saying to Giorgio, "I am an Independent," she couldn't have made a better impression if she'd tried.

After Shelley met Giorgio, the only people who interested her were that small percentage of long-haired, sandal-clad students who had been admitted to the then-experimental Honors College and who spent their time drinking coffee and studying in the damp, neon-lighted basement of Stratton Hall. Walking in and out of the Honors College lounge on Giorgio's arm, Shelley felt she was learning what was important. Through Giorgio, she heard about the mysteries of philosophy, the films of Truffaut and Fellini, the history of architecture, and the colors of Matisse and Picasso. She bowed humbly to what he could do for her, this deprived daughter of Middle Class America, too astonished at the world he offered even to feign indifference. It was plain she had lacked exposure to all things cultural. Having been brought up as her father's only child, she was a walking encyclopedia of car parts and Cowboy legends, of Sunday morning comics and of television Westerns with names like *The Fastest Draw.*

Her father had come to adulthood during the Depression, and so he had only been able to attend an airplane mechanics' trade school. But he had done well in the aviation company for which he worked, and had progressed to the position of supervisor, because he was one of the few good men in the business who managed to be already in the right place when all the other men came home from World War II.

So Shelley's going to college had never been a question of her desires, it had been the Law. "You are going to be something," her father told her. "You can be anything you want to be. A doctor. Maybe a lawyer. Even a Senator, Shelley. You're plenty smart. Just don't let anyone tell you otherwise."

Giorgio gave Shelley her first taste of classical music. "Not even Beethoven's Symphonies?" he asked her in surprise. She shook her head. Well, actually, she said to him, she thought she did know Beethoven's Fifth Symphony. Wasn't that the one they used at the end of the *Huntley-Brinkley Report?*

Giorgio gave her assignments. She put on ear-phones and listened to Mozart and Brahms and Beethoven in the School of Music for hours and hours. For her birthday, he bought her Leonard Bernstein's recording of the Seventh Symphony with the New York Philharmonic, telling her, "Now you will feel something, Shelley. Anyone can respond to Leonard Bernstein. Leonard Bernstein is so universal as to be almost, in a way, downright bourgeois."

It became one of Giorgio's favorite topics of discussion with others, how much Shelley had learned since she'd met him, how far she'd come. They would be sitting with his friends from the Honors College in the New World Coffee House and he would repeat how much she was learning, even if they only considered the music. Squeezing her hand under the table and smiling, he would tell his friends: "When she said that? About the *Huntley-Brinkley Report*? I thought I'd die!"

Giorgio told Shelley he would have preferred to go to Reed College or Lewis and Clark or Stanford if his family had had the funds. As it was, he'd had to settle for the Honors College at the University of Oregon. But he planned to get a scholarship for his graduate work, he said, and he would make sure he got into Berkeley for the Ph.D.

"I can't figure out why you're from California and you didn't even apply to Berkeley," he told her. "It would have been so easy for you, so cheap! You didn't need the grades and you wouldn't have had to pay out-of-state tuition. I can't believe you came up to the University of Oregon, Shelley. It's so flat and dull!"

They were having coffee in the New World after finishing an Italian midterm. Giorgio's major was art history, and he was taking Italian so that he could spend his junior year abroad. He propped his tousled, sandy head on one pale arm, and took a draw on his cigarette. "So why did you come up here, Shelley?"

She spread her hands, *God help me*, and made a frown. The truth was, she had come to Oregon the way she was not in a sorority—not because she had made a conscious choice for herself, but because she had been completely ignorant that she had a choice. Her father had insisted she go to college, but he had not cared which one, so long as she went far enough away from home to be independent. She should go somewhere out of state, he said, so that she could learn what it meant to be alone. *Expand your horizons,* he told her.

And so she was! "I needed to get away from my father," she said to Giorgio, summing up. She immediately regretted what had come out.

But Giorgio was interested. "Oh?" he said, leaning back. A slight smile tickled the blond hairs at the corners of his full, pink mouth. His face was still smooth, the color of cream except for two bright round red spots high on his cheeks.

"It fascinates me to think that you have a father," he said, his eyes assessing her as if she might have been a recently unearthed painting, a purported masterpiece, the whole value of which depends upon its authenticity. "It's as if you're just now discovering who you are. The more I watch your personality unfold, Shelley, the more it becomes impossible for me to imagine your having parents. What's your father like?"

Shelley shrugged. "Oh, you know," she said, and felt the guilt again, as if she were about to make a fatal omission. But fatal to what, she wondered? "He's been with this company that manufactures airplanes for years and years. Days, he works as a supervisor on an assembly line. Nights, he either watches cowboys and detectives on television while my mother sits there sewing or something, or else he goes out to the garage and works on cars."

She paused, still feeling that what she was saying was self-destructive, still not knowing why. "He rebuilds car engines," she said. "Only *American* ones. I mean, my father wouldn't be caught dead working on one of *yer goddamn bring us to our knees before they've finished with us Shelley Commie cars.*"

Giorgio laughed out loud. He told Shelley she was very amusing and that her sense of humor was one of the reasons he liked being with her so much.

Shelley blushed. She did not tell Giorgio that when she left for Oregon, her father said he was going to put a used VW together for her so that she could come home whenever she wanted to, because he and her mother would miss her now that she was in college, and they hoped she would be able to come home every now and then if she had a car. And later, he said, she could sell the damn thing if she wanted to, and she'd probably get three times what he'd put into it, not counting his labor of course, he said, but just the parts.

Giorgio took a long sip of his cappuccino. The steamed milk made the coffee a rich, patterned beige, the color of old pearls. And the color of his teeth, too, for that matter, because he smoked a lot. "Doesn't your father have any other hobbies?" he asked.

Oh Poncho! Oh Cisco! That's the way it was in them ole wagons, going West. Who was that masked man anyway? You know, Mr. Dillon, it just don't seem right, such a young lady over there working at Miss Kitty's, and that's a fact.

"Well, not really hobbies," Shelley said.

Giorgio waited.

"My father has this gift for telling stories," Shelley said. "You know. About the West and stuff."

Giorgio nodded. "What kind of stuff?"

She found she was getting excited. "Some of them are better than the ones on television. You know. Better than shows like *Have Gun, Will Travel* or *Gunsmoke*. My father's stories are about real Texas Rangers and outlaws. Stuff like that."

Giorgio leaned closer, his white face centered on his hand like a marble bust, *Head of a Noble Roman*, like those Shelley had seen in his art history book. "How fascinating," he said. "Good versus evil. Right always wins in the end. You have been brought up on the classic American fairy tale, Shelley." He touched her foot under the table with the toe of one of his Hushpuppies. "So that's where you get your ethics! You. The virgin of almost twenty, who will not lie down."

You all right, Miss Kitty? Did he hurt you? No, Matt, he didn't hurt me. But he would have, if you hadn't have come along right when you did.

Shelley looked down at her coffee and hoped to God that Giorgio couldn't see her face. He was bringing *that* up again. "There was one about my great-grandfather," she said, still feeling the tender pressure of Giorgio's foot. "My father's grandfather was a Texas Ranger."

You gotta remember the horses now, Biff, Slim, Shorty, Buck. Yonder's the only place this river's narrow. Iffen we don't ford this river now, we'll never cross.

"And because he was gone too long once on an assignment," Shelley said, "his wife thought he had been killed, and so she went ahead and married someone else. And when the Texas Ranger came back, he was only allowed to visit her and their son. And while he was staying there at his old ranch, with his wife and son, and his wife's new husband, an outlaw shot him. He crawled back to the ranch and died in Great-Grandma's arms."

Giorgio was wearing a big green sweater with holes in it. He had pushed the sleeves of the sweater up past his pale, hairless forearms. Shelley coveted that sweater. She wished he would give her a big green holey sweater just like that.

"I would love to meet your father," Giorgio said. He put his hand over hers and then withdrew it to light a cigarette. She thought with a thrill of desire and confusion, *O what he knows!*

"I think he'd like to meet you, too," she said. She brushed a soiled mass of thick, dark hair out of her eyes. Lately, her hair always felt dirty, and the sheer weight of it kept falling in her eyes. She was trying to let it grow so she could wear it long and parted down the middle the way Giorgio liked. But her hair wasn't cooperating. No matter how many times she brushed it to make it lie smooth along her back, she still didn't look at all like Joan Baez.

"I forgot to tell you that my father sings cowboy songs," she said. Then she added, "But remember, he doesn't know a thing about Bach or Brahms."

Giorgio threw his head back and laughed, revealing his small, pointed, tobacco-stained tongue. Later, he would kiss her under the eaves of the art building and she would taste the tobacco of his imported European cigarettes inside her mouth. He would touch her breasts that hid so sheepishly under her thick black sweater, and he would remind her that they could not go on forever like this, heedless of the presence of his desires. And then, dropping the issue of sex for the time being, he would compare Proust to Dante there under the eaves of the art building, and he would tell her about other major writers of the Western world they were reading and discussing in his Great Books class. They would sit there on a bench under the eaves for hours, safely out of reach of the silver rain.

Giorgio would say to her, "I can't believe you, Shelley—how much you've learned in the last six months. How far you've come."

* * * * *

In March, her father had to take a business trip. Something to do with comparing the quality of the competitor company's subcontractors to their own. He called to tell Shelley he was going to pass through Eugene on his way up north.

He stayed in a motel across the highway from her dorm. The motel, two stories of L-shaped orange cement buildings on a black asphalt parking lot, catered to the university clientele. A big green and yellow neon shield promised, *Special rates for parents and alums!* Shelley walked over from campus after her last class for the day. As she approached the motel, she saw her father, leaning over the steel railing outside his room. And though she wanted badly to have him put his arms around her, she did not run.

He pulled his tall frame up from the railing, raised a big hand in greeting, then walked slowly down the stairs to the place where she had stopped below. They stood there, her with her back to, and him facing, the academic world from which she'd come.

"Is your motel all right?" she asked. It looked garish and uncomfortable. It hit her that her father had been staying in places like this, whenever he went away on business, all her life.

He shrugged, letting his long smile tilt up one side of his thin-lipped mouth. "It's okay as far as these kinds of places go. You like your school?"

"Some classes are better than others," she said. She was aching to get on with the real reason he was there. "I like Italian the best, of course," she said. "The kids in the class are really neat." She tried to laugh. "Especially one."

"You mean your young man," her father said. "This boy named George."

The way her father said the name, *George* sounded suspiciously antique and out of touch, like *Harold*, or like *Rupert* perhaps, or worse yet, *Ralph*.

"Giorgio," she said, correcting her father. But the Italian name sounded phony as she spoke. "I mean, all of us in Italian class have changed our names. You know. To Italian ones."

Her father nodded. His eyes narrowed and he looked at her from one side with that look she knew so well. "And what is this *Giorgio* studying to be?"

Shelley cleared her throat. "I told you, Daddy. He's in art history."

"*Art* history," her father said. He was trying it out like a statement on his tongue. "Well," he said after a moment. "I suppose I'm a bit of a history buff myself."

Just over these hills, Biff. It won't be long, Old Timer. Here, take a sip of this here water. Easy now.

"It's not the same kind of history, Daddy," Shelley said. Her throat was dry. "George, that is, *Giorgio*, my friend, is studying the work of Renaissance artists such as Botticelli and Michelangelo and Da Vinci. Italian artists, Daddy. He's going to Italy to study them next fall."

"Really," her father said. She had the impression he had stepped back to look at her, and was not convinced. "Is your friend an artist, then, himself?"

"No," she said. "Giorgio studies other people's art. He's an art historian. He studies art to see what makes it great. You know—why a particular era produces a particular form of art. That sort of thing."

She felt foolish, caught in the position of informing her father of something he didn't know. But she went on anyway. "Take those pictures down in our rec room, for instance," she said. "The ones with the covered wagons that you like? Well, George would be able to tell you, if he were an American art historian, why that particular genre succeeded in a certain period of time."

Her father smiled and nodded, as though he were pleased to think he had begun to understand. "So George isn't American," he said. "He's an Italian then?"

"No!" she cried, and then frowned at her own exasperation. She started over. "His particular field is European art history, Daddy. Italian art history. In particular. To be exact."

"To be exact," her father echoed.

She paused, thought, *What the hell*, then hurried on. "Giorgio says that America is only just beginning to have any kind of art history of its own."

Her father stared over her head at the evergreen trees she knew were behind her on the campus across the road. "Can we ask this young man of yours to have a steak with us tonight?"

Shelley took his elbow, grateful to be back on common ground. "I could use a steak," she said. "And a nice baked potato with sour cream and butter and a great big salad, with whatever their house dressing is there on the side. We can give Giorgio a call from the restaurant."

* * * * *

That was the first time Shelley's father asked her if she would like a drink. They were waiting for George to come over from campus, and when he asked her, it was as if he'd been ordering cocktails for the both of them all her life. She sipped at her gin and tonic when it came and chatted with her father, murmuring, laughing, nodding her head in agreement and chuckling over the remembrance of good past times.

Almost like old lovers, she thought. She wondered if she was going to tell her father she would soon be sleeping with Giorgio.

But before she knew there had been a turn in the conversation, he brought it up. "This young man of yours," he said, looking down at the green cellophane pom-pom on the cocktail pick he was swirling in his glass. "Does he know how to take care of a virgin?"

A buzzing noise like some kind of insect filled her ears. *It's not what you think, Buck. I am not what I appear to be, you've got me wrong.*

"Nothing has happened yet between George and me, Daddy," she said.

Her father managed to glance up at her without moving anything but his eyes. "But something will?"

The buzz cleared. She shrugged. "Yes. It will."

"Well then." He signaled the waitress. "That means you and I should have another round."

* * * * *

When George arrived at the restaurant, he was wearing the big green sweater with the holes. Shelley had envisioned him in that sweater someday, a man relaxing in his leather armchair before a crackling hearth, an Irish Setter lying at his feet. An original Poussin landscape would grace the stairs. She would never nag her refined and intelligent husband about wearing that old sweater. She would never sound like one of those shrill housewives in the commercials that interrupted *Saturday Night at the Movies* on NBC. She would never cry her husband's name disdainfully, *Gee-yorge!*

"So you're Shelley's friend," her father said. He rose to take in his own powerful, brown right hand George's paler one. "Shelley tells me you're going to go on after graduation with further studies, is that right?"

George grasped Shelley's fingers on top of the table when he sat down. "Well, as I've told your daughter, sir," he said, "the whole point seems to me to be the Ph.D. Education separates the men from the boys these days." He hesitated, probably remembering that Shelley had told him about her father's three-year trade school certificate that didn't quite qualify as a degree. "In art history, anyway," he added.

All during dinner, George spoke to Shelley's father as if they were already married. He told her father, "Shelley is a remarkable person, Mr. Kruper. I should know. I've watched her, just in the time since I've met her, and I have seen for myself how much she's grown."

After awhile her father said he should be getting back to his motel, because he had to get up pretty early. He shook hands with George, and he told Shelley that he would see her in the morning if she wanted to have breakfast with him at the pancake house right there by his motel. He wished George the best of luck with his studies. He paid for the meal with his American Express card and then handed George a twenty-dollar bill. "Here," he said. "I'd like you to take Shelley downtown tonight to see a show."

Outside the restaurant, Shelley turned to watch her father go. As she and George headed downtown under a light drizzle, George lit a cigarette and handed it to her, then lit another for himself. Not having acquired much of a taste for cigarettes quite yet, Shelley drew on the Pall Mall carefully. Later, she would remember that cigarette as the first one she had ever smoked to the end, and the start of a pack-a-day habit she would keep for years.

George put his arm around her shoulders. "I like your father."

"He liked you, too," she lied. "I could tell."

George turned to her. "You really think so?"

"Of course he did," she said. "What do you mean? You think I'm wrong?"

George drew the hand that was holding his cigarette across his nose. "I don't know. It's just that your father is so, you know, *masculine*. So big. I see him out hunting deer or something. Bringing venison home to the womenfolk, you know? The classic husband and father. The great provider."

Shelley stopped short on the sidewalk. "Really? You see my father as a hunter, George? That's really strange. My father might like to watch westerns on TV, but he's so opposed to violence in real life that he won't even own a gun. And as for bringing venison home to the womenfolk? The classic head of the household thing? You've got him wrong there, too, I'd have to say. I mean, he's always paid for everything and all, always had a job, but he would never look at it like that. He's always said I could be anything I wanted to be. I don't think it's ever really occurred to my father that he was raising me any different than he would a man."

George laughed and started her walking again with a little hint of pressure from his thumb. "I don't mean any of this in a bad way," he said. "Maybe it's just hard for me to explain what it was I saw. I liked him. He reminds me a little of Jason Robards. Did you ever see Jason Robards in *A Thousand Clowns?*"

As it turned out, the only movie with another showing by the time they reached town was *The Sound of Music*. George said he didn't really feel like seeing a religious film. He wanted to turn back towards campus, maybe stop at a friend's apartment. He had a key to the apartment. And the best part, he said with a grin, was that the friend had already told him he would not be home.

But Shelley said she'd promised her father they'd go to a movie and she wanted to be able to tell him about it at breakfast. George groaned and stuck his hands in his pockets, but he went along. They sat through an uncut version of *The Sound of Music*, complete with scenes of young novitiates watching Maria's marriage ceremony from behind the pillars of the enormous church, with the result that there was no time after the movie to discuss the friend's empty apartment, and so they avoided, once again, the consummation that George said they had already been putting off unnecessarily for far too long.

* * * * *

The next morning Shelley slept through her alarm clock, and by the time she had jumped into jeans and a workshirt, and pulled her hair back into a greasy ponytail, and run across the highway to the pancake house to have breakfast with her father, he had already been sitting in the booth waiting for her for half an hour.

She smiled as she slid in across from him. "Well," she said, still breathless from her run. "What did you think?"

He poured her a cup of coffee and passed her the artificial

cream. "That stuff can't be good for anybody," he said. He flagged down the waitress. "Say, would you mind bringing us over a little *real* milk, please?"

He watched his hand stirring his own black coffee. "Actually," he said, "since you've asked me, Shelley. I think that boy is the poorest excuse for a man I ever saw."

Shelley fell back against the vinyl seat. The breakfast smells of the restaurant—pancakes and syrup and bacon and sausage and eggs over easy and toast and hash browns, even the little square tins of Smucker's grape jelly stacked up on the inside of the table on a carousel—all seemed to press in upon her until, for one awful moment, she wondered if she might be sick. She remained like that, propped against the tufted red vinyl, her arms limp, her mouth taking some old shape she tried to remember, but couldn't, some sort of expression she almost remembered, a little O.

Then she told him. "For your information, Daddy," she said, "I am going to marry that poor excuse."

Her father gave her a little wince, as if he didn't quite believe she was serious. She could swear he would say in a moment, *You must be kidding, Shelley.*

"But you liked him!" she insisted. "I could *tell* you did."

Her father was wearing a string tie with a turquoise Indian clip. He'd bought the tie years ago, on that trip they'd all taken together, at the same time he'd bought her the big brown boots with the mustard scrolls. His eyes narrowed and he shook his head. "That boy thinks he owns you. All that crap about art and music and paintings." He rolled his eyes toward the ceiling, clasping his folded hands against his chest in an unconscious *adorata.* "He'll chop away at your roots, Shelley. And if you let him, he's going to destroy all the basic, decent things you stand for. You won't be fit to sweep the floor with, by the time he's done."

Shelley felt herself begin to shake. "Basic things like what?" she said. "Like cowboy music? Like television? What basic things, Daddy? Tell me. What?"

Her father took a long sip from the coffee he had just poured from the thermal container on the table. The coffee was too hot, but Shelley knew he wasn't going to admit he'd burned his tongue. "A man's family," her father said, "is the only monument he leaves behind when he leaves the earth."

And that is when her ugliness came out. She told her father he was a bigot with a small, lower-middle-class mind. She said she was glad she was getting away from him. He only knew about car engines and cowboys and airplanes and about nothing else. At least George would be doing something worthwhile for the world when he got a job!

She slammed her fist on the table as she got up to leave. "For your information, Daddy," she shouted so loudly that everyone in the restaurant turned to stare, "I am going to sleep with Giorgio Simonds tomorrow night!"

* * * * *

Shelley did sleep with George, just as she'd said. She expected the earth to move beneath her, the way Hemingway had described it in a passage George read to her from *The Sun Also Rises* before they went to bed. But she was surprised to find that, unlike the fictional heroes, George did not draw blood. After she lost her virginity, she lay there, a little repulsed by the smell, wondering if the earth might move a little more the second time. George rolled over on one arm and drew her to his hairless chest, then lit cigarettes for them both. He said, more proudly than ever, "I can't believe it, Shelley, how far you've come."

The next fall, George went to Padova for his year abroad. Shelley transferred to Berkeley. She made up with her father, and since her parents' house was just down the Peninsula and she wasn't dating anyone because of the understanding she had with George, she went home almost every weekend, to watch cowboy shows with her father on Saturday nights. George wrote faithfully from Padova twice a week, describing museums and churches and restaurants and villas and little gardens—*grottos* as he called them—with leafy plants. He was also able to spend a lot of time, he said, thinking about their future together. He would marry her when they graduated, and then if she would help him to obtain his doctorate, he would see to it that she had the opportunity to get hers later on. He enclosed a long reading list. "I want to be able to talk to you about all of this," he wrote, "when I get home."

After awhile, Shelley became so involved in the protests on campus that she didn't have time to go home on weekends. She wrote George in Padova about the events at Berkeley, telling him how glad she was she'd moved to Cal. "I see people from Oregon on Sproul Plaza all the time who have transferred here," she wrote. "The other day I even saw a girl who lived on my floor there in the dorm. Her name was Jenny Alice—a strange girl, really, who kept to herself. But one time I delivered a letter to her that had come there to our dorm, and I remember reading her name on the envelope and thinking it was the kind of name girls have if they're from the South."

George wrote back that in Italy things were beautiful, and that they were how they had always been and ever would be, and that he knew what he was going to do with his life now, and there was nothing else.

They married the day after she graduated from Berkeley. Shelley got a secretarial job in the Political Science Department and George was accepted into the Ph.D. program in art history, just as he'd planned. He landed a good job afterwards with the De Cordova Museum. But he said there wasn't enough money now, or time either for that matter, for Shelley to go back to school, what with the children coming bing, bing one right after the other after he got his doctorate. And to be honest, he said, what would be the point?

"Be sensible, Shelley," he said, stretching out in front of the fireplace next to his Irish Setter, and wearing the holey green sweater, just as she had imagined him years before. "What would a woman with two small children do with a degree in art?"

When her father died, Shelley wished she'd taken a course or two in aeronautical engineering, just so she could have talked to him about a subject that interested him. As it turned out, she arrived at the hospital too late even to say good-bye.

"It's all right, dear," her mother told her. "Your father loved you, and he didn't suffer." But he was gone.

Lately, Shelley thinks a lot about that story about the Texas Ranger. The cattle rustler was caught, of course. The local people strung him up outside the town without a trial. But Shelley wishes none of it had happened in the first place. If only the Ranger's wife had waited until he returned. If only she'd seen that she didn't have to marry that other guy.

And the cattle rustler must have known all along he would be punished for killing the Texas Ranger. So why did he have to shoot him, and leave him to crawl home to die, a hero, in Lottie's arms?

Then Shelley thinks about Lottie's new husband. The one who leaves her alone in the house to face the Texas Ranger, while he goes out to hide himself in the second story of their barn. What will become of that husband? Whenever Shelley thinks of them, Lottie's new husband and the cattle rustler don't really seem as if they're two different men—the one pure evil, the other an innocent victim of circumstance. They have both become killers. They melt in one. Lottie's new husband is becoming more and more possessive of her all the time. He knows now that he owns her, with the Ranger gone. He can keep saying these little things, and she probably won't stop him, and then, after awhile, it won't really matter to her. He can keep picking at her, tearing her apart, saying how disappointed he is in her, and finally she won't hear him anymore.

He can tell her that if she would just listen to him, if she would be humble enough to listen and to follow his advice, if she would accept his plans for her, and be willing to listen, there would be no telling how much she might accomplish, how far she'd go.

KINDNESSES

I know now it wasn't just the proverbial affair with the married man in Boston that set it off. I'd had a series of semi-breakdowns before this one, and by now my family and I had come to know the symptoms very well. From the moment Nigel told me that he loved me in the stairwell of my apartment building on The Fenway, till the moment his wife, who had left him to go back to South Africa, discovered she was pregnant with their second child, I kept telling myself, *Lisa, you know this is ridiculous. You know better than to fall in love with a married man, let alone a married man named Nigel. Even if he weren't married, Lisa, you can hear the entire goddamn British empire in his voice.*

And I kept telling myself, *This really isn't enough by itself to do it, you know, Lisa. You know that, don't you, Lisa. If you will just stay calm.*

But in the end, I had to leave my job in Boston anyway. I spent two months with my parents outside Chicago. Then I flew out to California to stay with my sister Elodie for a little while.

When Elodie picked me up that night under the TWA sign at the L.A. International Airport, she was driving the 1939 Dodge she'd told me over the phone in Boston that she'd bought. She'd also told me what to do about the married man. *You write him a letter through inter-office mail, Lisa. Tell him: Put up or shut up. You give him an ultimatum, that's what you do. And if he doesn't come through for you in three days, Lisa, if he's too big a coward to do something about it, to make a choice, then you get the hell out of his sight and come out here. Tell him you're moving, but don't tell him where you are going. Just tell him you're about to disappear. That's what you do, Lisa, you hear me? Poof! A little mist, then nothing. Over, out.*

Like my parents, Elodie thought it was Nigel's fault. But I knew things were exactly as he had told me: *You were messed up before you met me, Lisa. It strikes me that you were standing there just waiting for something sad to come along.*

It was easy enough for my sister. She had *disappeared* a lot of times from a lot of men. Even during the time I'd been staying with my parents in Chicago, Elodie had managed to meet another one. He sat in the passenger's side of her '39 Dodge, a tall man with long legs stretching clear out under the dashboard. His curly blond hair stood out like a halo around his head, and everything about him was completely white, leaving me with the strangest impression he was some kind of angel. Elodie introduced him to me as merely *Roy*—offhand, like, "Lisa, this is Roy," when she picked me up.

I sat in the back seat of the Dodge with Mikey, my good, tow-headed nephew, who was all excited that he was about to turn eight years old. He'd been planning his birthday party, he told me, and now *I* could come. And I sat there wondering why Elodie hadn't told me that she'd met another man, and where I could go tomorrow, now that I'd just finished charging tickets on my TWA Getaway Card which, added onto the balance I already had there, would put me completely over my allowed amount.

Elodie caught my eye in the rearview mirror. "Look at the *lights*, Lisa," she commanded. "Mikey, pick out the Capitol Records Building, and some of the others, and show them to Auntie Lisa and explain the lights."

* * * * *

One of the effects this time of what my mother had called *your little illness, Lisa, but it won't last long*, was that I had a fear of going places, of going out. I was hoping I could stay inside at Elodie's after I got there, maybe sell magazine subscriptions over the phone or something, from her house, but then after I moved in with her and found out she wasn't working because the lawyer she'd been typing for had gotten mad at her for taking a week off to go to Mexico, just her and Mikey, and had cut her off, I felt like I'd be in her way if I stayed at home. Elodie's unemployment check and food stamps were only enough for her and Mikey, and I could see she wasn't ever going to bring herself low enough to ask anything on a regular basis from her Roy. That was how she was. So I saw I was going to have to pull myself enough together to get a job.

Elodie put me in the only other bedroom of the house, across the hall from Mikey, by myself, and she and Roy slept on the floor in the living room under a sleeping bag of Mikey's that they zipped out and spread like a blanket over my great aunt's quilts. I knew it was Elodie's way of saying, *Sorry I didn't tell you, Lisa*, that I had the bed.

After three weeks of reading through the want-ads of the Sunday *Times*, I pulled on the one dress I'd brought with me, a blue and white polyester mini with wide white cuffs, and I ate a bowl of Elodie's home-made granola, and I asked her if I could borrow the Dodge because I was going out.

I could tell she was relieved. "Sure, sure, Lisa," she said, wiping her hands on her baking apron and smiling. "Any time!" She was in the kitchen, with clumps of flour stuck to her face and to the counter and cupboards from one end to the other, because she was making oatmeal cookies with the sorghum molasses she bought in bulk from the food co-op. "Here," she said, removing four hot cookies from the baking sheet and dropping them into a brown paper sack. "In case you get hungry." She was careful not to ask where I was going, but I saw her glance at the fold-up want-ads section of the *Times*. She dropped two or three more cookies in the sack. "You'll be back for dinner, won't you? Roy's making his famous spaghetti. He makes all his own pasta. Over in Reseda, at his father's house."

She was full of respect for me. I saw now that I had arrived in her house, without knowing it, as a kind of hope. I had a flashback of my mother the day I went out looking for my first job up in Northern California where we lived back then. My mother hadn't really spoken to me much for days, while I lay on the back porch getting what I thought was nothing more than my usual tan. Occasionally, she would come out through the sliding glass doors and stand there washing the windows with a cool, thin smile. "You know, Lisa," she'd say. "You might just want to look into making a little money this summer. Making your own money is going to give you some self-respect." She kept this up till I went out. And when I came back with a job as a telephone operator, I was in. "Don't bother Lisa this early," I'd hear her saying all that summer to Mikey, who was a toddler then. He was staying with us because that was the summer Elodie was going through her first divorce. "Don't bother Lisa, Mikey. Lisa has to be fresh and alert this morning for her nice new job."

Elodie handed me the keys to her Dodge. "It might need gas," she said, placing some money in my hand. The money was crumpled up, two one-dollar bills. I knew that the bills had come back as change at the grocery store from the food stamps and that they were all she had.

"Thanks," I said.

I decided to try the local phone company first, because there was one right there in Topanga Canyon, and because I'd worked that one summer for the phone company six years before. I'd been *college-bound* the summer I worked at Pacific Tel in Palo Alto, and they'd treated us *summer interns*, as they called us, like we were really something. All the executives made a special point of saying they hoped we'd come back later to work for them and of using our names when they said hello every time we passed them in the green plaster halls.

I pulled into the driveway outside the beige stucco Spanish-style building of the phone company in Topanga Canyon and parked the Dodge. As I stood there staring at the phone company,

I wondered what all those executives would say to me if they could see me now.

"I'd like to apply to be a long-distance operator," I told the receptionist in the foyer of the phone company in Topanga Canyon. Her tightly permanented hair matched her flowered chiffon shirtwaist in shades of brown.

She led me into another room and gave me an application. Then she left me alone in there to fill out the application, and, when I had finished, to study the blue and green striped wallpaper and the blue plush armchairs, and the blue push-button phone display, and the pictures of employees shaking hands with their supervisors, and the framed certificates of merit that lined the walls. I concentrated as hard as I could on one gold-framed picture of a little boy about Mikey's age in a red and blue sweater, some employee's son. But I saw him growing up and going to work as an executive at the phone company, saying hello to his mother and all the college-bound summer interns as he walked the halls. And before the receptionist could come back to take my application, I found a door that said *Fire Exit Only*, and I slipped outside.

As I drove along the canyon highway to the Topanga Mall, I smoothed out the *Times* want-ad section on the seat beside me and breathed in the sweet canyon smell of sagebrush and eucalyptus blowing in through the open driver-side window of the old black Dodge. I thought of Nigel in his house in Hingham, south of Boston. I pictured him as he might have been right then, right that moment, wandering in the woods alone behind his house. I tried calling out to him. *Over here, Nigel*, I said. *Look behind you. By this maple I am standing. Or behind this rock.*

I thought of a dream I'd had once when I had a very high fever while I was growing up. I was at a birthday party in this dream, and the other children were making fun of me. I said, with a magician's voice, *Very well then, watch closely. I am going to disappear forever from before your eyes.* Then I woke up, just to prove I could do it, chuckling and pushing away my mother's hand with the cool washcloth she held to my forehead, proud that I'd disappeared from those nasty children with a little *pop*.

When I got outside the canyon, I stopped for gas, and while I was putting in two dollars worth at the self-serve pump I saw a pretty blonde girl standing near the station, on a stretch of Astro-turf that was just outside. She had her thumb out, hitch-hiking, and while I was paying the attendant in the little bullet-proof booth for my self-serve gas, I noticed a red Chrysler slowing down to pick her up.

I have this thing about red cars. I've had it ever since I was little, and I don't know why. You don't trust red cars unless they're Volkswagens, and even then, if it's a convertible, you can't be sure, although it's usually okay if it just has one of those little sun-roofs on the top.

I shook my head and opened my mouth to cry out to the young blonde girl not to take the ride, but my mouth was still full of the dry hot air of the canyon and I couldn't talk. Tomorrow, I thought, I would read through the L.A. *Times* and find some story about a blonde girl found dead in a Dempsey Dumpster behind somebody's apartment complex, all beaten up. I would call the police and tell them the last place I saw her, and the number on the license of that big red car. For now, I'd just have to be satisfied I could help them catch the guy. I didn't think I had it in me to save her life.

But as I got back in the Dodge and started up, I saw that the girl was shaking her head at the man in the red Chrysler, and stepping back, and then that he was angrily gunning his accelerator and driving off. I coasted over to where she was standing and cranked down the heavy window on the right-hand side. "Gee," I said to her when she looked up. "I'm sure glad you didn't get in that car. Could I give you a ride someplace?"

She looked about twenty, her pale hair pulled into two braids that hung down to her shoulder bones. She had nice green un-made-up eyes and a wide white smile, and I noticed she was carrying a thermos. "Water," she said, lifting it up to show me as she climbed into the Dodge. "I always have some with me. You never know, when you're hitch-hiking, do you, when you might get stuck. Thanks a lot. This is sure a neat car. Nah. Don't worry. I never get into a red car like that when I'm alone."

As we drove out to the Topanga Mall, I learned that her name was Phoebe and that she was fifteen, not twenty, and that she'd run away from her divorced mother, who lived with her lesbian roommate in Detroit.

"My dad's out here," Phoebe said, "and I came out thinking I could live with him. But once I got here, to his apartment, you know what I mean, he had this *woman*. Bleached hair and ruby-red lipstick, frosted pink polish on her toenails, gold chain around her ankle, that kind of stuff. And I thought to myself, *Feeb, you got out here all right on your own now, didn't you, and you don't need this kind of protection, do you, and if you can just find some way to make a living you'll be all right.* And so far, I have been."

She'd discovered EST, she told me, her second week. "Funny thing is," she said, "it was in this mall. The one where we're going. They had these display tables and I picked up some of their pamphlets and started reading, and it all made sense. Like, you stopped for me as a little kindness, you know? And I sort of figure that was the *objectification*, as they say, of all the kindnesses that were in my thought. Because I'm kind to people, too, see, I always am, and so, I just sort of expect kindnesses as something normal that will come around."

She told me she was going to apply for a salesclerk job at Joseph Magnin's she'd read about in the paper. I asked her which paper she'd read the ad in, because I'd missed that one.

Maybe she could tell I was worried about getting a job, because she said, "Shoot, why don't you apply for it too. No hard feelings. May the best man win."

She suggested that when we got to the mall we should break up. "Let's toss a coin," she said. "Heads, I go in first, and tails, you win." She tossed a nickel into the air, and when it came up heads, she seemed genuinely disappointed that I'd lost.

"Okay," she said. "I said I'd go if it came out that way, so this is it." She jumped down and threw up her hand in a little salute and hurried off.

It wasn't until I was getting out of the Dodge myself a few minutes later that I noticed she'd left her thermos of water on the seat. I had a feeling she'd done it on purpose. Probably if we'd decided I was the first to go into Joseph Magnin's, I'd have come back later and found the thermos with a little note. *Dear Lisa, Thanks for the ride, it was nice meeting you. Here's some water in a thermos. Because you never know, do you, when you might get stuck.*

As I smoothed down my dress and started walking across the parking lot, I tried to think about kindnesses. I reminded myself that the words *kindnesses* and *calm* both started with a little back-of-the-throat explosive, and so maybe if you knew one of them existed, you could count on the existence of the other one. I thought about Elodie and the sack of oatmeal cookies, and I thought about Roy making his homemade pasta at his father's house, and I thought about the room I slept in with the purple wall-to-wall carpet at my sister's house, and about the sleeping bag and my great-aunt's quilts laid out in the living room every night, and about good old Mikey the night they'd come to get me at the airport, him sitting there holding my fingers with one hand and pointing out the window with the other at the electric lights. *That one there's the Capitol Records Building, Lisa. And that's Westwood off in the distance. And over there's the Miracle Mile, and right behind it, in one of those high-rises, is First Western Bank.* I reached into my purse and squeezed the Indian head-band he'd braided for me the summer before while he was up at camp.

When I got to Joseph Magnin's, I stood in a long line of charge customers at a cash register, and when it was my turn to talk to the tan, middle-aged woman with the short, dyed yellow hair who was standing behind the cash register, I asked her very quietly where I could find Personnel.

"Through those double doors in back of you, honey," she said. She looked at me very carefully, and I grew conscious of the spreading wet places under the sleeves of my polyester dress.

"Thank you," I said. I tried to smile, but I was too aware of the stale smell of fear from my pale, parched mouth.

The woman raised her eyebrows and nodded. "Don't mention it," she said, and leaned over the top of the cash register.

As I walked over to the double doors I heard her say to someone behind me, "Jesus. Is Feinbaum still *in* there? Why doesn't somebody tell that woman she should just go home?"

I walked down a long creme-colored corridor with tiled floors, at the end of which was a little waiting room. Through the open door, I could see a woman with neat, salt-and-pepper graying hair. She was leaning over a desk, writing something down. The desk was covered with a large, bright pink blotter with red leather sides, and there was a matching container for pencils. A name-plate at the front of the desk said *Myra Feinbaum.* I stepped into the office and stood there for a moment, looking at the thick pile of papers. All applications, I thought dismally, for that one small job.

"Yes?"

Myra Feinbaum lifted her head, and I found myself looking into the unglamorous but friendly and attractive face of a woman about fifty-five with light brown eyes. "Have you already filled out an application with us outside?"

I don't know if it was Phoebe's thermos on the seat of the Dodge, or if maybe Myra Feinbaum didn't just remind me a little bit of my mother, who, after trying so hard those several weeks to help me, had given up, but when I opened my mouth to tell the lady behind the pink desk blotter that I needed very, very badly to find a job, and that I hadn't, in fact, already filled out an application, I began to my own great helpless embarrassment to cry.

"Oh no, no, that won't do at all," clucked Myra Feinbaum, moving quickly from behind her desk to close the door. "Here, dear. Sit down. Can I get you something? Some tea? Do you want an aspirin?" She reached over beside the pink desk blotter and handed me a box of tissues so I could blow my nose.

But the kinder she was, the more I buckled. I tried to tell her not to worry about me, that I'd be all right. But instead I sat there, my face in my hands, sobbing. And then I heard myself telling her everything that had happened to me in the last six months.

"I see," she said finally, after a long wash of silence. I was horrified. I wanted to sneak out of Myra Feinbaum's office, promising to see a doctor, a clergyman, a marriage counselor, anyone at all she suggested, but just let me out.

"So you *need* this job," she said, rising from the armrest of my chair where she'd been sitting with her arm around me while I sobbed. "Well, I think we can arrange something. Actually, I've already made my mind up to hire someone, a girl who came in just before you, but she's very young. Would you be willing to share the hours with her, perhaps, and just work part-time?"

* * * * *

You'd have thought I was some sort of returning war hero when I got home. "Don't tell them yet, till dinner," Elodie whispered, throwing her arms around me and putting her mouth against my ear. I could feel my shoulder blades cutting through my blue and white polyester against her arms.

Roy had made his home-made pasta, and Elodie's parsley-based meatless sauce was simmering deliciously on the big white stove. My parents had bought the house for Elodie because she and Mikey had been having a hard time finding a place to live, even down in Burbank, on Elodie's typing income, and my parents said they wanted their grandson to grow up in a decent place, somewhere with air and trees like we'd had when we were growing up.

The house was a green clapboard two-bedroom, one of those little tract houses built in former avocado groves during the Fifties when land wasn't worth so much. There was a big avocado tree right in front of the living room window in the small front yard. Elodie said that this was like the Garden of Eden here tonight, with all of us together, and God dropping the fruit of the knowledge of His provision in squishy little green nuggets right in our laps. When she dished up the spaghetti, she passed hot flour tortillas and Monterey Jack and guacamole made from the avocados from our avocado tree around.

"This is like one of those big feasts like the kings used to have," Mikey said, stuffing his mouth full of guacamole.

Elodie laughed, and I realized how much it depended on having a full stomach and a roof over your head, that kind of sound. "Lisa's got a *job*, everybody!" she announced. She beamed at me with pride, and everybody clapped. "My little baby sister went out in a single day and came back with a *very* glamorous job at Joseph Magnin's."

"Hey, hey!" Roy said, raising his glass of water to give a toast. "Joseph Magnin's, huh? Now that is *class*."

Elodie put her fork down and reached over to the phone table to pull out a pad and pencil. "The first thing we have to do," she said, "is make a list. We're going to have to pool our clothes, Lisa, so you'll have something sufficiently Joseph Magnin-y to wear."

My sister had been making lists for one thing or another all our lives. I remembered lists for summer camp, for back to school, for shopping, for improving boyfriends' dispositions, for taking steps to be more in control of her hectic life. As her hand left the phone table, I also remembered that her phone bill was overdue, and that it was subject within a day or two to a disconnect.

"Let's see," Elodie said, pursing her lips and thinking. "That blue and white dress you're wearing, for one, but with my blue shoes. And then, my crinkly Mexican cotton blouse with the embroidered flowers and your old white pants. There's some sort of stain on those pants, Lisa, right on your butt. Like you sat on some kind of grease or something. But I think with a little bleach and Boraxo we can get it out."

I had acquired the stain on my white pants the night Nigel told me his wife was coming back from South Africa. He picked me up in his car and we drove out of Boston on Storrow Drive and on up to Revere Beach. We walked on the polluted sand for about an hour, and at midnight I sat down beside Nigel under a sodium vapor light, the two of us surrounded by our own filthy circle of footprints, there on that wet black oily beach off Highway One.

* * * * *

I started to work at Joseph Magnin's a week later.

"This'll be your *assignment*," the blonde woman I'd seen the day of my interview told me. "You'll be in the Junior Section, and when you don't have any customers, you still try to look busy. Make sure the clothes are straight on the hangers. Make sure they're all right in there with their size. Or check the mannequins or something. Tidy up."

Just before I went *out on the floor*, as she called it, I asked her where Mrs. Feinbaum was, so I could just say thanks. She busied herself with some sales receipts, then gave me an answer without looking up. "Mrs. Feinbaum is on an extended leave," she said. "She came in to do this hiring, but she's supposed to be on leave of absence all year long. Her mother has been in the hospital, dying of cancer, and she was very close to her mother. But the day after she hired you, her mother died."

Then the blonde woman told me her name. "You can call me Joy. Come straight to me if you have any questions there in Juniors. Because while Feinbaum's on leave of absence?" She pointed to her hefty bosom. "I'm in charge."

When I got to Juniors, I saw Phoebe going through the Size Nines, straightening up the dresses and checking tags. She was wearing a new white Levi's mini skirt and a pink velour sweatshirt with a little cat design, and she'd taken her blonde hair out of the braids to let it hang in big loose wavy chunks along her sides. "Hi!" she said when she saw me. "I'm not surprised!"

A few minutes later, Joy led me away to learn how to put my sales number into the computer so I'd be sure to get my commission for all my sales.

* * * * *

After I got the job at Joseph Magnin's, Elodie signed up with a temporary secretarial agency. She was a fast typist, but the thing people always liked about her was that she didn't give a damn about other people's business. As she put it, *Live and let live.* So she was pretty popular at Harold Goode's Temps in Canoga Park.

We worked around each other's schedules, and around Mikey's school, so that one of us—Roy or Elodie or me—was always there in the house when he got home. One day, when it was my turn to look after him, he'd just finished his snack and was going out the front door to ride his bike, when he said to me, "Lisa, why don't you get a bicycle?"

He was standing there at the door with his hands wrapped around the rams-horn handlebars of his brand new bike. It had been a present for his birthday, or at least the money had. His father, Elodie's first husband, always sent him money for his birthday, because, he'd told me once when he called to leave a message for Elodie that the child support check would be late that month, he hadn't seen Mikey for a couple of years now, and he was more used to his own kids now anyway, who were a whole lot younger, by his second wife. So he didn't really know what a kid like Mikey, living out there in California with all those hippies, would really want.

Mikey had put his father's birthday check together with the other money he'd been saving, and gone down to a special store in Burbank and bought this bike. It was watermelon green, a ten-speed model, with specially made hand-brakes and a wheel-operated generator that ran safety lights. Mikey was very proud of it. He and Bobby Torres, the Chicano kid he palled around with after school, rode their bikes all over the neighborhood. So it was pretty hard for him to imagine that I might not really care whether or not I had a bike.

"I could get you one cheap," he said as I stood there behind the screen door that Elodie's four cats, sharpening their claws, had broken through.

"That's okay, Mikey," I said, trying to sound disappointed, as if I knew what I was giving up. "The bus through the Canyon is dependable enough, and anyway, your mom's pretty nice about loaning me her car."

But I could tell that Mikey, polishing an imaginary speck of dust off the watermelon green metallic paint-job of his ten-speed, was not convinced. "Hm," he said. "Well, see ya."

I sat down on the calico sofa in Elodie's living room. She'd bought the sofa at the Salvation Army and covered it with a yellow posy print from the discount store. I was careful as I sat there not to position my bottom too close to the broken spring. I turned on the T.V. and tried for awhile to watch *As the World Turns*, or one of those soap operas, but the handsome men with their careful English and tan, broad shoulders all seemed too much like Nigel, and the plots, which I'd heard the tired-looking mothers of toddlers discussing in the laundromat on Reseda Boulevard when it came my turn to do our laundry, seemed to me to be making something glamorous out of plain old hurt.

After about an hour I turned off the television and was wondering if I should splurge and order a vegetarian pizza for all of us, because it was my night to make dinner and I wasn't as imaginative as Elodie could be without using meat.

All of a sudden, Mikey clattered in through the front door and slammed it, adding a couple more inches of open air to the ripped-out screen. "Lisa!" he shouted. "Hey Lisa!" He was moving his arms in great big X's. "Come here and see!"

It was hard to get impatient with Mikey. He'd do things like break more of the screen, or throw a softball through a window, or leave one of the cats or dogs locked up inside so they'd go to the bathroom on the multi-colored tweed indoor-outdoor carpet while we were all away, and you'd want to get angry with him, you'd want to say, *Mikey, goddamnit, why the hell did you do that,* but then you'd just look at him, those dark ridges of sweat and dirt under the dirty blond hair above the deep blue eyes, and you'd think, *Okay, what's the use, anyway?*

"All right, all right," I said. "What is it?" As I followed him out the front door, I tried to be very obvious about reaching for the handle and pushing my hand through the hole in the broken screen.

But Mikey didn't notice I was annoyed. He was turning back and forth to look at me and running straight ahead, so that I was afraid he was going to fall right onto his face on the hard cement. "Will you just watch where you're going?" I yelled.

When we got out on the sidewalk, he threw his arms around my waist and pointed over at the grease-spotted driveway. "See what I mean?"

I saw two dirt-bikes lined up in the driveway, a girl's model with a red, white and blue plastic basket in front of the handle-bars, and then another, beside it, a smaller version for a boy, with a big printed license-plate at the back of the raised-up, pickle-shaped seat that said 83.

I guess I knew before I asked him, but I would not believe. "Where's your new ten-speed, Mikey?" I felt my chest getting tighter. I looked over at Bobby Torres, his white grin riding over a sea of mocha smoothness, his blue-jeans straddled over a bike like the other two. Beneath Bobby's bowl-shaped brown hair and round eyes that were dark and mottled as Sunmaids, his straight teeth gleamed. But he didn't say a word, not one, leaving the glory for Mikey.

"I exchanged it!" Mikey said. "I went in to the bike store and swapped it for two of these."

* * * * *

In March, Elodie got a sort of promotion. She'd started out at Harold Goode's Temps getting paid a dollar over minimum wage, but her supervisor always got such glowing accounts about her typing and filing skills whenever she sent her out on assignments that she decided to up Elodie's hourly salary to just one notch lower than the highest wage they paid at Harold Goode's.

"She said she didn't want to lose me," Elodie said over the celebration dinner we were all having. Celebration dinners were big with Elodie. She liked it when everyone brought something pot-luck. My donation to the dinner tonight was a large economy size bag of potato chips.

Mikey had invited Bobby Torres to join us, and his mother had sent over a Tupperware container full of re-fried beans. I'd invited Phoebe to come home with me from Joseph Magnin's after work, and she'd bought a five-pound box of chocolate chip cookies from Mrs. Field's. "I like your sister," Phoebe had whispered to me with her nice smile when Elodie came to get us in the Dodge. And I knew from the way Elodie didn't get going about the future doom of America because of shopping malls and chain stores and junk foods like cookies and potato chips, that she liked her back.

Roy came to the celebration dressed up in his ice-cream-man suit. He brought along three loaves of rye bread, a gift from his elderly father, who liked to bake. Roy's father had moved out to California from someplace in Appalachia during the Forties to be a citrus grower in the Valley, and now that he'd sold off all his groves to developers he didn't leave his house. Roy described him as a kind of hermit. He said his father liked what he heard Roy tell him about Elodie and Mikey, though, even though they'd probably never meet.

"My father says to tell you they don't deserve you," he said to Elodie, meaning not the four of us sitting around her table, but what they called the *personnel advisors* at Harold Goode's.

"Pooh," Elodie said, raising her glass of ice-water with long-fingered hands. "It's all just a matter of anatomy, when you come right down to it. I've just got typists' fingers, is all it is."

Phoebe looked at her own hands, lying in her lap, and turned them face up flat, so I could see the cross-stitch pattern, two trees with all of its branches, across her palms. "How does a person go about learning something like that when you aren't in school anymore?" she asked. "I mean, my mom always said to me, *Phoebe,* she always said, *you should learn a trade. Take typing. Take shorthand. That way, you'll always be able to make a living.* She always said, my mom did, *Phoebe, don't go into your life with nothing so you'll need a man.*"

Then she looked over at Roy and blushed, worried she might have hurt his feelings. "Not that men are so awful," she added. "Anyway, I could've worked in an office if I'd learned to type in high school, before I quit. Now I sort of wish I'd listened to my mom."

Elodie laughed. "Fifteen, maybe sixteen, and you're worried? Anyway, Phoebe"—she reached over and patted Phoebe's hand—"Joseph Magnin's is a *very* elegant store."

After dinner, Mikey suggested we all go to the drive-in with the Dodge. So all of us except for Roy, who worked part-time as a night-clerk in a 7-ll store in Burbank and was due at eight, climbed into the Dodge, with Elodie driving.

Sometimes Elodie could be very stubborn. As soon as the rest of us were settled, Phoebe up front next to Elodie, her thin arm extended up out over the window on the right-hand side, and Bobby and Mikey and I stretched out like gang-land big-shots in the huge back seat, Elodie insisted, in spite of the fact that we lived right next door to a freeway on-ramp and were almost out of gas, and only had exactly enough money added up among us to pay for tickets, on taking surface streets.

"Mom," Mikey said quietly in what I had come to call his reasoned voice. It was the voice with which he tried to get through to Elodie when she got this way. "Mom, listen to me. Look at the gas tank. It's riding a little above empty. If you take the freeway we can get on right here and then we can get off right next to the drive-in and we won't waste gas."

But Elodie wouldn't have it. "I've had enough of these goddamn California freeways," she said. "And this is *my* celebration, isn't it? Well, I may have to take freeways when I've got to be someplace by eight o'clock in the morning to start typing, but I'll be damned if I'm going to drive on them when I've got a choice."

We lurched backwards down the driveway as she hit reverse.

Elodie drove the Dodge down the canyon towards the sea. We rolled down all the windows and Elodie got us all to singing *Let Me Call You Sweetheart*, a song she'd taught me one summer when I was about Mikey's age and she'd gone to camp. When we got to the word *sweetheart*, the sweet air of the canyon, smelling of eucalyptus and wild sage and geraniums, rushed dry into the waiting vacuums of our open mouths.

I looked up front and saw Phoebe there singing next to Elodie, and I thought it was really something, when she'd had such screwy parents, and had hitch-hiked out here, and was having to make a living now on her own, that she could still be so happy, and be singing like she was, and I made a note to myself that later I would thank Elodie especially for inviting Phoebe to come along.

Everyone was having a good time, except maybe for Mikey. He was trying not to let anyone notice, but he was keeping his eye on the gas tank, I could tell.

And so could Elodie. "Come on, Mikey," she said finally, looking back at him through the rear-view mirror. "You're acting like your father. Can't you just for once step out onto the water and not worry about what's going to happen if you don't stay up? Trust me, will you? I've been getting you around in this Dodge without any problems, haven't I, for the last six months?"

Mikey sank back against the plush velour cushion of the big back seat and crossed his arms. He never liked it when Elodie said he was like his father, and I sort of sympathized with him about that. It was a lousy way to win an argument, was what it was.

We were still on Topanga Canyon Boulevard, almost to the place where it feeds onto the coast, when the gas gave out. I hadn't ever been in a car that had run out of gas before, so I was surprised to see how it happened, how it felt. I always thought that when a car ran out of gas it coughed and spluttered first for a minute or two and then maybe kept on leaping forward in little fits and starts. But that wasn't at all how it happened. One minute Elodie was driving along full speed at forty, all of us singing and waving at all the other people in the other cars, and the next minute we were slowing down inside this incredible silence, just going slower and slower, and Elodie pumping the accelerator and getting nothing, and, in the end, hardly even getting the Dodge over into the right-hand lane before it completely stopped. People were swerving around us and honking. One man made a sign, *screw you*, outside his window, his arm straight up.

"Shit," Elodie said. "I knew it. I just *knew* it. Decent people can't even go to the movies anymore without something going wrong."

I held my breath, afraid Mikey was going to say *I told you, Mom,* which would send Elodie into one of the self-justification speeches she'd been famous for in our family since she was a child. They were always admirably complex and eloquent, and no one had ever dared argue with her while one was going on. I reached over to pinch the loose skin on Mikey's elbow—a silent signal I'd learned from my mother that meant *you'd best shut up*—but then I saw that he wasn't going to say anything anyway. He just sat there, staring straight up at a button that was dangling by a thread from the torn red velvet ceiling, his lips pressed tightly together, the muscles working hard inside his jaw.

"Well," Phoebe said in a cheery voice. "We can't just sit here now, can we?" She pulled open her door and started out. "Come on, guys," she said, motioning to Bobby and Mikey and me in the back seat. "Elodie can steer the car while we all push."

But Elodie was already out of the car, walking. Head down, hands shoved into the pockets of her big blue skirt, she slung her legs forward, one two, one two. She was marching away from us, right back up Topanga Canyon, exactly in the direction from which we'd come.

"What are you doing, Mom?" Mikey called, his voice going up and down. "You're not just going to leave the car here, are you? Mom! This car is *famous.* Somebody'll come along and rip it off!"

But Elodie kept on walking, till the rest of us finally started to follow.

"Mom?" Mikey said when we all caught up.

Elodie stopped by the side of the road, her hands on her hips, and I thought Mikey was a whole lot stronger than I was for being able to continue with what he had to say after her freezing, *"What?"*

"You gotta let other people help you sometimes, Mom," he said. He gestured over at Bobby, who was standing there, his brown eyes very wide. "Tell her, Bobby. Tell her that story about the woman who always gets herself in trouble in your mother's church."

But Bobby shook his head and would not speak up.

"Okay, then I'll tell her," Mikey said. "Listen, Mom. In Bobby's mother's church there's this woman, see. They call her Our Lady. She's Our Lady of Durango, or Our Lady of Guadeloupe, or Our Lady of whatever place she shows up in, but also she's called Our Lady of Sorrows, because she's always sad. And she goes around, see, and she's been going around like this for years and years, *centuries* even, sort of like a ghost, and she goes to these different places and she acts like she's having these horrible problems, right out there in the open, you know, right in front of everybody, so she can give people a chance to help her. And that's how she finds out what kind of person they really are."

He stopped then, absolutely certain he'd made perfect sense. Elodie, who for all her love of trips to Mexico had definite ideas about the official stand on birth control by the Catholic Church, cocked her head and studied Mikey for a minute. She had been known to break into spontaneous lectures on family planning and *religious interference in the bedroom,* as she called it, or, for that matter, on the evils of fashionable women who insisted on wearing leopard or sealskin coats, or on the relationship between big business and world hunger. But I could tell this time she wasn't going to go into one of her lectures, from her voice.

"Mikey," she said. "Could you maybe tell me what Our Lady of Sorrows has to do with the five of us trying to go to the movies and then ending up here down by the ocean because we ran out of gas?"

Mikey pulled himself up to his full height and squared his shoulders. "You should give people a chance to help you," he said. "Because for all they know, Mom, you might just *be* Our Lady of Sorrows. Only this time you're Our Lady of Topanga Canyon, see. And you've come down here to see how they're doing, and it's their last big chance."

I felt something growing in my chest, something old and

welcome and familiar that had been gone too long. For the first time since I'd left Boston, I began to laugh.

* * * * *

I had *disappeared* from Boston in the middle of November, and it was the end of December by the time I'd left my parents' condo in Illinois. Every now and then I had to remind myself of that, because November and December seemed to have moved so slowly, and then, after I moved out to Elodie's and went to work at Joseph Magnin's in the Topanga Mall, time, which everyone says cannot be altered, moved very fast. I remember hearing something about that on the UCLA radio station while I was living with Elodie. Some scientists in the physics department there were studying Einstein's theory of relativity, and they were discussing the possibility that time became less and less relevant as we disengaged ourselves from matter and let ourselves start moving at the speed of light. I didn't understand their theory, but I thought it might have had something to do with what was happening to Elodie and to Mikey and to Roy and me.

Then one Saturday morning I was watching cartoons with Mikey in the living room, and remembering that I was going to have to put something to wear together later that afternoon because I had to work, when I realized it was already the end of April. The cannas that some past tenant had planted under Elodie's living room window were beginning to bloom. If you looked closely you could see columns of holes in graduating sizes where the snails had eaten through the unfurling leaves. And the avocado tree was already starting to get another set of buds.

Mikey was whistling a tune to go along with the cereal advertisement he was watching, and I closed my eyes.

After a few minutes I realized he was standing there next to me, his hand on my left shoulder. I opened my eyes and saw him leaning over my face, studying me as if he had me under a microscope, like a special bug. "Lisa?" He looked very happy with what he saw.

I frowned up at him. "What are you staring at, Mikey, if I may ask?"

"I can *see* it," he said. "I can see it there for myself. And you're all right."

* * * * *

I guess it was June, or maybe the first part of July, when I told Elodie I was going back to Boston.

I was sitting on the quilt-covered box springs in the front bedroom where I slept, and Elodie was standing behind her ironing board, pressing a red flannel shirt she'd made for Roy. I remember that she was humming. I remember that I considered telling her that the buttonholes on a man's shirt were supposed to be on the left side, and that she was going to be giving Roy a shirt that had buttonholes on the right like a woman's, but instead I told her I was moving back.

She stopped, steam-iron in mid-air. "You must be crazy." It took her a full minute to feel the weight of the iron and to set it down. "How are you going to get back there? What are you going to do when you get there? You can't just walk into that same office and start working right there in front of that man after what he put you through. You can't go back there, Lisa. You're not *well* enough."

I dug my nails deep into the stuffing of the quilt. "Yes," I said. "I am. And I can. And I know exactly how I'm going to get there, too." I took a breath. "I'm going to drive."

Elodie unplugged her steam iron and came over to sit beside me on the bed. She took my hand. "Lisa." She said my name with deliberate slowness, as if I'd gone off somewhere already and wasn't sitting right there beside her, and she was trying very hard to call me back. "You can't do this, Lisa. You're just now getting better. And you know how men are. He won't leave you alone. He'll be knocking at the door of whatever little hole you find to live in with the stupid little amount of money you'll be making, and he'll keep saying he *needs* you. He'll keep saying he's *missed* you. He'll keep telling you that you brought *poetry* into his life. And he'll keep that up, and keep that up, even though he's got a wife he's already told you he won't be leaving, and probably another goddamn baby by now, too, and a nice warm house."

I thought it would be pretty useless for me to rub it in about her and Roy—how he'd been living there, ever since I'd come, the two of them sleeping under Mikey's sleeping bag on the living room floor under my great-aunt's quilts. I wanted to ask her, *So who's paying for that, then, huh? Which one of us decided that what this house really needed was another man?*

But as if she were reading my thoughts, she said, "It's different, you know, between me and Roy. He isn't taking advantage. He isn't married. He hasn't promised me something he knows in his heart he will never deliver. He hasn't lied."

She stood up, but she did not let go of my hand. She held it between both of hers. I will never forget how warm and safe my hand felt at that moment inside her hands. "Roy *can't* take advantage of me, Lisa," she said softly. "Don't you see that? Because I'm not like you. I'm a hell of a lot harder. Lisa, what I'm trying to say is that I don't crack up."

When I didn't answer, she went on standing there, holding my hand and kneading my fingers.

"Oh shit," she said after a few minutes. Then, in a tiny voice, "All right."

* * * * *

Roy helped me to get the loan for the car. He drove up the next day in his big green truck when I got home from working the morning hours. Elodie was down at the farmers' market, getting vegetables in the Dodge. I could see by the fact that Roy was all dressed up in his white Mexican shirt and clean white Levi's, with his hair all slicked down to hide the halo, that he and Elodie had talked this over, and that it was her way of giving me her blessing, even though she made her point, when it came time for us to do it, of being out.

"Pacific Finance," Roy said when I asked him if he knew where to start. We drove on down the freeway to Canoga Park. "Under the square they've got that says *Current Salary*," he said as we walked up to a corner building with black glass windows, "write down the amount you were making before you left Boston. Under *Extra Income,* put down the money you're making here for the part-time work you're doing now. They won't ask any questions. They're looking for suckers. They *want* you not to be able to make the payments. So you go along with them, see, you take advantage of them, and they give you the money with a phony smile. And then you just make damn sure you pay them the amount they don't ever expect you to give them. Whether or not you eat, you see that these bastards get their goddamn payment *every month*. You got all this?"

I did exactly what he told me, and he was right. I was interviewed by a small, round, tired-looking man with a balding head. I told him I wanted to buy a used car so I could go back *home* to Boston and *resume* my job. "Jeez, kid," the man said, "I wish I could do that. I wish I could get out of this place and go back East."

I walked out of Pacific Finance with a check for eight hundred and fifty dollars, and Roy and I set out to find a car.

But before we started, Roy and I drove through the McDonald's drive-up window and bought Big Macs and chocolate shakes and two large fries. "Don't tell Elodie, will you?" he said, handing me my white bag with the golden arches. "I go along with her, eating vegetarian and all, but if I didn't hit one of these places every now and then, I think I'd starve."

"Thanks, Roy," I said, and dug down in my purse for some money.

"Forget it." He shoved my hand away with the money. "This is my treat. Now we'll just pull over here in this park and thumb through your used car section there till we find a buy."

* * * * *

We bought a light blue Pontiac wagon, fifteen years old. The front windows had been soaped with the message, *Stick shift with rust, runs good!* Roy said it was good camouflage to get something stodgy that no one would notice, rather than *your typical hippie number, you know, Lisa, an old V-dub bus or something, 'cause the cops'll see you crossing the country alone in one of those and you'll be in trouble, pull you over and ask you do you know what yer doin' all by yerself here little lady, and away you'll go.*

The used car dealer promised to throw in a full tank of gas and two new front tires. He said he'd deliver the Pontiac to Elodie's house that evening, at which point I should be prepared to give him cash.

"You let her buy a *Pontiac*, for God's sake?" Elodie said to Roy when we got back. Roy and I were doubled over, giggling like kindergartners. He had his arm around my shoulders. I'd lost another fifteen pounds since getting to California, and it was just about all I could do to hold him up.

"It just smiled at us from the showroom," Roy told her. "Aw, come on now, Elodie, it's okay. If you don't like the color when you see it, the salesman said no hard feelings, they're real proud of their Mercedes down there, and so, when the guy delivers it, if you don't like it, rather than argue with their customers they'll take it back."

Elodie shook her head, but she was smiling now. "You two are both just plain crazy. I'll go put dinner on."

Roy nudged me with his elbow in my side. "Sure hope you've got a lot of that there pasta, Elodie honey," he said in a loud voice as she walked away. "Because me and Lisa are *real* hungry. It's awful hard, you know, finding the right kind of food, healthy nourishing vegetarian food and all of that, when you're out shopping all around Southern California for the perfect car."

* * * * *

That night, after the used car dealer had delivered the Pontiac, the four of us sat out on Elodie's front porch steps and listened to the avocados dropping from the branches of the thick old tree.

Mikey was leaning back, whistling. Every now and then his whistling would be punctuated with a little *plop*. "There goes another one," he'd say, and we'd all laugh.

"It needed *four* tires," Elodie said after a little while. "You just said two."

The Blue Blazer, as Mikey had christened it when we all took it around the block for a little drive, seemed to glow by its own light out on the driveway, its second-hand surface, despite the rust-spots, polished up by the used car dealer to a hard, high shine.

"The tires are part of why we got it for such a bargain," Roy said. I could see the two of them sitting next to each other in the dark. They were holding hands.

"He was damn lucky to get rid of that car," Elodie said. "And if it gives her any trouble on her way back there, I'll sue that bastard through his teeth with the lemon law. Anyway, Lisa, I'll loan you my Sears credit card, and you can get tires for the back, too, and charge them. I don't think Sears has this address yet on their computer. When they get it, we'll have to start paying, but that'll be awhile. They'll have to send it around and get it back from about three different places. We've got about two months."

I stood up and went inside and brought out the presents I'd bought at Joseph Magnin's after work that day.

"Are you out of your mind completely?" Elodie said. "How are you planning to pay for all this stuff?"

But I could see she couldn't resist the Lady Olaf clogs I'd bought her. They had cork heels, and navy perforated leather upper vamps. "They'll stay on your feet even when you're shifting," I told her. The clutch was really heavy on that old Dodge.

"And anyway, Mom," Mikey said, as he took apart the bright red, white, and blue plastic boxes-within-boxes I'd bought for him in the culinary-arts-and-living section, "she gets a discount. Plus, she only has to pay for it a little at a time, like you do. She doesn't have to pay for it all at once." Then suddenly he jumped up and ran out into the darkness. I could hear him, squishing the rotting fallen avocados between his toes.

"He's going to miss you, you know that, don't you?" Elodie said. "Do you think it's fair, what you're doing, the way you've come out here and let us all care about you, and then one day you decide you're half-way healthy and off you go driving out of here back to Boston like a fast blue streak?"

Roy laughed. "She'll probably get to Boston in the Blue Blazer, all right," he said. "But I don't think anyone but you would ever say she was going to get there like a fast blue streak."

I told them about Phoebe at Joseph Magnin's and what she'd done.

"You know how you put your sales number into that computer when you ring something up?" I asked them. "Well, I found out today that Phoebe has been putting my number in instead of hers, every time she went to the register to ring a sale. They only tally up these commissions we get outside our salaries once a quarter. I wouldn't have known about it till I got my final paycheck in the mail in Boston, except that today Joy, this woman we work for, kept patting me on the back and calling me Tiger, and saying they'd have had to move me to Fine Apparel if I'd stayed. And she said I'd be getting this fat bonus in my paycheck after I left. I couldn't figure out what she was talking about, because I'm really not such a hot-shot when it comes to sales, but then I saw Phoebe. And it dawned on me. She'd been using my number to ring up all her sales."

Elodie reached over and ran her hand over the back of my cotton rib T-shirt. She started massaging the bones along my spine. I could feel her fingers exploring the ridges that spread out either side of my backbone like rungs on a ladder. My sister had always been good at giving a massage. Once, I heard one of her men say of her, before I was old enough to know what he meant, that Elodie had the gift of *healing hands*. I imagined her now leaving patterns on my back forever, her flat palms printing out the good designs, my shoulders glowing with the shadowy tattoos impressed upon them by the old cooking scars along her thumbs.

"Thanks for everything, Elodie," I said.

Roy stretched out behind us on his back. In the dark yard, the avocado tree answered with another *plop*.

"I didn't realize you were getting so goddamn *thin*," Elodie said, pushing me away from her with the flat of her hand.

I felt as if she had thrust me forward to walk along a precipice, alone. I felt like I had as a kid, when she'd made me walk in front of her along the curb, the two of us pretending there was a fathomless canyon on either side. *The difference between walking along this curb and crossing a real canyon, Lisa,* she'd tell me, always the older, wiser, sister, *isn't the distance there is to the bottom. The only difference between this curb and a canyon is your fear. So if you ever have to cross a real canyon, keep your arms out for balance, and don't look down.*

Now she was saying quietly, "I think it might be a good idea, Lisa, if maybe after you get back to Boston, just for a little while, you ate some meat."

Carnegie Mellon University Press
Series in Short Fiction

Fortune Telling
David Lynn

A New and Glorious Life
Michelle Herman

The Long and Short of It
Pamela Painter

The Secret Names of Women
Lynne Barrett

The Law of Return
Maxine Rodburg

The Drowning and Other Stories
Edward Delaney

My One and Only Bomb Shelter
John Smolens

Very Much Like Desire
Diane Lefer

A Chapter From Her Upbringing
Ivy Goodman

Narrow Beams
Kate Myers Hanson

Now You Love Me
Liesel Litzenburger

The Genius of Hunger
Diane Goodman